THE BELLE CRÉOLE

CARAF Books

•

Caribbean and African Literature
Translated from French

Renée Larrier and Mildred Mortimer, *Editors*

THE BELLE CRÉOLE

MARYSE CONDÉ

TRANSLATED BY NICOLE SIMEK

UNIVERSITY OF VIRGINIA PRESS
CHARLOTTESVILLE AND LONDON

Originally published in French by Mercure de France
© 2001 by Mercure de France

University of Virginia Press
Translation and afterword © 2020 by the Rector and Visitors of the
University of Virginia
All rights reserved
Printed in the United States of America on acid-free paper

First published 2020

ISBN 978-0-8139-4421-0 (cloth)
ISBN 978-0-8139-4422-7 (paper)
ISBN 978-0-8139-4423-4 (ebook)

9 8 7 6 5 4 3 2 1

Library of Congress Cataloging-in-Publication Data

Names: Condé, Maryse, author. | Simek, Nicole Jenette, translator.
Title: The belle Créole / Maryse Condé ; translated by Nicole Simek.
Other titles: Belle Créole. English.
Description: Charlottesville : University of Virginia Press, 2020.
Series: CARAF books: Caribbean and African literature translated from
    French | Translated into English from French.
Identifiers: LCCN 2019047816 (print) | LCCN 2019047817 (ebook) |
    ISBN 9780813944210 (hardback ; acid-free paper) | ISBN 9780813944227
    (paperback ; acid-free paper) | ISBN 9780813944234 (epub)
Subjects: LCSH: Guadeloupe—Fiction.
Classification: LCC PQ3949.2.C65 B4513 2020 (print) | LCC PQ3949.2.C65
    (ebook) | DDC 843/.914—dc23
LC record available at https://lccn.loc.gov/2019047816
LC ebook record available at https://lccn.loc.gov/2019047817

Cover art: Compilation (background: iStock/peeterv; dog: Freepik/@enola99d;
man: Fotosearch/Diomedes66; woman: Adobe/Christin Lola)

CONTENTS

TRANSLATOR'S ACKNOWLEDGMENTS

This translation benefited immeasurably from the generosity of many who gave their time and insightful suggestions on multiple drafts. Thanks go first to Maryse Condé and Richard Philcox for their inspiring work, their hospitality, and their openness to the project. At the University of Virginia Press, Eric Brandt shepherded this book to completion with skill and care, and I am grateful to him for his enthusiasm and counsel, as well as to Helen Chandler, Mildred Mortimer, Renée Larrier, Ellen Satrom, Susan Murray, and the anonymous reviewers for their expert guidance and feedback. I am particularly indebted to Eleanor Matson and Maeve McCracken for their assistance studying the novel, reviewing drafts, and debating translation strategy, and to the Louis B. Perry Summer Research Endowment at Whitman College for making this work possible. Chetna Chopra and Gaurav Majumdar pored over the manuscript closely and offered invaluable comments and recommendations. Thank you so much for your friendship and support! I would also like to express my deep gratitude to Bruce Magnusson and Lauren Theisen for their advice and constant encouragement, and to Rhonda Simek for sharing her ideas and incredible excitement about the project. Zahi Zalloua has been unwavering in his devotion and his belief in me, and thanks are not enough to capture my love. To my father, I can't tell you how much I wish you had been able to see your suggestion in print. I think of you and cherish the time we had together every day.

THE BELLE CRÉOLE

For Amédée

Now is the time of the assassins.

—Arthur Rimbaud

AFTERNOON

1

The country was suffocating. From the North to the South, it was hot, steaming hot, worse than any dry season in twenty years, complained those who had the strength to recollect. The meteorologists claimed that this inferno and the dust clouds that came with it were traveling from the coasts of West Africa, or more precisely from the Cape Verde Peninsula, and portended further abominations: all manner of furious rains, winds, and Category 4 hurricanes, which would come pelting down on the country nonstop as early as the month of July. Old folks and dehydrated infants were dropping like flies. In the Saint-Alban region, the ground had split open, and from thousands of cracks in the earth, tightly packed columns of insects had come marching out, fleeing the hellish depths. The tall windows of the courthouse formed sharp cutouts of blue, crackling with electricity and dotted with white splotches against which, as if drawn by the hand of a child, stiff green palm fronds stood out. Inside, the fans beat the air vainly like mournful birds. Everyone was drenched in sweat: the guards, the lawyers, the judges, the witnesses, the accused. Great beads of perspiration bathed every protocol of justice. Crowded into their box, the jurors were mopping themselves. The four women stirred the air, heavy as a wet blanket, with small, palm-leaf fans. Perpetually dressed in a navy-blue suit, the fattest one, whose languid eyes hadn't left Dieudonné for a second through the four days of the trial, seemed to be having difficulty breathing. The previous day, everyone had heard the closing arguments; after one last burst of fireworks in French-French, Matthias Serbulon, Esq., had taken his seat. He was a young man, already bald on the top of his head, unfortunately, wearing his remaining shoulder-length hair tied back in a less than orthodox ponytail, and, underneath his robes, a Giorgio Armani suit. Despite his appearance, he was the son of an austere political dignitary, founder of the PPRP, the defunct party for *lendépendans*. Dieudonné didn't like him much. From their very first meeting, in the canary-yellow prison visitation room, he hadn't cared for the way Serbulon had put a protective hand on his shoulder and pulled out his Creole, as if Dieudonné wasn't capable of understanding French. He didn't recognize himself in the picture the lawyer had worked hard to paint of him as the pitiful victim. No more, for that matter, than he did in the one the public prosecutor had drawn of him as a coarse and dangerous brute. And Mr. Serbulon had gotten so familiar as to relate how he, too, had done one stupid thing after another back in the day. Dieudonné had not been fooled. Most likely, while he was in law school, the young Matthias Serbulon had gotten drunk a few times, rolled a few joints, and fondled a pair of more or less consenting tits. Nothing more serious than that!

However, this lawyer that he deemed rather unlikable had found words fit to convince. The jury came back with a verdict that, truth be told, Dieudonné had not dared to hope for. His friend Rodrigue had just gotten slammed with twenty years. He had everything to fear. The country had seen more than enough of this young generation that didn't know how to do anything but kill, rob, rape, and burn, these youths with ex-orbitant dreams the size of special effects in the movies. And yet, if he had taken a page from his father's playbook and put the whole of society on trial, invoking colonial domination and its trail of evils, Mr. Serbulon had skillfully managed to spice up this overcooked stew with ingredients that transformed it completely. The result: this spectacular acquittal, tempered only by a few months of community service. What exactly would that entail? Come on! This wasn't the time to ask for details. Nobody had a clue what that meant. Dieudonné found himself squeezed, almost smothered against the flabby chest of his grandmother, Arbella, and, taken aback by his own emotion, he kissed her wrinkled cheek, soft as blotting paper, for the first time in years. For there was little love lost between them. She was no doting grandma, Arbella. However, that day, Dieudonné understood that the poor woman had done what she could. Not much. Not her fault. With no hard feelings, he also embraced his mother's older sister Fanniéta—his godmother, in keeping with tradition, who had so often predicted that he would end up in jail—as well as her partner, Magloire, the only member of the family Dieudonné liked, and, finally, all of his cousins. He spotted Ana's blonde braid but—surprise of surprises!—she kept her distance. For the photo for *France-Caraïbe* news, he willingly took up the appropriate pose by his lawyer's side. As he headed down the courthouse stairs, the burning air on his cheeks and the shouts in his ears from the crowd contained behind the shields of the riot police tortured him. Hundreds of hands were waving like butterflies; jumbled voices declared their satisfaction. Had he become a hero without knowing it? In his stupor, his feet missed two steps, and he nearly collapsed to the ground. A television crew from Martinique had dispatched its technicians and set up its cameras, for the angry staff at the local station had been occupying its headquarters for a good month. This time, Dieudonné placed himself a little to the back, almost outside the frame, and the picture offered up on the evening news was one of a young boy, timid and awkward, too tall and muscular for his clothes. You would think he had grown and filled out even while in prison. Yes, let Serbulon show off and parade about. This victory was his. It was the triumph of his intelligence. Dieudonné himself was just a minor character with no real say at all. At the same time, a feeling was starting to blossom within him that resembled happiness. He was free. But another thought instantly besieged him. Free? That meant what? Free to do what?

Concretely, for the time being, freedom meant the lingering diesel fumes, the hawkish sun soaring above his head, the Saint-Jean-de-Obispo Cathedral at the bend in the road, gargantuan and graceless, and the stench of trash strewn about, up and down the sidewalks, for the sanitation department was on strike, too. It had been months now. Those city-dwellers who hadn't sought refuge with their *bitako* cousins in the countryside took turns cleaning up this garbage and burning it in huge bonfires out in the mangrove past the Lothaire bridge. Dieudonné was astonished by the changes. During the eighteen months he had been locked up awaiting judgment, the demolition workers had lost no time. They had leveled the Rancil post office housed in one of the rare dwellings dating back to the beginning of the century, and an ultramodern luxury apartment building with balconies and terraces had taken its place. It was christened "Tropical Garden." The country was in its death throes, spilling its lifeblood out all sides. But exoticism was going strong. At the corner of Rue Camille-Auguste, the Noblécourt grocery store, the "largest supermarket in the Caribbean" as the ads had trumpeted when it opened some two years before with a parade of majorettes through the neighborhood, had resigned itself once and for all to closing its doors. Twice, its security guards had been fatally wounded. Today, it had lost its luster. Its walls were stained and striped with all manner of graffiti slogans, some simplistic or even vulgar—"Blan dèro" (Whites Out), "Fwansé foukan" (Fuck Off, French People)—others nobler, attesting to a wholesome education—"Revolution or Death," "We shall live free or die martyrs."

In the middle of the small family group, the silhouettes of Fanniéta and Magloire moved off in the direction of the Place des Écarts, before skirting it prudently. A sign of the times—bad times—under the century-old sandbox trees, once the pride of the town and an attraction for tourists who came from afar to contemplate them, there were no more babies asleep in the arms of their *das* wearing madras head scarves and stiffly starched aprons, no more baby buggies as majestic as the carriages of olden days, no bourgeois children decked out and primped with devotion, trundling along, knock-kneed. Instead: police officers. Police on patrol, two by two, revolvers on their hip. The sea, with its violet gums, bore scents of decay. In another sign of bad times, the tourism bureau, towering at the edge of the square in a magnificent home with a garden and courtyard bequeathed to the state by the Boyleau-Peyrellac family, had been vandalized time and time again, its clapboard shingles torn off, its tile roof dismantled, its windows gutted, and its statues decapitated, to the point that it had definitively closed. But what tormented people the most were the dogs. The Place des Écarts had become their rendezvous point. One fine morning, a throng had emerged from every neighborhood in Port-Mahault, from every district and even adjacent towns, a frenzied herd, emaciated and mangy, baring hostile fangs in menacing rictuses. Some galloped around at all hours of the day, through the once carefully raked walkways bearing graceful botanic names: Allée des Lataniers, Allée des Bauhinias, Allée des Musendas. Other, more homebody types had taken up residence in the concert gazebo, where they continually made love, the females whining revoltingly while mating. Obviously, all of this came with reeking piles of excrement, hard and dry like those of goats, dropped just about everywhere on the lawn, or, at the other extreme, bile-colored purees spread around the gerberas and the areca palms.

Dieudonné and Arbella climbed into Mr. Serbulon's gleaming BMW. The lawyer stopped at one of the rare service stations still open for business, and the attendant, in his red uniform with a flower-shaped seashell stamped on the middle of his back, recognized him as well as his client. He showered effusive greetings on the latter, as is proper for a hero of the people, a thief with honor, a crooner, or a movie star, and once again, Dieudonné wondered if this fervor was really meant for him. Somewhere along the line someone had mixed something up.

After raising her five children in a hovel by the canal, Arbella, in her old age, had been relocated to Morne Julien. The municipality had taken a half hectare of land covered with gooseberries and Spanish tamarinds, a paradise for truants and lovers, and converted it into a housing project: four rigid, towering, six-story pyramids, surrounded by a thick wall resembling that of a prison. Seated in a booth where a fan spun uselessly, two popular-militia volunteers dressed in faded fatigues were checking visitors' IDs. They, too, recognized the lawyer and his client. They stood up to salute the first with respect while avoiding the eyes of the second. No doubt about it! If they had been part of the jury and it was up to them alone, they would have made an example out of this good-for-nothing. He would have become old bones in prison, old bones kept safely behind bars. But these days, people made up excuses for every crime, pardoned every heinous act. As a result, criminality dogged the country from north to south, spreading and multiplying thick as weeds.

Good Lord, what terrible times these were! One after the other, the country's services were shutting down, like the organs of a body in failing health. Heart, liver, lungs, spleen. The most spectacular strike had been that of the hospital nurses and nursing assistants. It had ended when the doctors, in desperation, had lain down on the scorched lawn and refused to touch even a drop of water until emergency services, at the very least, were operating again. The problem was that no one knew what to do with all the dead. The refrigerated storage units at the morgue were overflowing. To prevent decomposition, cadavers were being covered with bars of ice. The most unpopular strike had been the city services walkout. For months, in Port-Mahault as in most municipalities, the sanitation department was no longer functioning, and trash was piling up in the streets, in gutters, on the sidewalks, and wherever there was room. It was impossible to obtain birth certificates, death certificates, or any personal records. Children were being born to unidentified parents. The dead were burying the dead. No marriages could be registered, which meant that more and more people were living together unwed, and the priests were predicting an influx of belated *béni-rété* ceremonies when everything went back to normal.

In Arbella's living room, boiling hot behind its closed shutters, Mr. Serbulon took a seat facing the Sony wide-screen television. It had been a present from her eldest son, who had emigrated to the Côtes-d'Armor. Another son managed more or less to earn his living in Marseille. The third daughter had married a man from Dominica she had met in Guadeloupe, and now she lived in Toronto, where she'd had to switch to English. That's the way families were today, dismembered and flung to the four corners of the planet! In Arbella's case, this dispersal manifested itself in the disparate character of her furniture. Besides this state-of-the-art television, there was a three-seat black leatherette sofa from the second son, a fan and a garnet-red velvet recliner equipped with vibrating massage from the daughter in Toronto, as well as a traditional mahogany pedestal table, a gift from Fanniéta. The lawyer took off his jacket, revealing the patches of sweat on his shirt, loosened his tie, and then seized the old lady's hand, as she had started to cry. Tears of relief? Gratitude? Probably both at once, we might wager. In a hodgepodge of reassuring words (once again, he had pulled out his Creole), he swore to her that never again would her grandmotherly heart suffer what it had suffered. From this day forward, he would be the father, the big brother, the uncle that Dieudonné had never had. If he had been paying attention to such claims, Dieudonné might have had cause for concern about the future being prepared for him. But he wasn't listening, knowing that these were words without weight or consequence, hollow promises as empty as the wind or a dream. In a few days, Mr. Serbulon would forget him and everything would go back to normal. Unemployment. Loneliness. Boredom. Boredom. Loneliness. Unemployment.

Because she was no longer there to transform his life.

The door opened in a burst of laughter. The group of relatives arrived with Magloire and Fanniéta, who were brandishing a bottle of champagne. Magloire popped the cork extra loudly and spiritedly since the liquid was warm. Four hours of electricity per day, rotating sector by sector. No one could chill anything or even preserve it longer than a day. Everything went bad. Baby formula for the infants, plain yogurts for the elderly. When the round of champagne was done, Fanniéta spread out the embroidered tablecloth reserved for special occasions, while on a charcoal cook stove—the only place to buy butane now was on the black market, too expensive for those on a budget—Arbella started reheating the inescapable colombo curry. Soon, saffron-yellow and creamy, spiked with cubes of eggplant and bilimbi, it bubbled in the soup pot next to a dish of white rice studded with red chilies. Colombo was part of every celebration. Birthdays, baptisms, marriages . . . Only on Christmas did it take a day off, replaced by pork stew and pigeon peas. Throughout the country mealtime talk generally revolved around the same stubborn problems: the strikes, the shortages, the break-ins, the murders, the rapes. People lamented the state of things. People worked themselves into a fright. Thanks to Mr. Serbulon's presence, the conversation avoided this rut. He joked, regaled his audience with anecdotes from his trials, moved them with touching stories, and had them roaring with laughter.

Meanwhile, Dieudonné fought to suppress his nausea. He had always hated the very smell of colombo. The guests were guffawing, but he suddenly felt extremely worn out. For him, what would tomorrow be made of? Where was he going to sleep tonight? Where would he stay in the days after that? Would he have to go back to living with Arbella? He really would have liked to turn his back on all these people, get on a plane, and head for Jamaica. In jail, the Ramah Jah family, locked up for having followed the biblical precept and grown ganja instead of sugarcane, had extolled to him the splendors of Negril. The sand was white as cotton. The Rasta-men freely banged blonde Americans who gave them mixed-race children they nourished with the milk of their breasts. Yes, but in Jamaica people speak English, a language that his trimester at Jules-Verne Junior High had completely soured him on. For the prosecutor had lied through his teeth; there was nothing illiterate about Dieudonné. He had even successfully completed his school certificate. Until that fateful year of 1989, his education had rolled along without any bumps or complications. Not first in his class, but not last either. Despite those fits that took hold of him and transformed him into a zombie. The neighbors suspected it was *mal kadik,* and urged his mother, Marine, to have him seen by the hospital. When she finally made up her mind to do it, after a round of visits to various *kimbwazè,* a doctor from the mainland had explained that what they were dealing with was a genetic disorder. A genetic disorder? In plain language, that meant a disease that can't be cured. Even so, out of pure formality, he had prescribed pills that cost an arm and a leg. But it was obvious that he didn't really believe in what he was doing.

For people in the Americas, 1989 is the year of Hurricane Hugo. The Terrible One sowed desolation all the way up to the USA, where it made the Carolinas cry. It buried Martinique in shrouds of mud and practically wiped Guadeloupe off the map. For Dieudonné, Hugo was one of the most unforgettable events of his childhood. He was just over ten years old. Since her house on Morne Lafleur was about as solid as a cow pie, Marine had taken refuge with Fanniéta, who at the time was working as the manager of a high-rise apartment complex built to last. Under her sturdy roof Fanniéta was also sheltering her companion of the moment, Élie, and her string of children, along with Arbella and two of her friends. While the old women sang hymns, told the beads of rosaries blessed in Lourdes, and cried at each rant of thunder and howl of the winds, Élie, Marine, and Fanniéta relived all of the tribulations caused by the long line of cyclones visited year after year upon the country: Betsy, Flora, David, Allen. They agreed that Hugo's malice surpassed them all. During this time, the young people, ten or so in all, had gathered in the bathroom. Élie's three boys had pulled the clothes off of Hélène, Fanniéta's eldest daughter, and had taken turns on top of her, one after the other, in front of her younger brothers' smirking eyes. Dieudonné had not dared admit that he knew nothing of womankind, and so, beset with terror, he had tried to imitate the others when his turn came. By that point, Hélène, who had been smiling and docile at first, had had enough and wasn't going along with it anymore. She was whimpering, scratching, writhing, and twisting around every which way, exhibiting her plump stomach, her slender thighs, and her bloody pubis under a sparse bush of hair. So, Dieudonné had charged forward with his head down like a bull in the arena. However, the whole thing had ended abruptly; he had come up short and burst into tears, while around him his audience jeered at him in contempt:

"Makoumè! Makoumè!"

Nine months later, Hélène gave birth to a little girl. Stung by her mother's slaps, badgered by her grandmother's pleas, and scorned by the neighbors, she had still refused to open her mouth, going only so far as to name the newborn Huguette, as if in defiance.

Just the same, the children had found other, more wholesome ways to amuse themselves that night. Back in the living room with their elders, they had cut out peepholes in the sheet of plywood protecting the picture window, and by the glow of the lightning bolts they watched everything from roofing sheet metal to tree trunks, parked cars, and catamarans in the marina spinning like tops in the wind. Around midnight, a wave higher than Chauve Mountain had unfurled, drowning the neighborhood with its raging waters and mounting an assault on the windows. Abruptly, in the morning, around seven o'clock, everything had become calm. The freshly washed sky started shining again, and the sun sparkled between the last tiny, tiny drops of rain.

A few days after that memorable September night, the catastrophe that was to change Dieudonné's life unfolded. Marine, ever active, got up on her roof to reattach the shorn-off sheet metal herself. All of a sudden—was it a dizzy spell? Did her foot slip on some wet leaves? We will never know exactly what transpired. The fact remains that she fell crashing down like an overripe breadfruit right at the feet of her terrorized son. The neighbors had come running, flocking around, curious and concerned; the ambulance had arrived at top speed; the injured woman was transported to the hospital. After her fall, she lingered for five years, paralyzed from head to toe, hunched up in an armchair, living through her eyes, which ate up her now-gaunt face. Then she ended up dying, and Dieudonné, who had never met his papa, found himself all alone in this world.

One could say that Marine had not had a good life. She was a beautiful black woman, though, with sapodilla skin, as they say, and thirty-two pearly teeth. The only thing she lacked was luck. Good luck. For a time, she had run a little *lolo,* which had caved to competition from the supermarkets and other megastores. Then she had tried her hand at selling at the street market, but she had neither the gift for smooth talk nor the stoutness needed to go toe-to-toe with the matriarchs. So she had hired herself out, as if she hadn't received her *brevet* certificate from Sadi-Carnot Junior High, and she started cooking for strangers, washing their dirty laundry, scouring their floors. As for men, she would hear nothing more about them. They had worn her heart thin, and her body too. Some of them had eaten up what little money she had. All of them had hurt her in every sort of way, so much so that she had determined to raise the son she had reaped from one of them all by herself, without anyone's help. Behind closed doors, the family would whisper that if she had wanted, she could have lived out her days in the lap of luxury, because Dieudonné's father was not some nobody. Far from it, on the contrary. But Marine didn't take advice and stubbornly did as she pleased. One year, she found work with the Cohen family: the husband, a pilot for Air-Alizés, the wife, a teacher at Saint-Esprit Junior High, and their three children. That was the sunniest period in her life. The Cohens, who were from the Pyrénées-Orientales area, didn't just behave like good bosses. They also tolerated her sensitivity, her mood swings, her outbursts—anyone would think they were afraid of her—and, above all, they adored her little boy. The proof being that he called them Mama and Papa. They took him to the doctor regularly and bought him his medications. They took him along on cruises and, putting flippers on his feet, taught him to dart this way and that in the belly of the sea. These mountain-dwellers had fallen passionately in love with the ocean. Thanks to scrimping and saving they had bought a large, 35-foot sailboat, perfectly organized to maximize space. They had christened it *La Belle Créole* and sailed all the way to Antigua, St. Martin, St. Barth, and the Grenadines. For entire days and nights they drifted on their cockleshell, between the blue of the sky and the foam of the waves! Their ears resounded with the blast of the enraged winds! Their eyes drank their fill of the open sea in its incalculable vastness. Alas! The good luck of some makes for the misfortune of others, goes the well-known popular saying. After years earning miserable pay at Air-Alizés, Vincent Cohen was offered a job as a pilot for Swissair, an international company far more prestigious than the rickety collection of crates that was the local fleet. Gathering up his wife and children, he bid the country adieu and sold everything he owned. Only the monohull had remained, docked at the marina, the residue of former dreams. In these times of crisis, no one wanted to buy it. What is inexplicable is that, once outside the country, the Cohens gave Dieudonné no further sign of life. No more cards at Christmas, no more cards at New Year's. Which proves that this second popular saying is also true: out of sight, out of mind. As a result, in thinking back on these years of his life, the boy wondered at times if he hadn't dreamed them.

Because of his mother's illness and then death, Dieudonné's seizures increased. Sometimes, he awoke deafened by the clamor of a freight train barreling under his skull. Other times, he was so weak that he lay prostrate on his bed, unable to open his eyes and curled up like a fetus. He was mercilessly crossed off the school rolls because of his absences. Searching for relief, he realized that crack took the edge off his pain. (On this point, however well inclined he was toward him, Mr. Serbulon had not believed him: that he was ill, not a depraved junkie.) He had discovered the powers of the magic powder. All he had to do was fill up his nostrils and inhale, inhale until the earth became round again, filled with colors, flavors, and fragrances. It was Rodrigue who had introduced him to crack. The police had nicknamed Rodrigue "Public Enemy No. 1." Mr. Serbulon never called him anything but "The Angel of Evil." Picture a *chabin,* with very light skin, golden hair cutting a jagged silhouette above a pronounced forehead, and eyes like two deep pockets of seawater. Rodrigue and Dieudonné lived in two neighboring cabins on Morne Lafleur. Their mothers, who had known each other since their school days, had given birth to them the same day, the same year, in the same hospital. On their birthdays, neither one of them had the means to offer her kid a cake with frosting or a party with friends to help blow out the candles and sing a chorus of "Happy Birthday." At best, they planted a kiss on their foreheads before hurrying off to their inglorious work. So it was that one April 14th, Rodrigue had gone into a supermarket and, right under the guards' noses, had come back out with an eight-slice apple tart, some Paris-Brest pastries, and bottles of cider. For good measure, he had also carried off two cured Toulouse sausages and some white bread, which he adored. That was his first real theft. Up to that point, he had only pinched some ballpoint pens, erasers, and compasses at school like everyone else. After this success, nothing could stop him. He started stealing bigger and bigger items: refrigerators, television sets, washing machines, stereo systems, cars, and, one time, a truck. In addition, he became a dealer. He bought crack from Colombians on Bonne-Marie Island and resold it to eager adolescents at the gates of school grounds. On top of all this, he was always surrounded by girls, attracted to his white skin like flies to honey. A good dancer too, and a rapper when he was in the mood. But now his luck had turned. A week or two before Dieudonné, he had gone to jail for a crime that the jury could not forgive, and they were making him pay a high price for it.

Marine's death had serious repercussions. Dieudonné had to leave Morne Lafleur, where he was born, where he grew up, and where he had suffered alongside his mother. In a word, he had to abandon his home and all of his memories. Because, at the age of fifteen, how could he take care of himself? Wash his clothes? Buy shoes? Life is stitched together by scores of these mundane necessities. First he had lived with his godmother, Fanniéta. But, following Hélène's complaints, she had quickly pushed him out the door. Next, Arbella, who did after all have a sense of family loyalty, had pitched in. She had bought a pull-out sofa that she squeezed into a corner of her cabin, and, honest to God, Dieudonné didn't sleep too badly there. But the old lady grumbled if, upon returning from sunrise Mass, she found him snoring, and criticized him for every little thing. Because he was no longer going to school, because his crook of a friend Rodrigue visited him too often, because he wolfed down food like an *alouvi grand falle,* because he stole the 100-franc bills she kept hidden in her dresser for safekeeping. After a few months bearing this cross, he began to wonder whether he could share Rodrigue's room. But Rodrigue lived in cramped quarters with his mother, three little sisters, and two younger brothers. That's when he had an inspiration: the *Belle Créole!* The *Belle Créole* was just lingering there at the end of the dock with her berths, her galley, her dinette, and a "For Sale" sign hanging around her neck. Getting more and more dilapidated, more and more neglected, since the agency that was supposed to be taking care of it had packed it all in and gone back to the mainland.

The Mégisserie marina was located at the back of Saint-Christophe Bay, a stone's throw from the capital, Port-Mahault. A marina is the rudeness of dry land transformed into a flowing wave. On this liquid brow, shifting and shimmering, the great sailing boats, monohulls and multihulls, jostle past one another in their impatience to get the hell out to open sea, and the catamaran, which comes from Sri Lanka, ferries dreams on its slim moorings. Saint-Christophe Bay formed a perfect arc, as if drawn with a compass. On the right, travelers could admire the rising mauve bulk of Haute-Terre and the Chauve Mountain volcanic crater, ever shrouded in smoke. On the left, the uneven line of residences in Sainte-Marie and Marbelle, low and white in the sultry *pié-bwa* thickets. Straight ahead, the proud ocean, which knows no limits. In the past, the Mégisserie marina was a floating city, a Hong Kong crowded with junks. Then pleasure boaters had deserted the country. Little by little, the waves of the sea regained their empire of peace. Dieudonné almost cried when he saw the *Belle Créole*. The pride of her owners and apple of their eye was at present a painful sight with her rusted hull, her paint flaking off in leprous patches, and her rigging in a pitiful state. Rats, roaches, spiders, and ants caroused in every corner. Mud daubers had built their mud nests smack in the middle of the dinette. The showers were no longer working in the head. The toilets were clogged. Dieudonné spent hours brushing, scouring, lathering, and rinsing everything with bucketfuls of seawater. At the end of the afternoon, he settled into the aft berth, the very same one he had shared back in the day with David and Benjamin Cohen. And it was as if past and present had come together again. As if Marine wasn't under the ground. As if he had become a kid again, and, honest to God, a kid no unhappier than any other. He arranged his treasures. A photo of Marine disguised as a *jablesse* for carnival. One of himself as a baby in Arbella's arms, chubby and cute in his romper. Another of David, Benjamin, and Rebecca Cohen, naked as jaybirds, tanned and curly-haired like little Arab children. A poster of Manhattan, the huge square windows of its skyscrapers blinking wide-eyed in the night. Then he went to bed. Unfortunately, at the start of the evening Rodrigue turned up, flanked by a pair of cheap beauties in glitzy *sousoun klairant* dresses perched high on wedge heels. He criticized the place and pronounced it a pigsty, though this didn't prevent him from holing himself up in the forward berth with his conquests and making them squeal with pleasure, one after the other or both at the same time.

Around midnight, Dieudonné couldn't stand it anymore and jumped back out onto the dock. He himself never made love and didn't really miss it much. The whole effort of seduction was beyond him. He didn't know how to give the right compliments, joke, or dance. In his company, women, at first drawn to him because of his physique, grew bored and, disappointed, left him high and dry.

At that time, despite the rise in thefts, Port-Mahault wasn't really dangerous. Curfews were unknown. There were no armed police patrols, no security guards stationed at the door to every bar and restaurant. People could stroll around as much as they wished in the Mégisserie neighborhood and ogle the tourists scarfing down platters of seafood. No bones about it, those folks treated themselves to a good time. Soon, foggy with rum ti punches, their stomachs heavy with crawfish, they would be off dancing awkwardly to the sounds of zouk. Yet no one mocked them; they were gods to whom all was permitted. Still, among the batch Dieudonné couldn't help but pity the single women out alone: jittery, talking too loudly, they would splutter with laughter at the least little thing. Sometimes, he would follow them all the way to the doors of the nightclubs and stand guard to wait. Some would come back out hanging on the arm of some stud in a tight dress shirt, his Levi's hugging his butt and his cock. The others came out empty-handed. These he would trail behind without trying to approach them, even when they turned their heads and shot him inviting glances.

2

That first night was the night he met Boris.

It had started to rain. One of those showers that just drop on you without warning, soak everything in their path from every blade of grass to every *pié-bwa*, and then disappear just as they came. He had run to take cover in an abandoned bus stop. A homeless man seemed to be sleeping there, wrapped up in bits of sky-blue plastic. At the noise Dieudonné made shaking himself off and swearing, he stuck his head out, furious, but then, undoubtedly softened by the presence before him, he had greeted him in a flowery French-French and introduced himself:

"Boris Gamel. Man of letters. French and Creole poet. For I write in both languages. Yes, I know it is good form to use Creole alone. But for my part I consider Creole and French to be the two sides of my personality, the southern slope and the northern slope. Why, then, would I mutilate myself by writing exclusively in Creole? I am the author of *Dé mo, kat'pawol, Confluence* . . . to cite only my best works. Edited with care by my own hand with the Bon Vent printing press—an auspicious name, bidding me 'Godspeed.'"

If it hadn't been raining so hard, all this gabbing would have chased Dieudonné away. He didn't like to talk. He especially didn't like people who talked, filling their mouths with words and sounds. For years on end, it was in silence that he had cared for his mother. They had pierced a hole in her throat for her thin voice to come through, muffled and gravelly. She never used it, directing her son instead by looks and signs, and thanking him in the same way.

Just a year before, Boris had been a pretty average guy: a beat-up Japanese car in the garage, a two-bedroom apartment, furnished well enough, in the Fleurie complex. His only distinguishing feature was that he was a poet. At the bookstore where he was responsible for the textbook section, he followed after hurried mothers, schoolchildren, and high school students, thrusting his poems into their hands. At every opportunity, he would recite them. On Saturdays, he would show up at the Poet's Circle. Then the wife he adored left him. We don't know exactly what prompted this abandonment. (Besides, do we ever know why people split up?) The couple seemed close. People assume, with no proof whatsoever, that she got tired of a husband who put all his ambitions into literature and wasted their household income on printing costs. Luckily, Boris and his partner, Ixaura, had no girls or boys. That made one less child of divorce in the world, at least. Because of the dramatic turn in their relations, Boris, heartbroken, had quit his job at the bookstore, even though he was their prized jewel, and had fallen into rum. He plummeted rapidly. In less than a year, he had quarreled with his family, fallen out with his friends, who reproached him for his sudden excessive drinking, and ended up on the Mégisserie docks. Curiously, once there he no longer touched a single drop of alcohol. But alcohol was in him and refused to loosen its grip. He seemed always to be drunk. He accosted drivers stopping at the Texaco station next to the marina, which was open twenty-four hours a day, forcing his drivel into their hands. People were frightened by this man who wouldn't have hurt a fly.

Did Boris have talent? This sort of question shouldn't be asked, because it has no answer. For some, he was an unsung national bard, the only true champion of popular culture. For others, a weak rhymester and a first-class bore. What is clear is that, from that meeting on, Dieudonné, who had no other friends besides Rodrigue, gained a second one. The contrast was striking. Rodrigue talked only break-ins, hold-ups, and armed robberies. His role model was a certain Fernando Diaz, who had brought the Santo Domingo police to their knees before fleeing first to Montreal, then New York, where he was still on the run. Boris was an idealist, for a time a militant activist, and still a fervent nationalist. Often, at the end of the afternoon, curious onlookers gathered around the bus stop and Boris, thrilled, would address them in a schoolmasterly tone. He would recite his poems, or else the many aphorisms he was brimming with, to the delight of his audience:

"The intellectual in this country is like a zoo animal, born and raised in captivity. Accustomed to being hand-fed by others, he can do nothing by himself."

Or another:

"Our country is like a bird without wings. Incapable of taking off, and still less of soaring. It drags us all down into its mud."

Or, he'd hold forth on the authors he admired, expressing his passion for two geniuses, one English and the other Chilean, Shakespeare and Neruda. Among the works of the first, he had a particular fondness for *Othello, The Moor of Venice*, the tragedy of a man who had gotten up the courage to kill the woman who had betrayed him. He recited, with a somewhat questionable accent but with the right emotion:

It is the very error of the moon,
She comes more near the earth than she was wont
And makes men mad.

Of the other, he favored the *Canto General* and declaimed, with just as questionable an accent:

El jaguar tocaba las hojas
con su ausencia fosforescente,
el puma corre en el ramaje
como el fuego devorador.

As a general rule, he was dismayed by Dieudonné's indifference; the latter rarely opened his mouth and had no more interest in poetry than he did in robbing people.

In fact, what exactly did this guy care about? Mystery of mysteries!

As far as character traits go, the only thing that one could pin down about him was his attachment to the sea.

Every day that God creates, Dieudonné would arrive at Le Goulet and swim the distance to the cay twice, in that moment of silence before the first Mass, when the town was still sleeping, and no beachgoers had yet left their Friday's track in the white sand. The early-rising fishermen launching their boats would see him cross himself piously and drink three mouthfuls of water three times in keeping with custom before making his first strokes. They especially admired the way he could swim so long in the deep. Sometimes, anxious, they thought he would never resurface. And then he would reappear where you didn't expect him, a black comma on the white foam of the waves. Next he'd alight on the beach skirting the cay, taking a breather for a few minutes before setting off on the return trip and then starting all over again. The whole thing lasted an hour. Charmed, the little *chabine* who ran the shop at the corner of Rue du Général-de-Gaulle would watch him replenish himself with food, ravenous after so much exertion. He was so attractive, she thought. In her opinion his body rivaled Arnold Schwarzenegger's, only darker, of course. What she particularly liked was that he wasn't vain about it at all and didn't swagger and flex like the usual neighborhood muscleheads. When he ordered his two codfish sandwiches and a double café au lait, his voice was measured, a murmur. He always thanked her effusively. What she doesn't admit is that to her great dismay he never responded to her advances. Killer smiles, knowing *koudzyé*, swaying hips: nothing worked.

You'd think he didn't have eyes to see.

If you had asked Dieudonné and he had managed to explain himself, he would have responded that first he had lost the Cohens, his adoptive parents, and then his mother, Marine. Only the sea had never abandoned him. Whenever he needed her, he always found her in the same place; boiling in the dry season, cool in the muggy rainy season; always quick to wrap herself around his body and greet him with the moist kiss of her mouth.

One could also note—and such a thing is surprising in this boy who everyone agreed appeared so sweet, so reserved—his love for *kokdjèm*. For a time, he owned twenty or so. When he was living with Marine, you might think he raised them to support his invalid mother, because a *kokdjèm* that wins cockfights brings in a lot of money. However, you could see that it wasn't necessity alone; he threw himself into it with a passion. He spoke to them as if they were living people. Once a week, he rubbed their plumage with tafia spirits blended with cinnamon and nutmeg. Then, he coated them with lemon. Once a week, he gave them egg yolks to eat, mixed with corn and banana, and added guinea pepper to warm up their blood. He wasn't satisfied until his *kokdjèm* were so mean that they attacked his hands when he fed them and tried to rip them to shreds with their beaks. Every Sunday, he would choose two of the most ferocious, trim their tail feathers so they wouldn't gather sand, and clip the tips of their wings too. Then he would take the bus to the Marylebone cockpit. Marylebone is the most renowned cockpit in the country, where the bets can reach colossal figures. Dieudonné's *kokdjèm* didn't need steel spurs in order to win all the fights. One of them, which people had christened Lucifer because of his blood-red color, took fourteen victories in a row. This earned him a half-page spread in *France-Caraïbe*.

That was the first time Dieudonné appeared in that newspaper. There is even a photo illustrating the article: in it, one can see a teenager, very tall for his age, his facial features still taking shape. Will he be an angel, or a beast? The Good Lord alone knows. Dieudonné's circle of relations didn't care much for this *kokdjèm*-rearing. When Fanniéta took him in, the first thing she asked him was to get rid of those satanic creatures, those beasts of hell. He obeyed, sold them, and got a lot of money out of them, but Rodrigue recalls that he cried his eyes out. During the trial, Mr. Serbulon carefully refrained from mentioning those moments when his client, amidst a din of roars and insults, indulged in this bloody sport.

People might have imagined that it concealed some vicious core, some violent nature.

3

Once the colombo was eaten, after a reasonable period of digestion, Mr. Serbulon put his Giorgio Armani jacket back on over his increasingly sweat-soaked shirt and cheerily asked permission to get on the road. It was his way of taking leave. He embraced Arbella and Fanniéta warmly, shook everyone's hands heartily, planted himself in front of Dieudonné, mock-stern and brotherly at the same time, and commanded:

"I want to see you tomorrow morning at seven o'clock in my office."

What he would do with Dieudonné, what he would say to him when he saw him Matthias really didn't know. No one could say what counted as community service. Without waiting for an answer, then, he sprinted down the stairs. His BMW was waiting placidly for him in the shade of a mango tree. As soon as he sat down behind the wheel, he felt his eyes fog over. A terrible fatigue bent him over double, like a spent old man, and he rested against the leather cushions to catch his breath. Over! It was over and he had won! He felt as if he hadn't touched a single glass of whiskey or eaten a red snapper soup or banged one of his mistresses for ages and ages. As if it had been forever since he had admired the sun rising or setting behind Dominica from his splendid terrace or feared the oncoming storm as he watched the sky darken. All the while, in his oblivion, the days had added together to form weeks, and weeks had added up to months. In truth, he had been appointed by the court and had taken this case on without much enthusiasm before understanding what it could mean for his career. However, as soon as he saw Dieudonné, he was seized with affection for him and had promised himself he would save him. His youth. His fragility. How vulnerable he seemed. Very quickly, he had realized that this wasn't an easy client. After months of meetings, he barely knew the sound of Dieudonné's voice. At first, he had pleaded with him or admonished him, depending on the moment:

"Talk to me! Talk to me! My God! How do you think I can do this if you keep your lips sealed like a safe?"

Then he had resigned himself to Dieudonné's silences, understanding that it wasn't stubbornness, bad will, or impertinence. Dieudonné was trying. Yet he didn't know how to present the facts, explain them, connect a cause to its effect. So, he had gone to work all by himself, constructing the real based on his imagination like a novelist, patiently building and rejecting various versions of the drama. When, finally, one of them had satisfied him, he had schooled his mute client:

"Now listen and listen good! This is the way it happened, you hear me?"

He would remember that moment forever. They were sitting facing each other in a visitation room reeking of pine-scented disinfectant mixed with bleach, himself perched on a hard iron chair, Dieudonné seated on a no less uncomfortable stool. Working from his notes, he had spoken for more than an hour, choosing simple words, precise words suitable for a story that was on the whole banal, unworthy under other skies of making front-page news. For, at the end of the day, everything could be summed up in a few sentences: tired of being humiliated, a lover gets rid of his mistress. What endowed it with symbolism was that the whole affair was taking place in this country fresh out of slavery (well, maybe not so fresh, one hundred and fifty years on), that the mistress was white, and a *békée* moreover, and the lover was black. The mistress was rich, and the black man, her gardener, without a penny to his name. When he had stopped talking, Dieudonné, who had listened without moving a muscle, his expression inscrutable as usual, had lost his impassivity. He had stared at him with his *kako*-colored eyes, too light for his skin. Then he had turned his face to the wall, his chest suddenly heaving with hiccups, with sobs. Serbulon had decided to take this first display of emotion for the confession he no longer hoped would come.

Now that everything had been brought to completion, Dieudonné had been acquitted, and not even the Good Lord in heaven himself could reopen the matter or reverse it, Serbulon was tortured by the private conviction that he had been wrong all down the line. What had he misunderstood, deciphered incorrectly? What piece of the puzzle had he placed upside down?

He left Port-Mahault and dashed off at breakneck speed down the road, which at that hour was mostly free of traffic. He loved speed. Not because it gave him a sense of power as it does for the common populace. On the contrary. Because it made him remember his fragility. At eighty miles an hour, he was at the mercy of a careless child, a stray dog, a roaming cow popping up right in front of the hood as they always do, a flat tire, or an angry driver bent on proving his virility at all costs. Because of this, at the end of his race he always extracted himself from his hot rod sweating with relief. A roadblock had been erected near the Sainte-Marie Cemetery, facing the tombs, which, in the sunlight, resembled oxpecker birds scattered in the undergrowth. Formerly, Sainte-Marie had been a tourism gem: swimmers, windsurfers, tick-ridden dogs, and dinghies jockeyed with one another for space on its beach. Today, the sun poured its oil onto a deserted, white-hot sea, where it sizzled in a blaze of sparks. A line of exasperated drivers advanced haltingly while the police meticulously verified identities. Recognizing the lawyer, they, too, jokingly stood to attention before bursting into applause. Mr. Serbulon made an effort to smile.

Like all those who had recently entered the middle class, Matthias Serbulon had followed fashion and retreated as far from Port-Mahault as possible. He had built his house in Château-bon, on a piece of land that had belonged to his grandparents.

Rocky and covered in *razyé*, it had seemed to these farming folks fit only for grazing their goats. Twenty years later, the real estate developers going over the country with a fine-tooth comb had discovered that Châteaubon had a stunning view of the San Diego archipelago and, behind it, when the weather was good, of Dominica. In a snap, fortunes were built. The stony ground became peopled with villas of paradise, while, by dint of watering, Haitian gardeners made it bloom with roses and azaleas. Tapping on his remote control, Matthias opened the gated entranceway chiseled out of the thick wall studded with barbed wire. Despite such precautions, Châteaubon received regular visits; Matthias himself had been burglarized six times. At the sound of the car, Joséphine, his latest mistress, a pretty panther with black-nail-polished claws who had been a model back when she was living in Paris, hurried out, full of pride and talking excitedly. Phone calls from her friends had alerted her to her man's triumph. She cooed, proud as a peacock, thinking of her girlfriends who must be envious.

"The telephone won't stop ringing. Your dad . . . Martinique. Paris too . . ."

With a curt gesture, he cut her off. For months, Joséphine had tolerated his brusqueness, which she attributed to the concentration required for a tricky case. She was hoping that on this day of glory he would be relaxed and in the mood for laughter. Apparently he was nothing of the sort. Men! Matthias sat down on the veranda that wrapped around the villa, indifferent to the panorama that drew cries of admiration from all his visitors. Today, this molten sea was blinding him, despite his tinted glasses. Besides, this stunning view was starting to tire him. Why hadn't he gotten himself a traditional rustic house with a view of the mountain? He poured himself a whiskey to wash away the taste of Arbella's warm champagne. Nowadays, even in the most modest of homes, champagne had taken the place of rum and no one served you a good punch flavored with guineps or gooseberries anymore. That art was dying like all the rest.

He could feel it, he had been wrong all down the line. How was it possible? He had been methodical and had left nothing to chance. In this case, unfortunately, there were few witnesses.

No family, no close friends in tears. Not even any upset neighbors. A handful of prim members of the local white community, embarrassed by all this publicity, had assembled at the Saint-Jean-de-Obispo Cathedral to follow the procession to the cemetery. He had questioned the servant, whose statements had only bolstered his conclusions. Clearly she had little sympathy for Dieudonné. Were she to be believed, it broke her heart to have to witness his humiliation. She was waiting for some surge of revolt, hoping for it. However, though he hadn't consciously lied, wasn't his view of the facts influenced by the country's singular history, by the relationships between ethnic groups? What clues had he neglected? There were indeed those two bullets that the ballistics expert had discovered, one lodged in the wall, the other in the bedpost, which could mean there had been a struggle. But when he asked, Dieudonné had shaken his head frenetically. There was also that lover the painter, who had come to spend Christmas and New Year's with Loraine. But he had returned to New York before the drama unfolded and Matthias hadn't seen the use in summoning him. He suspected at present that this was a mistake. Perhaps he could have shed some new light on things. At first, Matthias had been proud of his line of argument, which he deemed Césairean, or even Fanonian. The cruel *békée* mistress. The defenseless slave. The mistress humiliates and wields the whip. One day, the slave frees himself. By killing. A baptism in blood. Now, this melodrama that had won the credulous jury over so well seemed to him to lack imagination. His actors had done no more than play out the old stock roles, donning costumes that tradition had worn thin. He had made a mistake: a modern drama, an entirely modern drama lay behind this screen with its hackneyed motifs.

On the stand, Rodrigue, to the smirking laughter of the *malnèg* men among the audience, had not hidden the fact that his friend had no taste for women. They made advances toward him because he looked so fine, a real athlete despite his young age, strong build, standing straight and tall as a *pié-bwa*, but he didn't pay any attention. Was he afraid? persisted Serbulon. Afraid? No! For him it was just a trivial thing that didn't seem to gnaw at him like it gnawed at men of all ages. Even so, this boy whom everyone unanimously described as timid and awkward had dared to set his sights on this filthy-rich *békée* and had burrowed himself a place in her bed. Even supposing that she had made the first move, she hadn't forced him. You don't force an erection. What kept the two of them together? She didn't just humiliate and subjugate him. At times, he spread her legs and administered the supreme proof that he was the master and she, nothing but a female.

At that moment, Joséphine emerged suddenly on the veranda, alongside Matthias's father, Pierre, who was having trouble hiding his discomfort at finding himself in this company. Pierre had braved the heat and driven two hours from Anse-au-Sel in his antediluvian Citroën. A basket of Amélie mangoes in hand, he couldn't wait to congratulate his son, his dearest possession in the world. In his youth, this founding member of the PPRP had been an extremist. He professed the deepest scorn for the electoral path, repeating the old refrain, "Elections are scams for idiots." People had reminded him over and over that this wasn't Cuba and good old Chauve Mountain wasn't the Sierra Maestra, but in vain; he dreamed only of guerrilla warfare. For this reason, during a palace revolution ten years earlier, he had been removed from the governing body of the party he had founded. He was a former doctor, married to one of the first women social workers in the country, who had died giving birth to Matthias. During their marriage, the couple's political opinions had seriously hobbled their financial success. Settling in the poor and pebbly North, they had spared no effort, instead opening their wallets too often to assist their clients, toiling farmers in need and swimming in debts. After the death of his wife, Pierre had continued to follow his calling, hardly distinguishable from those in his care, barely lighter-skinned, barely better shod, barely less disheveled. Everything about his son's lifestyle offended him: the luxury he surrounded himself with, the women he went out with and continually changed up, he who had lived in worship of a dead woman's memory. He didn't care for his profession. For him, lawyers were faithless, lawless beings who used their talents to defend murderers. Even Nazi war criminals. Even the perpetrators of the Rwandan genocide. Nevertheless, Matthias's success today fulfilled all his desires. It seemed to him that for once, in the age-old battle between the oppressor and the oppressed playing out incessantly the whole world over, his son had obtained justice for the weaker party and made his rights prevail. And so, he wanted to convince himself that Matthias, who, to his great dismay, had always refused it, would finally accept a career in politics. Today more than ever, what the country needed was a leader. The role that the father had never been able to land would be played by his son instead. Matthias returned his embrace half-heartedly. At a time like this, his downbeat attitude and his morose air were stupefying. But such was the boy's nature. As a child, the day he had swept up all the first-place prizes at the school awards ceremony—and was buckling under the weight of all the gilded books—he got upset over trivial things. When he had taken his place on the platform, he whined, his shirt wasn't crisply ironed. And also, these books with the golden edges, Victor Hugo, George Sand, Guy de Maupassant, weren't the ones he wanted. He preferred comic books or science fiction novels. *Dune,* for example, which he had already read six times. Pierre, disappointed, entreated Joséphine for a rum, neat. Whiskey, gin, champagne . . . Out of principle, he refused to swallow these white man's drinks and would only touch rhum agricole. When Joséphine brought him a bottle of Feneteau, he poured himself a glass large enough to knock out an ox, let the liquid burn his mouth and throat, then, with moist eyes, he turned to his son, exclaiming:

"Your mother must be proud up there!"

Thirty-five years she had been underground, yet he always called her as his witness to everything that happened to him. Matthias didn't answer. It was always painful for him to think about this mother who had chosen to leave the world at the very moment he was entering it, and who was always smiling, eternally youthful, as if nothing had happened, on every page of every photo album. Another reason he had liked Dieudonné was that they were both orphans, afflicted with that wound that will not heal, that never lets up. Deep inside himself, Matthias adored Pierre, the most generous and affectionate of fathers.

However, he had never wanted to be like him, nearing the end of his life penniless, or almost, clinging to a community and a narrow strip of land, turning over the soil again and again like a forced laborer. Because of him, Matthias had grown up in the most difficult conditions, dressed like a peasant, walking on foot under the sun because his father refused to buy himself a car. Because of him, until Matthias left to finish his studies, he had never been to France or England or any of those capitalist countries that his father condemned, returning year after year in khaki shorts and a *bakoua* hat to the same summer camp for kids in Santiago de Cuba. Now he dreamed only of traveling, of discovering the world—Africa, Asia, America, Oceania. If it had just been up to him, he would have set up his practice at the other end of the earth. One of his classmates at law school in Montpellier worked for the International Court of Justice and traveled regularly to Arusha. He, on the other hand, was here pleading divorce cases, negotiating custody arrangements, defending hotheaded neighbors killing one another with machetes, and, best of all, live-in boyfriends who had raped their girlfriends' innocent little daughters. Being lucky, this was the second time his name had come to the country's attention. A few months earlier, he had obtained an acquittal for a murderous mother he defended who had taken her twins with Down syndrome and doused them in gasoline, then set them on fire. However, he had learned to keep his dissatisfactions, his doubts, and his questions to himself, since Pierre wanted him to be a man of certainty and righteous thoughts. He asked him only, "Tell me what you think. What should we do with him now? The court is full of talk of 'community service.' Believe me, nobody knows what that is. One of my acquitted clients got lucky: he's packing Bouteille pineapples for a small cooperative of plantation owners in Salins. Another is cutting and weighing banana bunches."

Pierre had his own opinion on the matter. "He has to learn what side he belongs to—he doesn't seem to know. We are the descendants of slaves, of Africans. Making love to the daughter of those who whipped us in the cane fields and humiliated us is out of the question."

"Indeed, but what else?" Matthias replied mockingly.

Pierre, oblivious to the irony, continued, "Next, he has to learn a trade."

Has to! Has to! Still sardonic, though the other didn't perceive it, Matthias insisted, "Which one? The unemployment rate in this country is thirty-five percent."

Pierre made a long face. "He'll have to give tourism a try! It's the only field with any openings! Mind you, in my day, I did write a lot against tourism." Ten years earlier, he had, in fact, paid out of his own pocket to publish a pamphlet: *We Will No Longer Be the Brothels of the West.* "But today, you have to admit there are no other options for our young people!"

Suddenly, his voice became tinged with sadness, for this was a striking admission of failure. It meant resigning oneself to belonging to a people of lackeys. Matthias was about to remind him that it had been several years now since the tourists had deserted the country. But then he felt guilty for spoiling his joy at the occasion. For once, his father, usually so critical of his way of life, was radiant. Matthias turned to Joséphine and, mustering an enthusiastic tone, ordered, "Go get some champagne! We're going to celebrate!"

Joséphine obeyed and moved off, her hips swinging with a sensuality, *mi ta-w, mi tan mwen,* that made Pierre lower his eyes.

"Make an exception," Matthias begged him. "Have a glass with me. For the occasion!"

Pierre acquiesced with a nod, grumbling, though, that he shouldn't mix drinks. He was still planning on going back to Anse-au-Sel that night.

"Oh, come on!" said Pierre. "You can sleep here."

When Joséphine returned, father and son were holding hands, at peace. The setting sun reddened their skins, and their faces seemed painted for some mysterious ceremony.

The country was split into two factions. The fortunate, who possessed generators, and the unfortunate, who did not. Obviously, Matthias belonged to the first group: the bottle of Veuve Clicquot that Joséphine brought was chilled to perfection.

DUSK

4

The weather had cooled off, for the dethroned sun had begun its descent into its abyss. In the already faded light, Dieudonné considered the patchy fabric of rooftops spread out below the windows. Under these roofs, in this jumble of houses, he had not a single friend who cared about him; not a single woman waiting expectantly for him, desiring him. Rodrigue was out of the game; he had years to go in the Basse-Pointe prison. Where was Boris? He had come to visit him early on, when Dieudonné had first been remanded. Ever the talker, he was full of solemn, grandiloquent words:

"Didn't I tell you both, you and Rodrigue, that you were heading for hell down different paths? Now look! The two of you in the darkest depths of the pit."

Moreover, he was agitated and uneasy in the company of all these bad boys. Feverishly, he kept asking Dieudonné, "What did that guy do? And that one?"

After a few awkward visits, he had disappeared. Some time after that, some prisoners had cut his photo out of a *France-Caraïbe* page that someone had used as wrapping paper for a package, and the wildest tales had started going around. Prisons and psychiatric hospitals are alike as two drops of water: everybody there paints reality in the colors that please them and Dieudonné wasn't having any of it.

He nearly cried out in his loneliness and turned toward Arbella. "Grandma, I'm going out."

Where was he going? Around him, everybody's ears pricked up. He took pity on his grandmother's look of panic, and to calm her, murmured, "I'm just going for a quick walk, Grandma. I won't be gone long."

He started down the dusty, narrow spiral of the staircase. At the sight of him, some children who were playing stepped aside and mumbled hello. By contrast, two busybodies chatting on the landing quickly dove back into their homes. The militiamen on watch at the entrance fixed him with a distrustful stare. Where was he going? What kind of fast one was he thinking of pulling now? Dieudonné sighed. From now on, he'd have to live his life as an object of admiration for some, hate and terror for others. He had no truth of his own; he was nothing but a carnival *bwa-bwa,* festooned in frippery, dressed in the fantasies of his compatriots. His hands in his pockets, he walked down Morne Julien, filling his lungs with the growing sweetness of the dusk air. At the same time, curiously, he missed prison and the safety net it had woven around him.

Two years earlier, Basse-Pointe had replaced the old jail located in the center of Port-Mahault. Following a bloody mutiny that had ended in the deaths of three guards and four inmates, the government was left with no other option than to open an investigation into the goings-on in this land so remote that nothing much was known about it. The inquiry revealed that, along with the one in Cayenne, in French Guiana, Port-Mahault's jail was a disgrace, a veritable hell. So, the government built this penitentiary, the largest and most modern one in the Caribbean. No more than four people per cell, each equipped with a color TV and stereo, so that everyone could drift off to sleep to the music of Kassav or Kali, whichever they pleased. Each cell had its own bathroom with a shower and sink. Copious meals were served three times a day, and not just cheap root vegetables and green bananas. There were workshops on plumbing, carpentry, and basketry. People planed wood, and a soft mat of sawdust covered the floors. Or, you could operate the computers donated to the prison by charities, and gain familiarity with email. Dieudonné hadn't learned any of that, but no matter. Safely sheltered behind these guarded concrete walls and electric fences, he had rediscovered the camaraderie of his school days. Everyone fought and dreamed together as one. Nobody judged anybody else. When he had arrived at Basse-Pointe, the prisoners had clustered around him:

"So, what happened? Tell us!"

But he had retreated into his memories and his timidity was mistaken for arrogance. After that, he hadn't really made any friends. Rodrigue, though, bombarded him with questions non-stop during yard time. Because he was fuming. In prison, their statuses were reversed. He was no longer the god, the boss. He was an ordinary delinquent, an armed robber and a murderer to boot—in other words, a common criminal. But his timid vassal Dieudonné had laid hands on the untouchable forbidden goddess, had deflowered her before sacrificing her.

Well anyway, in less than two years they had managed to deface the country even further. Engineers from Europe had built a corniche road surrounding Port-Mahault bristling with streetlamps straight as ramrods. To accomplish this, they had razed the Justinien neighborhood, wiping out the cabins of the destitute marring the space and uprooting the *pié-bwa*—scarlet flamboyants, yellow-fronded catalpas, guineps, white cedars. On the four-lane desert thus created, the gleaming toys of automobile technology jostled each other: Japanese, French, and German cars. He put out his thumb to hitch a ride. Nobody stopped, for, in the twilight, the wary drivers kept their doors locked. Luckily, the distance separating Morne Julien from the Mégisserie neighborhood is not too sizable for a good walker.

The marina had deteriorated even further. Pools of tar and diesel lapped the docks, staining the surface of the water with greasy black trails. The last remaining proprietors had seen an opening and run off to those other islands that still made good places to dream. Hooligan vandals had decapitated the streetlamps and darkness had started to drown the forest of masts, sullen phalluses half-erect in the air. When it came time to turn toward the bus stop and the Texaco station, Dieudonné's feet disobeyed him. They forked off to the left. And so, brought back like every murderer to the scene of his crime, he understood that this search for Boris was in reality just a pretext. A way of getting closer to what was once the burning core of his life.

The Allée des Amériques, an unoriginal paradise of bougainvillea and hibiscuses running perpendicular to the Mégisserie dock, was quite sought after by well-to-do *métros,* or main-landers, CEOs of banks, commercial firms, and major corporations. With their swimming pools and bay windows, their houses displayed that standardized luxury style that architects dub with the meaningless label "Californian." In front of villa 18, a "For Sale" sign beckoned alluringly. However, it was clear this was purely routine, that the sign itself had no real confidence given the foregone conclusion that, after a drama like that, no buyer would come forward. Once he had pushed open the gate, Dieudonné saw that the grass was tall, the mussaendas had not tolerated eighteen months of abandon nor the inferno of the recent dry season, and the hibiscuses had been scorched to death. He squatted down under the withered and yellowed dwarf coconut trees while images from the past came back to slap him in the face.

Loraine Féréol de Brémont was the only daughter of a *béké* with no male descendants, whose family, back in the day, had managed three-quarters of the country's land. She had gone through three unhappy marriages—all with Europeans, because she hated everyone in her own caste, who returned the sentiment. She was still a very beautiful woman, though definitely not young anymore, about fifty and a little heavier for it, and always covered in gold. The craziest rumors went around about her. A first cousin, a *béké* from Martinique, had supposedly been her lover but had hushed it up for fear of scandal. Supposedly the couple had produced a monstrous child with the head of a dog, who was hidden away in a clinic in Miami. If Loraine was a disgrace to the *békés* because she drank like a fish (some said it was since her husband left; others said no, she had always been like that), and because, without any proof whatsoever, people maintained that she collected one-night stands (generally young men, naive and well equipped), some couldn't deny that she had a big heart. Always helping compatriots in need, in bankruptcy, or in distress, without ever caring that they were darker than she was. Always standing godmother to children of all colors. Always financing AIDS research, school scholarships, and literary prizes.

Of course, when he started working for her, Dieudonné wasn't aware of any of that. One morning, he had knocked at her door looking for work, just as he did at all the houses in the neighborhood if there was no German mastiff or Doberman loose in the yard: prep cook, courier, laundry worker. Most of the time, people sent him packing. At best, they would have him wash their car in return for spare change. For, unlike Rodrigue, who scoffed at him, Dieudonné had an aversion to danger but no problem with hard work. No job seemed too arduous or too humble if it allowed him to get by. He had worked on the docks emptying containers and transporting bags of rice and cement and casks of oil. Surprise! Loraine had listened to him, inspecting him from head to toe with eyes gray like the rain. Then, she had made him her offer in her low voice, hoarse from too much booze. Actually, as it happened, the Haitian responsible for tending her garden had just gone back to Petit-Goâve. His job wouldn't be complicated. He would have to water the mussaendas, a plant that never gets tired of drinking, work the soil at the foot of the crotons, trim them, cut off all the dead branches, spray the ailing hibiscuses with a special treatment, and, once a week, mow the small patch of grass. All of that for 500 francs a month. It was no jackpot she was offering. Far from it, but he was startled to realize that, for her, he would have worked for free. Dumbfounded, he stood before her while an unfamiliar feeling banged furiously on the door to his heart. Between them, things had developed very slowly.

The very next day, she had started offering him nylon tracksuits, one white, one orange, one blue, and he had gathered that she didn't care for his worn-out clothes. An old pair of jeans. A faded T-shirt. A baseball cap. In the beginning, the villa's interior was off-limits to him. He would get his gardening tools out of the garage, toil away under the sun the entire morning, and leave at one o'clock. He only ever went into the kitchen, his head dripping with sweat, to drink a glass of ice water. Then she got in the habit of setting out some leftovers for him for lunch. She enjoyed good food, and every day her servant cooked up scrumptious little dishes for her, and that is how Dieudonné became acquainted with eggs Florentine, salt cod brandade, ratatouille Niçoise, and jellied trout. He learned how to reheat his plate in the microwave. Then he washed it and set it on the dish rack to dry. After a few weeks, at her request, he entered the living room to shampoo the carpet. The house surprised him: it was a veritable museum. For, unbeknownst to him, Loraine, who had studied painting in Paris, was a patron of the arts. For a time, she had taught at the École des Arts Plastiques, which had deeply shocked the country. With all her money, what did she need a salary for? She insisted that the local painters' works were a thousand times more valuable than the ones by Haitian Naïve artists, so overrated; she bought their pieces and resold them at a high price to foreign merchants, especially Americans. At times, she planned private receptions, and, seizing the occasion, buyers rushed to her home. Apart from that, she received no visitors. In the living room, this mess of forms and colors on the walls made Dieudonné uneasy and he kept his eyes off his surroundings, as if he were being assaulted by graffiti or obscene inscriptions. He made an exception for two paintings. The first one was small, and all done in shades of brown. What did it represent? He thought he recognized a silverfish. Or was it a moon crescent? The white foam of the sea. Or was it clouds? The other, larger, very large, represented a leaf. A giant banana tree leaf. Or was it a face, its veins symbolizing features, a nose, a mouth? The second month, he ventured deeper, into the office. When he entered the bedroom, it was with the feeling a believer has exploring a cathedral. Yet the place had nothing solemn about it. It was supremely cold because of the air-conditioning. Dirty clothes had been thrown on the floor. Jars of face creams, uncapped, sat in a row on a dressing table of very ordinary make, at the foot of a mirror without a frame, an oval eye on the wall. Only a rocker, a mahogany bed imprisoned in its mosquito net, and a chest of drawers resembled the rich pieces that you see in the display windows of the last master craftsmen. You could sense that these were the remainders of the precious furnishings of a family scattered to the four winds. Dieudonné did not even notice the small safe in the wall to the left of the bed.

Apart from him, there was only the servant, Amabelle, in the house, a surly *zindienne* who never said hello to him and spent all her time on the phone as soon as Loraine was out of earshot. After a while Dieudonné gathered that her companion had dumped her for a girl from Dominica, and a good friend was keeping her up to speed. Once a week, the "Blanc Impec" van collected or dropped off the napkins, sheets, and dishcloths.

At Loraine's, the days followed one after the other, as identical as twins.

Up at dawn with the rainbird's song, her eyebrows furrowed, she would be tapping away on her computer keyboard, a glass and bottle of whiskey within reach. What was she writing? A novel? Poems, like Boris? Dieudonné struggled vainly to decipher the phosphorescent lines on the greenish screen. At half past noon, she ate lunch, her eyes glued this time to the news broadcast. At two o'clock, she shut herself up in her room for a siesta that dragged on until five. Then, suddenly concerned about getting some exercise, she would slip on some jogging clothes, head out down the Allée des Amériques, and stride across the entire length of the Mégisserie dock. Soon out of breath, she would sit down on the benches at the Jean-Bart Square and stare at the waters of the bay, which, as the dusk descended, took on the sadness of her eyes. She would walk back up the Allée des Amériques at the hour when the German mastiffs and Dobermans would start showing their white fangs over the tops of the hedges. Once she got back home, she'd start drinking again, huddled in front of the television until midnight, then fall asleep, her mouth open. When did Dieudonné first offer her his arm for her afternoon walks? The sea breeze stirred the almond trees; they would take a slow pace coming back, oblivious to the watchdogs' chorus, and happiness started to blossom in him like a fragile flower. When did he first start running to the Texaco convenience store in the middle of the night to buy her alcohol? Thanks to her second husband, who was Scottish, single malt Clynelishes, Dalwhinnies, and Glen Grants held no secrets for her. Yet when she was out of those, she'd knock back anything. When did he first start showering her with care and attention? Reheating her dinner. Setting a place at the table for her. Turning on the TV, flipping through the channels, turning it off. Putting Loraine to bed. Undressing her. Slipping a silk nightshirt over her beautiful ravaged body. Her dejected breasts sagging with the weight of their nipples.

Her stomach with its curves like a gourd. He got in the habit of sleeping lightly, so, so lightly, like a mother with a feverish child, for her nights were always occupied by the same bad dreams, by the same sorrows. He fixed himself up a bedroom in the garage, between Amabelle's ironing board and washing machine. And, in serving her this way, he imagined he was serving Marine, brought back to life. He felt he had returned to the time when his mother was still alive, prostrate in her chair like a mummy, communicating with him only with her gaze, always bright with tenderness. Their relationship always followed a strict routine, never deviating. All day long, neither of them spoke to the other, as if they were both staying in their places. In the evening the floodgates opened and she confided in him endlessly, rehashing the same old wounds, her speech becoming more and more slurred and her voice less and less audible as the night wore on. He soon understood that she was just as alone on this earth as Marine had been. Her parents, dead for years, had never loved her, she complained. Her sister Florelle, nine months older than she, had been taken away by leukemia at the age of fifteen, and since that time, she could no longer tell which of them was living and which was dead. Her or me? She had no children. Her entire family had disowned her. For his part, Dieudonné hardly opened his mouth. His own melodramatic troubles, the departure of the Cohens, the illness and death of his mother, weren't the garlands of flowers he wanted to adorn her with. He would have liked to chase away the clouds that snuffed out her joy, to entertain her, make her laugh. He had no material to work with except the cruises from his childhood. He embellished them. At times, they landed on desert islands, inhabited by nothing but scentless thorns and wild goats. They dropped anchor in bays with unknown names and swam in their white-sand waters. One night they were drifting with the stars as their guide when they hit some coral reefs. The hull was punctured. Quick, quick as a flash, they had to take the dinghy to get back to shore. They set up a tent for the children. The adults slept curled up in the fine-grained sand, as white as rock salt.

Dieudonné liked the mornings best. When he came back from his daily swim at Le Goulet, Loraine was already awake. He busied himself helping her get ready for the day. The bathroom opened onto the garden. The bird-of-paradise flower beds, the hibiscus bushes, and the salts he perfumed the bathwater with carried the scent of oleander. Loraine let her head fall back, doleful, while he led the sponge to her most secret parts. When his caress became too indiscreet, she would open her eyes again and give him a little smile of complicity, as sweet as the day that was taking shape beyond the slats of the shutters. Next, he helped her choose clothes from her closet, laid them out on the bed, and helped her slip them on. She liked to wear white. Linen. At times, too, she dressed all in black as if she were in deep mourning.

He also liked the beginning of the night. For hours, while she snored, he would flip through the photo albums she kept in her dresser. He couldn't care less about the pictures of her family: her *béké* father, looking very dignified decked out in a high, stiff collar and pith helmet; her mother as a young bride in a long, lacy gown, the puffed bodice cinched at the waist with a wide ribbon bow, standing on high heels, her right hand leaning on a high-backed Voltaire armchair; her sister, an overly pudgy brunette. His eyes went straight to her: as a little girl, a teenager, a young woman. So beautiful at twenty, her hair in her eyes, smiling broadly at this life that was to disappoint her so.

Only one time was there a change to the routine, even though one can say that in love, there is no such thing as routine. The same gestures and words repeated a thousand times bring the same rapture each time.

Yolande Féréol de Brémont had just died in her eighty-second year. She was Loraine's aunt on her father's side and, in keeping with tradition, her godmother, the only relative she had kept any contact with. They would call each other twice a year, at Christmas and New Year's. They would send each other flowers on their birthdays and congratulate each other on the beauty of their bouquets. On the Day of the Dead, they'd decide together what wreaths to get to honor their many late family members. Yolande Féréol de Brémont lived in Saint-Léger-des-Feuilles, a mountain town on the other side of the country at the edge of the dense forest where, because of the cool weather, plantation owners had once built their homes. More recently, the black and mulatto bourgeoisies had invaded it with their flashy houses in reinforced concrete, their blue-toned swimming pools and their Jacuzzis, but there remained a dozen villas built of wood, antique and dilapidated, surrounded by thick, messy gardens—for everything grew in Saint-Léger-des-Feuilles—sitting at the ends of walkways lined with dwarf coconut trees or royal palms. To get to the wake and the burial, Loraine undertook laborious arrangements to rent a car and ordered Dieudonné to accompany her. He was thrilled, because while he had crossed the Caribbean Sea with the Cohens, reaching Grenada, the Grenadines, and Grand Cayman, and also made some forays into the Atlantic Ocean, at home he had barely seen anything outside Port-Mahault. They left around four o'clock in the afternoon, the car stuffed with a provision of whiskey bottles, and rushed forward at 25 miles per hour to attack the foothills of the mountains. Even so, Loraine drove with a fairly steady hand, all the while relating a series of anecdotes about the deceased woman.

"She's the one who should have been my mother. Like me, she was a rebel, a troublemaker. Since she had fallen for a mulatto, her parents shut her away in a convent for ten years when she was twenty years old. When she got back out, she moved in with a black man. Some people say they were secretly married. Unfortunately, like me, Yolande was sterile. The couple never had any children."

Dieudonné drank in this countryside that was so new to him, these banana plantations, this vault of tree ferns, this canopy of venerable trees, their axils eaten up by creeping vines and wild pines. The air turned from cool to almost cold. Rain started to fall, stopped, and fell again. Fog enveloped everything. They arrived at the deceased's home at nightfall. A couple of *zindien* servants in their seventies took their luggage and silently led the way to the stairs ahead of them. Everybody was well acquainted with Miss Loraine and her train of black gigolos. This one would last no longer or shorter than the others. In the garret, the room they gave them was as bare and austere as a monk's cell, but endowed with a splendid view of the sloping mauve bulk of the mountains and the sea, who reigned supreme here, too. A balcony overlooked the tangle of *pié-bwa*.

While Loraine rested, Dieudonné thought it best to go down to the sitting room, which had been transformed into a funerary chapel. It was when he crossed the threshold into the space lit with hundreds of candles, where, half-covered with a mound of flowers, the body seemed to wait for final kisses from the living, that he realized what an enormity his presence was. He was in the way, unwanted. Around him, there were nothing but white people, *békés,* some having traveled in from the neighboring island, exhibiting their creased parchment skin, their dull heads of hair, and staring at him with their washed-out pupils in mute disapproval. Besides their color, what was striking was their age. No young people or children. All of them were well over fifty years old. It was as if this was a gathering of the last survivors, the increasingly hoary, fragile, and threatened guardians of a time that would never return, but which remained firmly anchored in their nostalgic hearts. He almost fled, but a woman with a diaphanous complexion authoritatively pointed him to a chair, so he took his seat, trembling all over.

Two hours later, Loraine joined the assembled mourners, stumbling along on stiletto heels, a shiny belt around her waist, in heavy makeup and a dress that would not have looked out of place on Gloria Swanson in *Sunset Boulevard.* She greeted a good half the room effusively, pulled up a chair noisily, then started singing more loudly and off-key than anyone. She was tipsy, drunk, plastered. However, Dieudonné, who knew her better than the others did, could tell that whiskey wasn't really playing much of a part in these excesses. She meant to stir up trouble, make a scandal, provoke rage. Sadly, she failed to hit her mark. Everyone watched her without anger, with a kind of resigned patience, as if they knew that despite her escapades and tantrums, she belonged to them, their daughter and sister, forever marked with the indelible stamp of their shared origins. Loraine took part in the wake for a long time. Around one o'clock in the morning, she crossed herself before taking her leave and conspicuously giving Dieudonné orders to follow. Ashamed, he didn't know what to do with himself. He obeyed, however. Before going upstairs, he wandered through the first-floor rooms. Here and there, a few rugs covered the worm-eaten floorboards. Mirrors gaped on the walls. Apart from that, the house was curiously empty, all the furniture, knickknacks, and costly paintings having disappeared. Had they been sold? Was Yolande bankrupt? Where had the legendary Féréol de Brémont fortune gone? He ventured into the garden, the last remaining treasure, where beds of gardenias and roses dropped their petals. When he joined her in the attic bedroom smelling sweetly of turpentine, honeysuckle, and that inimitable scent of the mountains, Loraine was already snoring in her luxurious lace nightgown. He spent the night on the balcony, wrapped up in a blanket to protect himself against the chilly wind blowing down from the heights.

The next day, Yolande was laid to rest. The family crypt, a majestic piece in black-and-white marble hidden among the causarina trees, stood in a small, badly maintained cemetery invaded by guinea grass, beside the church, where *békés,* primarily, lay in repose. On the tombstones, long aristocratic names recalled former splendors and glories. Loraine wept a long time.

"You can't understand. It's as if I were the one who died," she whispered in Dieudonné's ear as they got back into the car. "No one loved her. No one loves me. Neither of us is leaving anyone to carry on after us."

5

There was only one shadow over this happy period.

No one knows how, but Loraine acquired a puppy. One fine morning, Dieudonné found himself face to face with a little creature who took no time exercising a despotic power over the household. All hours of the day, Loraine smothered her with kisses, petting her and showering her with sweet nothings. At night, she put her in a sort of bassinet lined with cushions of silk and velvet that she placed by the side of her bed. After giving her some skim milk enriched with egg yolk, she would hand-feed her beef filet slices or kibble made with chicken. It was a pretty pathetic and strange spectacle to see this usually cold, reserved, and even sullen woman suddenly dissolve into utter sappiness. This puppy wasn't one of those baby behemoths, fleshy and muscular, that her neighbors on either side could have sold her, easily trained to guard, attack, or even kill. It was a ridiculous female Spitz, that she christened Lili to top things off, hardly bigger than a rabbit, with reddish-brown fur streaked with black and as silky as a child's hair, that hung down over her quick, piercing, boot-button eyes. For reasons known to her alone, the stupid beast took a dislike to Dieudonné. As soon as she spotted him at the other end of the yard or somewhere in the house, she would bark, yip, and growl herself hoarse, baring tiny but very sharp fangs set close together in her gums, as well as a rough, blood-red tongue. At times, she'd get bold enough to approach him, and, audaciously, make as if to latch on to the leg of his tracksuit. If she woke up during the night and saw him entangled in the bed sheets, she would almost suffocate with rage until Loraine, to please her, dismissed her companion. Dieudonné, sick with shame, returned to his bench in the garage. Lili's behavior made Loraine laugh until she cried. In stitches, she would try to get the horrible yappy mutt to calm down.

"Oh come on, my little *doudou*, leave him alone! Are you jealous? You know you're my one and only love!"

It was Amabelle's job to take Lili out to do her business, walking hunched over and shaking her derriere all the way down the Allée des Amériques. While she complied without a word, it was clear that she had the utmost repugnance for Lili. How did she manage to cleverly offload the task onto Dieudonné? However it happened, in addition to escorting Loraine, he now found himself putting Lili's leash on and walking her around the neighborhood. Nothing was more humiliating for him. Overcoming her animosity, Lili was content enough to follow him quietly. But once outside, she'd take off like a shot, making Dieudonné run too. Then, without warning, she'd zigzag every which way, or else she'd stop, squat, and pee on a bougainvillea, or, even worse, painfully relieve herself of a dark, fetid turd while Dieudonné was forced to stand there and wait. Like Amabelle, like everybody in the country, Dieudonné feared and despised dogs. It goes way back. In the plantation days, dogs hunted escaping blacks, tracked them down, and made the maroons bleed on behalf of the Master. Besides, everyone knows that Spirits love turning into dogs, taking the form of the age-old enemy in order to play their malicious tricks. Worse still, they were animals only good for a laugh, or pity. As the days wore on, the hatred Dieudonné felt for the puppy reached its peak. He couldn't stand seeing her constantly curled up at Loraine's breast or on her knees anymore. He couldn't stand seeing Loraine covering her slobbering little mouth with passionate kisses, letting her eat off her plate or lick the bottom of her glass. Those affections should have been reserved for him. And yet, she never showed him anything but harsh condescension.

One late afternoon, then, he took Lili to the *Belle Créole*. Soon, the sky would be losing its electric-blue color and turning mauve. The waves of heat would be dying down. A strong breeze was rising, rippling the surface of the water. The languid boats were finishing their nap and readying themselves for nighttime. He knew that, because of the profusion of all manner of rodents, Boris kept rat poison in a cupboard in the galley. He carefully mixed the pink granules with a bit of ground beef that had been left lying around and put the concoction in a saucer that he set in front of Lili. At first, accustomed to oh-so-finer foods, the little beast sniffed at this dish with disgust. In the end, she must have liked the smell of rot, because she attacked it voraciously, licking her teeth over and over to finish off.

Death was practically instantaneous. Lili vomited up a bloody puree, let out a few hoarse whines, then fell down on her side, her four legs stiffening. Silence. When all was done, Dieudonné wrapped her body in a plastic bag and shoved it in one of the trashcans on the dock.

Then he came back to the Allée des Amériques with a jumbled story about how Lili, capricious as usual, had slipped away from him. Since she had shot off like an arrow right into the middle of the street, she had been squashed by a car. Dieudonné could tell by her expression that Amabelle didn't believe a word of his tale, but the account threw Loraine into a frenzy of cries and tears. He had a world of trouble preventing her from rushing to the scene of the accident. Then she shut herself up in her bedroom. When he came to join her, she revealed the key to her sorrow, in one of those sad soliloquies that she alone knew how to give so well.

"Everything repeats itself! This isn't the first time this has happened to me. You see, I'm cursed. When I was little, maybe five or six, we were spending our vacation at our Saint-Léger-des-Feuilles property when someone from the family gave me and Florelle a dog—that one was all white and curly, she was a kind of poodle. We called her Lili. We used to take her everywhere, even to church. We adored her. You won't believe it, but one afternoon our best friend Sophie came over to play with us and her chauffeur backed over Lili right in front of our eyes. He never even said he was sorry."

Her tears seemed to have no end.

For weeks, Dieudonné was unable to savor his victory. He was unable to get close to Loraine to drink from her waters. She refused to eat and drowned her pain in whiskey. Always more whiskey. Amabelle was constantly picking up empty single-malt bottles. As a result, by nine o'clock she'd already be asleep with her mouth open in front of the television, indifferent to the fortunes and misfortunes of the blonde American women who usually enthralled her. He would carry her to her bed, change her clothes, then watch her sleep for hours on end, his heart torn between tenderness, possessiveness, and remorse for the crime he had committed.

It goes without saying that once Dieudonné started working for Loraine, his headaches vanished. It was as if her gaze, her scent, her rare smiles, everything about her produced a drug more magical than crack, more powerful than any other remedy. Boris, sagaciously, advised him to take care. Everyone knows woman was created for man's perdition. Even more than black women, white women are vicious, dangerous, rattlesnakes. He assembled a series of examples.

"Eve was Adam's ruin. Helen caused the Trojan War. Cleopatra finished off Antony and Caesar. La Malinche screwed Cortez and that was it for the Incas. What is there exactly between you?"

Dieudonné tried to describe the feeling that was transforming his life, that was suddenly giving it a goal, a meaning, a direction. Then he realized that all Boris wanted to know was if he was sleeping with Loraine, and he closed up. It wasn't anybody else's business.

6

This extraordinary bliss lasted almost a year.

About a week or ten days before Christmas, when—a premonition of the drama to come?—the poinsettias were dropping tears of blood onto the flower beds, a taxi ground to a halt in front of the villa. A young man carting suitcases and a gigantic crate got out of it. The stranger was handsome. About thirty. His hair was as golden as Dieudonné's was black. On the other hand, his skin was almost as dark. In short, he was one of those unclassifiable mixed-race people who have all manner of bloods mingled together in unequal proportions. White. Black. *Zindien.* His eyes sparkled, and he seemed to be drawing himself up in challenge to the world despite his small height, for he was short. He greeted Dieudonné warmly as though he had chanced to come across an old friend he'd lost touch with for ages. His whole person radiated with devastating charm—devastatingly irresistible, like a child, but also literally ravaging, you could sense, deadly, lethal. When he saw him, Dieudonné, who had never envied anyone, was seized with an uncontrollable desire to be this stranger, to slip into his skin, to live by the rhythm of his breaths, his heartbeats. At that moment, Loraine, who had been on the lookout, came hurrying from the veranda. The man threw his arms open in a deliberately melodramatic way. She fell into them and they kissed and nuzzled one another without restraint, right there in front of Dieudonné's eyes, as if he didn't matter any more than the faded flowers, dried-up branches, and trampled ground in the surroundings did. His ears peeled, Dieudonné soon heard that the man's name was Luc, pronounced Luke, and that he was a painter who had emigrated to New York. Where had he come from? From Morne Vert, out in the Salines region in the middle of nowhere, a place whose only claim to fame was undoubtedly him. No sooner had he arrived than he opened his crate and started hanging up his works. What paintings! Disturbing shapes, some whimsical, curiously ornate, others geometrical, cubes, rectangles, and pyramids, displayed against murky greenish, bluish backgrounds, the offspring, you'd suspect, of someone unwell, someone unhealthy. If Loraine commented on each canvas admiringly, joyful and animated as he'd never seen her before while nonetheless repeatedly refilling her glass, Dieudonné, his feather duster in hand, was thinking that if someone had given him some paint and brushes, even he could have put them to better use. At one moment, Luc sidled up next to him and asked him, conversationally,

"You like it, man?"

Dieudonné didn't know what to say. Luc smiled his inimitable smile.

"You know, the hardest thing is to never ask that kind of question. To not give a damn about other people's opinions. To shut yourself off from others. Part of our training involves going to museums and copying the masters. So you do some Ingres, you do Manet, you do Picasso. I spent a year at the Academia San Carlos in Mexico City. So after that, I was doing Diego Rivera. I used to replace the peons with black peasants, and Zapata with Ignace or Delgrès and that was all there was to it. Only now am I starting to be myself."

It was the first time in years that anyone had spoken to Dieudonné as if he were an equal. Loraine always had a note of derision in her voice when she talked to him. Boris spoke to him with the kind of tone you'd use with a child. Rodrigue, like he was some naive type who refused to understand how the world worked. As for Amabelle, she ignored him. He looked at Luc with astonishment and gratitude. But Loraine had started to come over. By mutual agreement, they moved away from one another as if they had committed some forbidden act or one that they didn't want to share with her.

Around noon, Loraine and Luc disappeared. Amabelle served him his meal, but Dieudonné couldn't touch it. A pain that he hadn't felt in a long time wrenched his head, his stomach, and his heart too. All afternoon he kept watch, stretched out in the garage. But Loraine and Luc didn't reappear.

Tired of waiting, when the sun set in its daily orgy of blood, he went to take refuge on the *Belle Créole* where, other than the brief spell with Lili, he hadn't set foot for months, and ran into Boris, who was taking cover there from the bad weather. That year, the rainy season had come early. Ever since September, the rains had been falling and falling, filling the flat-bottomed ravines to overflowing, swelling the waterways, and transforming the dry *razyé* into swamps. Boris, bright and chipper from making some good sales to tourists, was cooking himself up a little morsel. He looked up.

"You're making quite a face! Did she dump you? She found someone else? It was bound to happen. That woman is a factory, you know!"

Boris didn't know anything about Loraine, but repeated with conviction all the gossip dished out about her. Since Dieudonné refused to respond, he added:

"On my advice, Gérard Benjamin is going to pull the trigger and launch the municipal employees' strike in every service sector. Not just in Port-Mahault. In Laglaine, Dieurif, Fonds-Grandbois. Across the whole country! Things are going to heat up."

Gérard Benjamin, whom everyone called by his nickname, Benjy, was the secretary-general of the PTCR, the union responsible for the proliferating strikes. Already, the traditional politicians were accusing him of embarking on the path to *lendépendans* while the leftist intellectuals, seeing in him their only hope, were rubbing their hands together and fawningly calling him Benjy the Red. What nobody knew about was Boris's influence over him. Benjy and Boris were kin, in the sense people in this country take kin to mean. Most importantly, they had sat side by side in class all the way from nursery school to the end of junior high, had sampled the same thighs, swayed to the same slow dances, gotten hammered on the same rhum agricole, and, throughout it all, Benjy had looked upon Boris as his god. Despite the disarray Boris's life was in, Benjy had never swerved from his opinion. On the contrary. In a basely materialistic world, he considered Boris to be a victim of his idealism and his purity. Benjy visited him every afternoon at the same time, ferociously chased away all the busybodies besieging the bus stop, and gravely asked his opinion on everything. Boris would answer, throwing his weight around as usual. Then he'd go whisper in Dieudonné's ear that he was the one true boss of the PTCR, since Benjy had never read anything but comic books and—O shame!—hadn't even cracked open *Das Kapital.* Dieudonné, for his part, had no time for Benjy. As soon as Dieudonné saw him anywhere around, he'd disappear. Benjy and Boris bored him with their speeches. Always going on about how he belonged to the oppressed class. Oppressed by who? By what? He had been born in the wrong cradle, bad luck! Luck's not debatable. It's a matter of chance. It smiles on some and takes away from others, that's all! He came back out on the deck while Boris went on pontificating:

"No doubt about it, what we need to get us out of the situation we're in is a leader. But if they think Benjy's cut out for that kind of job, they're mistaken."

Where were they? What had they been doing all day? Loraine had no family, no friends, no relations, no one to visit and nowhere to go!

The dinette was soaked. He leaned against the boom. In the fog, a dented moon hanging from the tip of her mast, the monohull swayed with the ocean swells. On the other side of the bay, the lights of Petite-Anse blinked like distress signals. A Boeing rumbled above his head and he followed it with his eyes. In eight hours it would come back down to earth and land at Roissy Charles de Gaulle Airport. The City of Light. The Champs-Élysées, the most beautiful avenue in the world. The Eiffel Tower, arrow of steel, marvel of technology. The Pyramid, strange and surprising gem of the Louvre. Bizarrely, none of these clichés that people filled their mouths with stirred his imagination. Paris, now that was a place with no appeal for him! Where he would have liked to go was Hollywood, because of some of the films he'd seen on television.

Mercilessly lacerated by the lashing rain, he had to go back into the galley to take cover. Boris had pushed his plate aside and, his pen in his hand, was putting the perfecting touches on his latest creation. Admirable Boris! Even without a future in sight or, at times, much of anything in his stomach, he had never stopped writing, convinced that one day his poetry would bring him love, glory, and beauty, conquering the world like the work of his masters, Shakespeare and Neruda.

Dieudonné squatted down in a corner. One question, repeating like a snippet of music on a broken record, preoccupied his mind. Where were they? He was burning with the fires of jealousy. At the stroke of midnight, Rodrigue burst into the dinette. For once, no cheap beauties at his side. Instead, two fierce-looking youths, sporting dreadlocks scorched like tobacco leaves. One of them opened his gunnysack to reveal an arsenal: two 6.35mm Beretta pistols, a 7.65mm Walther PPK, and a sawed-off shotgun, so-bering, murderous weapons of the kind you see at the movies. Despite himself, Dieudonné approached the table. He had never seen a gun, other than the jewel inlaid with mother-of-pearl that Loraine set at the head of her bed every evening. She claimed to have taken shooting lessons with one of her husbands. But Dieudonné didn't believe a word of it. That little toy was only good for purging her fears. Rodrigue's weapons had an entirely different look to them. They seemed real, and out of place in these anodyne surroundings, on this Formica table next to the leftovers from some meager dinner. Rodrigue explained that he had bought the lot from some Dominicans for a very steep price and lowered his voice: he was plotting a feat that would go down in the annals of the country's history. He was going to sack Mil-lénium, the big electronics store, jam-packed with gifts in this holiday season—computers, cell phones, stereos, laser discs. The plan? A well-oiled machine. An associate would wait for them at the wheel of a delivery truck, ready to roll. Another would be standing by at the helm of a speedboat, which was already hidden and waiting in a cove near Port-Mahault. Then it would be Dominica, first stop! Next, la dolce vita for us in Florida, or, even better, in California! Beverly Hills! Rodrigue's bragging had a knack for getting under Boris's skin—the two men couldn't stand each other—and he took it upon himself to lecture him pedantically. The Bible said it: he who lives by the sword shall perish by the sword. Violence only begets violence. Granted, the country was gangrenous. But the cure was to be found in political solutions. Rodrigue laughed until he cried. Tired of these same old discussions, Dieudonné jumped out onto the dock. The rain, worn out after its own violent fit, had eased up. It enveloped him, warm on his shoulders. He ran all the way to the Allée des Amériques. The house was plunged in darkness. Dieudonné tried all the exits: doors, windows, and garage were locked. Rejected, excluded, he sat down in the garden. In the dark, the ylang-ylang embalmed his lost happiness.

It must have been two or three o'clock in the morning when he heard the sound of her laughter, she who so rarely laughed. Then he spotted the glow of her hair as she advanced, stumbling, on Luc's arm, whereas he was the only one, he thought, that she could lean on. At the same time, parallel to this thought, so to speak, he couldn't keep his eyes off this Luc, whom he should have hated for misappropriating his possession, for stealing from him, but whom he didn't hate, seized as he was by a violent emotion and drawn like a magnet to every one of Luc's movements. The couple took the walkway bordered by hibiscuses and dove into the house, slamming the heavy doors shut and turning the bolt with a sharp click that seemed to rap out "Scat!" as if he were a dog. The rain started falling again. At first, a tiny, tiny drizzle. Then a rage, trampling the lawn and the flower beds with all its strength, whipping the shrubs. A clap of thunder shook the still air; then came the flash of the lightning, bluish and blinding.

Had he been wrong to believe that she needed him, as much as Marine had once needed him?

When he came back to work the next day, they were both still asleep. And he pictured the bedroom sanctuary that he only entered tremblingly, dimmed by the closed shutters, and them, in the middle of the unmade bed. She woke up first, came out on the veranda, and shot him a glance in which he thought he could detect a sliver of remorse. Luc on the other hand appeared a few hours later, smiling, naturally easy, and openly friendly. On this point, as on so many others, Mr. Serbulon had run roughshod over the truth. To Dieudonné Luc had never shown any contempt or arrogance. Quite the opposite. From the very first days, he had tried to build a rapport with him. Had made it clear to him that, with respect to Loraine, the two of them were on the same page, on the same side. At times,

Dieudonné let himself go with the flow, and, with one-word answers, responded to his advances. Other times, worried, he closed up. As if he were afraid. He didn't know of what.

The very first day after he arrived, Luc made it clear that he would not hear of Dieudonné eating all alone, standing like a horse in the kitchen, and assigned him a spot at the table between himself and Loraine. So Dieudonné sat, paralyzed with timidity, handling his silverware as if it were made out of lead. If only Luc had then ignored his presence, it would have been easier. But no, throughout the entire meal he goaded him, forcing him to participate in the conversation.

"Tell me! What do you think?"

Loraine showed signs of impatience. "Leave him the hell alone! You can see for yourself he doesn't think anything."

"Sure he does," retorted Luc, smiling encouragingly at Dieudonné. "It's just that he's not used to expressing himself."

Visibly, Loraine didn't care for this tone of camaraderie, and by contrast treated Dieudonné more and more like an underling and a nuisance. But Luc did only as he pleased. At lunch one day, as they were finishing up with coffee, he begged Dieudonné to take him to see his boat. When the latter hesitated, Loraine turned on him and ordered him, savagely:

"Do what he tells you. Got it?"

Then she left the room and slammed her bedroom door behind her. With a heavy heart, Dieudonné obeyed. At that hour of the day, the sun was blinding. The two young men were stepping on their own violet shadows clinging underfoot. Luc went over the monohull from top to bottom, neglecting neither the head nor the sail locker, feeling the cleats and the stanchions, and leaning over the handrail. However, it was clear that none of that interested him. What did he want? Ultimately, he asked, "How did you become a skipper?"

"I did sailing school," said Dieudonné proudly. "Up to Level Orange. Then I practiced with Vincent Cohen."

Seated in the dinette, Luc fixed him with a gaze that made him uneasy, as if he were evaluating him, sizing him up. Finally, he remarked, "You could earn a lot of money with that. Hire yourself out for cruises!"

Dieudonné shrugged his shoulders. "To what tourists? Nobody comes around here anymore. The last boat rental agencies are closing."

Luc sighed. "Hell of a country we've got here! As for myself, I don't think I'll set foot here again. Nobody has the money for my paintings anymore. Nobody's interested in them anymore."

In an instant, happiness flooded Dieudonné's aching heart. So he'd have Loraine all to himself! Luc got up and continued, switching topics, "Personally, I hate the sea. Once, I went to visit one of my aunts in Marjane. When we crossed the strait, I puked all my guts out. I thought I was going to die."

Abruptly, he leaped like a cat onto the dock as if the *Belle Créole* bored him stiff. From the blacktop, he shouted, "Adieu! Enjoy your freedom. I'm a slave."

What did he mean?

Curiously, Dieudonné wasn't mad at Luc for evicting him from Loraine's heart and her bed. At the end of the day, it was natural that she would prefer Luc to him. He was so superior in every way: more handsome, more intelligent, elegant, made unique by his creative gift. Little by little, Dieudonné got used to his paintings, discovering a secret beauty in them. His favorite was a study in every shade of gray, representing a shape that could be that of a woman seen from behind or a tree eaten up by epiphytes or a fanciful animal. Nevertheless, these considerations didn't prevent him from suffering. From suffering torture.

7

Dieudonné stood up, surprised by the suddenly mournful color of the weather.

He didn't have a watch. Was it already curfew? Every night when he was in prison, police cars would unload groups of boys, and girls too, whose only crime was to have lingered too long on the streets. They'd rough them up. They'd park them in cells with the most hardened criminals. Sometimes they kept them twenty-four hours without giving them anything to eat or drink and you could hear them crying loudly, calling for their mommies like little kids. He imagined with a sort of happy feeling

that maybe a patrol would arrest him and he'd be back again
in the warm bosom he had lost. Alas! There were no uniforms
on the horizon. The police didn't waste any time patrolling a
neighborhood like this: the security systems, the dogs, and the
private guards outdid them. He started listlessly back down the
road to town. As he was about to get on the freeway, a ribbon
of black velvet studded with the headlights of cars, he changed
his mind and turned back. The Texaco service station of old,
formerly a modern palace with its lights and its "boutiques"
stocked with bottles of mineral water, cartons of cigarettes, and
bags of potato chips, was abandoned, surrounded by a ring of
by rusty barrels. Ironically, its neon lights were still glowing,
proclaiming "24/7." In the bus stop, an old man with a beret
pulled down over the dirty wool of his hair was settling in. In
response to Dieudonné's question, he gave a laugh.

"Boris? You must be the only one who doesn't know where
he is. He's the only thing you hear on the PTCR's radio station,
Radio Solèye Lévé."

Dieudonné pressed him. What did he mean? What happened?

"Where've you been?" said the elder, shocked by his ignorance.

A few months earlier, the old man related, Boris, as usual,
was hassling some motorists filling up gas to get them to buy
his latest volume. But this time, it happened that these were
no ordinary motorists. It was an Italian television crew from
Bologna, come to film a report on Caribbean malaise. Why do
Paradises spoil? Why do they become Hells? This uncommon
homeless man, this fervent political activist, a smooth talker
who wrote verse and quoted Shakespeare and Neruda—even if
his accent was bad—was worth interviewing. So, they parked
their cameras in front of the bus stop. Over the course of the interviews, Carla, a very well-known journalist back home—she
wrote articles for the *Corriere della Sera*—had become besotted
with Boris. So she had let Alitalia leave without her. Then she
had pulled Boris out from where he was and set up house with
him. Boris, who now had a mouth to feed, had once again put
his neck under the yoke of employment. When all was said and
done, he had taken over the directorship of Radio Solèye Lévé,
Sunrise Radio, the PTCR's independent station, which nobody

listened to. Thanks to him, it had eclipsed Caraïbes-Diffusion, the channel with the most listeners in the region, famous for its *Jeux de Midi* noon trivia games. Imagine! A host would distribute prizes of 2,000 or 3,000 francs to anyone who knew how to arm himself with a good dictionary and answer questions like, "Where is the source of the Garonne River?"

What a godsend for the droves of the unemployed! At Radio Solèye Lévé, every morning starting at five o'clock, Boris would give his editorial perspective. At noon, he'd analyze the local and international news. In the evenings, he'd reward his listeners with some verses from Neruda, Nicolás Guillén, Césaire, or Derek Walcott—you know, poets from the Americas! In his defense, it must be said that he never read his own poetry, and some people were sorry he didn't. Modesty? Dieudonné stood there, dumbstruck. So the outrageous rumors he had heard in prison were true. Boris had changed. Truth be told, it was an edifying story. The triumph of man over adversity. The poet had been right to hitch his wagon to a star, to keep the faith. Faith in what exactly? The future? Existence? Himself? Despite this good lesson in endurance, Dieudonné felt miserable, forgotten, deserted once more. His last remaining friend had turned his back on him. He held back something that tasted like tears, murmuring, "Do you know where he lives?"

"Well, that I don't know! Go ask at Solèye Lévé!"

With that, the man's eyes started shining like two fireflies. He half-rose from his blanket, exposing his knock knees.

"Hey, I recognize you! I kept looking at you and looking at you, telling myself I had seen that face of yours somewhere! It's you! You're the one who . . . !"

Frightened, Dieudonné took to his heels, pursued by the old man's excited shouts.

8

Ana contemplated Werner sprawling out luxuriously in his bassinet, as babies like to do.

It had been a hard day. She had taken him for a walk along the waterfront. But the sharp breeze gusting in fits and starts had irritated him. His forehead was soaked in sweat. She'd had a hard time getting him to sleep, despite an herbal bath of pressed soursop and marjoram, a recipe from his godmother, Eudoxia. He fussed and squirmed, his head on fire, as if he might have malaria. Her child's beauty delighted her. She attributed this quality entirely to his father, not believing that a person as ordinary as she could have created this perfection. She was waiting expectantly for Dieudonné. She knew that before the night was over he'd come to her. Just like the last time, because he had nowhere else to go. Snatches of biblical verses danced in her memory. The Son of Man has no place to lay his head. She would be that place, his rock, and would pull the door shut behind him when he joined her and Werner and hold him prisoner. Forever.

Ana lived in Lakou Ferraille, in Cadenat, an old fishermen's neighborhood curled up in Port-Mahault's flank. Rowboats dozed on the black sand, between the bumpy trunks of the almond trees. Chewing on tobacco just as black, fisherman with hair grown white with age chatted about the country they had lost to time. In the old days, ah! the old days, this land was a paradise. Families were made in the Good Lord's image: Joseph, Mary, Jesus, a donkey. Locks and keys were unknown. People lived with their windows and doors open. Perverted guys were those who enjoyed women and rhum agricole too much. But today, ah! today! Sons straddled their mothers. Fathers, their daughters. Brothers, their sisters. People got killed for a piddling 50-franc bill. Nobody wanted to do honest work to make money.

Lakous have practically disappeared in our times, replaced by the HLM and LTS housing projects that municipalities churn out. In the past, there were many of them in working-class neighborhoods, inhabited by the needy, who would squeeze together into a single room: papa, mama, kids. The bourgeois scorned them. However, these were clean and generally God-fearing people. Their children were often at the head of their class. At present, the surviving *lakous* were haunts for prostitution and drugs. The police had their eye on Lakou Ferraille in particular. Not just because of a good dozen *bòbò* ladies who had arrived from Santo Domingo, always looking to stir up scandal and make a racket. Not even because of the dealers—who were from Dominica, those ones—up at dawn with the rainbird's song busying themselves with their shameful traffic. The police suspected two tenants of belonging to a gang of armed robbers with blood on their hands. In a word, the place had a bad reputation. But Ana, who, with her means, could have chosen to live her life in any other setting, had fallen in love with the sea's navy-blue garlands festooning the windows, with the breadfruit tree, so, so tall and straight like the pillar of a peristyle, with the bell apples that ate up the facades and the louvered shutters painted gaily in orange. Nearly seven years before, she had arrived from Iowa State University, where she was completing a master's in ethnology, to study the oral traditions of the Caribbean. In less than six months, she had learned Creole. In less than two years, she had wrapped up her research, for she had attended every *lewoz,* every wake, every *gwo-ka* festival, and every *Chantez Noël* possible and imaginable. She had even stepped across the sea to go all the way to Petite-Terre, all the way to Ladiame, tiny island refuges, quickly discovering that she was tracking an imaginary dreamland, a mythologized land, yet still persisting in her unreasonable quest. When it was time to leave, though, she couldn't pack her bags. Some je ne sais quoi held her back. Next, Dieudonné and then Werner had entered her life and tied her down tight with bonds she could no longer break.

In Lakou Ferraille, Ana enjoyed an unusual status. She was the only white woman, even if, among the Dominican *bòbòs,* Eudoxia had skin as light as hers, and she was also the most fortunate. Consequently, her room was the largest, the best furnished, and the best decorated, flowering with all manner of potted plants, and a hammock swaying on the balcony. Until Werner's birth, whenever they were broke, the *bòbòs* knew that at her place they would find a square meal and an open pocketbook. Even the dealers relied on her for her stock of Alka-Seltzer on the days they got hammered. Ana had never set foot in Basse-Pointe prison because she didn't want that to be the way Dieudonné found out about the result of their night together. She had limited herself to sending him packages month after month: jams, sardines packed in oil, canned tuna fish, and jars of cassoulet to supplement the sad, everyday jail fare, Folio paperbacks that he probably didn't read, and menthol cigarettes that she had seen him smoke one time.

Ana's life had started out happy (like Dieudonné's), before taking a turn toward mourning and loneliness in 1989 (just like his). However, there were differences. For Ana, it wasn't Hugo that set that year apart. 1989 was the year the Berlin Wall fell. Even today, you can see films, hear stories, and read accounts of this great victory. THE END OF COMMUNISM. Historians celebrate the reunification of a nation cut in two. But even though she was born in Berlin, in Ana's eyes 1989 was just the year her parents died. Her father had always been sickly—jaundiced, short of breath, heart problems. That winter, which was no rougher than any other, he had finished. And so her mother lost her will to live. Without a thought for her two little girls, she too had left in turn. There followed letters, phone calls, and endless family conferences, the outcome of which was that Ana and her little sister were sent to live with an aunt who had married and immigrated to Iowa twenty years before. Up until that point, Ana didn't know how much she loved Berlin, with its avenues designed for majestic military parades, its squares in summertime, shaded like forests, and the solid weight of its buildings, heavy as cathedrals. As a child, you don't realize things like that. She had noticed it after being transplanted to the middle of what seemed to be a vacant lot, barbed here and there with houses so alike you could confuse them, buried under feet of snow in winter, imprisoned by wheat the rest of the year. A rustic church, no movie theater, a single drugstore, a McDonald's, a Pizza Hut. At school, the farmers' children, with their big ears and cheeks the color of beets, laughed at her accent. On top of that, her aunt's husband drank his fill and, when he was drunk, beat his wife, his two daughters, and his two nieces indiscriminately. Things hadn't gotten better when she left for college. Ames, a joyless city, fearfully closed in on itself. She was stuck in a law school track that didn't fit her temperament well when she met a Caribbean man who had come, who knows why, to study engineering at this third-rate school. He was just as lost

as she was, just as alone on campus, and their two lonely lives
had flowed together. Even if this great love turned brown in
autumn, it had flowered green all summer. Because of him, she
had switched from law to ethnology and had started studying
orality, the masters of the word, griots, storytellers, folktales,
wakes, *tambouyé* drummers, *mayolè, kimbwazè, doktè fèye,*
this whole folklore of beings as unreal as the elven tribe of the
Erlking whose adventures her grandmother used to tell her stories about in the old days.

She had met Dieudonné at the Sphinx, a nightclub in Le Goulet where—for once—she was trying to have a good time. He
was there with Rodrigue, and she with Julia, a compatriot from
Pittsburgh and one of Rodrigue's conquests. Right away, he had
attracted her because of his reserve, his silence, his sensitive air.
As the evening wore on, she got bolder and had indicated by
her glances and her smiles that she wasn't indifferent to him.
But he had remained distant, absorbed by the music and the
movements of the dancers. On top of that, at midnight he had
vanished like a real Cinderella. As soon as his back was turned,
Rodrigue grew generous with the specifics. He related in minute
detail how Dieudonné had made his way up from the garden to
the bed of a wealthy *békée* from the marina. This Loraine had
an Ali Baba's cave of a house. In a safe at the head of her bed she
had gold and silver jewelry, French francs, and other currency.
Alas! Because of his feelings for her, Dieudonné had declared this
juicy burglary off-limits. He claimed it would fail, since Loraine
slept with a loaded gun in arm's reach. Ana burned with passion
listening to this tropical version of Lady Chatterley's love affairs.
And so she started hanging out with Rodrigue, even though she
usually avoided him because of his interminable stories about
armed robbery and drugs. And one weekend, she got acquainted
with the *Belle Créole*. Such an odd idea, living on a boat! Obviously, this guy didn't do anything like other people. It's true that
he was never there and, in his absence, Rodrigue acted like he
was master and commander himself. Night after night, he got his
friends together: dealers, unskilled petty thieves, humble murderers, their pockets stuffed with easy money, hungry for girls.
During their drinking sessions, where the flow of booze never
dried up, the game was who could boast of the nastiest tricks

played on the police. Ana didn't care for this. No more than Boris, who, calm as an iceberg in this muddle of laughter and blather, kept on scribbling his poems, all the while grumbling that he who sows the wind reaps the whirlwind. At first, given his misogyny and his political opinions, Boris had snubbed the American woman. Quicker than a flash, Ana had turned him around. How a little flattery can change your man! She had only to compare his poems to those of Rainer Maria Rilke and Walt Whitman, her idols, and offer to translate them into German and English, for Boris to morph. When pushy men got too forward with Ana he made them back off. If it was dark, he would escort her back to Lakou Ferraille.

In Rodrigue's case, Boris's somber predictions came true soon enough. A few days before Christmas, on a peaceful night, the sky riddled with stars circled round a beatific crescent moon, Boris and Ana were chatting in the dinette when two police cars, sirens screaming at full strength, had poured out their cargo of men in navy blue at the foot of the monohull. They invaded it, ferreted out a Rodrigue dripping with urine, hidden unbeknownst to them in the forward cabin, and slapped a pair of handcuffs on his wrists. Two of his accomplices had already flipped on him: he was the murderer of one of Millénium's security guards. In their fury, the police officers almost carted off Boris. Luckily, one of them, who was well read, recognized him from the photo on the cover of one of his books.

It was the day after this sorry evening that Ana found herself face to face with the one she had given up hope of seeing. He looked like someone in mourning, sitting with his back against the boom, and though he greeted her, it was obvious he didn't recognize her. She'd had weeks now to mull over her line of attack:

"A boat that no longer goes to sea is as sad as a bird that can't fly."

He acquiesced. "It's not that I don't want to cast off. But it's been docked so long that I wonder what state the sails are in. I'm afraid they'd tear as soon as you tried to raise them. Plus the roller furling systems are shot. And the VHF radio too."

Abruptly, he started describing the *Belle Créole* in her former splendor. The cruises, the dusks reddening the waves, the string of islands, his favorite, St. Barth, a shell planted in the middle of the azure. And she understood that for him, too, happiness was anchored in the never-to-be-regained days of childhood. The very next day, she hurried back to the docks again. Just like the night before, he was sitting on the deck at the foot of the mainsail, as lifeless as a zombie, his expression distraught, visibly going through hell. She managed to drag him to a greasy pizzeria with decor aping American fast-food joints. Suddenly, pushing aside his four-seasons pizza, he drilled into her with his impenetrable eyes and exclaimed in a tone of indescribable pain, "She thinks I'm no better than dog shit!"

"Who does?"

The only answer he gave was to break down, his head falling into his arms on the table. Ana had never seen a boy cry. Far from scorning him for this weakness, she stretched out her hand and her fingers sank into his thick, black shock of hair, crudely chopped short. He shook himself out of it, stood up, rejecting her caress, and ran stumbling down the street decorated with paper lanterns for the holiday. She gave up any idea of following him.

Christmas was coming, but nobody's heart was joyful. For the last month, the PTCR's men were on strike, blockading Port-Mahault and Ferry. Consequently, the champagne, salmon, foie gras, and all the little treats the locals loved were nowhere to be found, and certain intellectuals, despite their leftist leanings, began to see Benjy in a less favorable light. In addition to the strikes, violence was mushrooming. One evening, a commando unit in ski masks had entered a restaurant in Le Goulet and cleaned out all the diners' jewelry and wallets. Another evening, a gang of criminals with faces in plain sight had done the same in a dance club. No one dared go to the Alhambra Cinema Theater anymore, even though a film with Denzel Washington was playing, for fear of getting hurt or getting their car stolen.

Curiously, Ana saw Dieudonné again very soon, two days later, on Christmas Eve. She had invited her fellow Americans to Lakou Ferraille, along with Boris, who, she thought, must be feeling pretty lonely in his bus stop. As long as she was living in Iowa, Ana had persisted in considering herself a foreigner in the United States, an outsider, a late addition among late additions.

She had learned French, and then Creole, the idiom of a dominated people, in order to break with the English language that
had assaulted her as a child. However, setting foot in this country was all it took to show her what world she really belonged
to at the end of the day. It wasn't the cold or the gloomy dome
of the winter skies that she missed, or the exuberance of the
wheat fields in summer. It was something else altogether. From
that point on, her skin clothed her, as conspicuous as a uniform.
References that she couldn't share engulfed her being. She who
had never been very popular during adolescence, who had never
been on Miss University's court, now found all the males losing
their heads over her just because of her blondeness. And yet,
far from satisfying her, this metamorphosis terrified her. Like a
moss transplanted into full sunlight, she longed for the shade
and the damp. In a word, everything made her foreign. At the
same time, she couldn't make up her mind to leave.

Despite everything going on in Port-Mahault, the mood in the
lakou was festive. The dealers were taking a break and smoking
a harmless tobacco. The *bòbòs* had planted a tree draped with
garlands of all colors in the middle of the courtyard. Every day,
before heading out to turn tricks at a grueling pace, they would
sing Advent carols. On Christmas Eve, when the parish priests,
out of caution, were no longer celebrating Mass at midnight
but at five o'clock in the afternoon, they had donned veils and
mantillas and all gone together to the Saint-Jean-de-Obispo
Cathedral, under the direction of Eudoxia. They had gone to
confession and taken communion, marching as one to the Holy
Table. Now Eudoxia was playing a series of Natividad CDs
on her state-of-the-art Sharp, and the women were singing the
refrains in chorus. Their voices, strangely childlike, decorated
the night with silver bells. Ana had had no choice but to give up
turkey, chestnuts, and cranberries for blood pudding, Dominica
yams, and pork stew. Her country was not completely absent,
though: in a pie, one of her friends had substituted squash for
pumpkin. When Boris arrived followed by Dieudonné, she was
so surprised and overjoyed that all her blood, in turmoil, had
flooded into her heart, then abruptly back out again, leaving her
frozen stiff. Dieudonné was no more merry or talkative than

usual. He sat down near the door, his face turned toward the outdoors, as if he were listening to the commotion of the *bòbòs*. Inevitably, the conversation turned to Rodrigue, who everyone knew was a thief, but who they were just finding out was a killer too. What a nasty mess he had gotten himself into! That morning, a crowd had protested outside the central commissariat, demanding they make an example of him. The murdered guard had been a father of three, and his wife was pregnant out to here with their fourth. The Americans were offended. That the streets of New York, Chicago, or Los Angeles were red with blood, they could accept. But not those of this country, a paradise on earth inhabited by tender, generous, and naive souls! And they started citing the bad influence of American-made series, sitcoms, and films. For his part, Boris shrugged his shoulders and once again blamed the politicians. Dieudonné alone stayed out of the debate. Soon, he complained of a headache and went to lie down on the daybed.

"What's wrong with him?" whispered one of the girls.

"It's because of a woman . . . his mistress," explained Boris. "She doesn't want to be with him anymore."

They all contemplated this figure consumed by love. Ana and the other women were envious. What magician had figured out how to light his fire? Why did she keep her knowledge secret? Dinner was lively. During dessert, Boris recited his poems amidst an admiring silence. Someone ventured to say he was truly the heir to the masters of the spoken word. Boris puffed up even more when Ana compared him to Walt Whitman. Around four o'clock in the morning, everyone parted company happy. By then, brimming with alcohol, the *bòbòs* had forgotten the sanctity of the night and were bickering. Ana closed up all the windows and doors. Then, she undressed and stretched out next to Dieudonné. Boris had tried vainly to wake him and had left him where he lay, like a tomb effigy. At first, Dieudonné took her convulsively in his arms. Then he opened his eyes and, realizing his mistake, turned over to face the wall.

Ana dissolved in tears.

When she awoke in the full light of day, the bed next to her was empty.

You can say that Ana was waiting for love as the earth waits for rain in the dry season. For her sister and her classmates in Iowa, sex had lost all its mystery by the age of twelve. But Ana was repulsed by the pimply teenagers who straddled them on the back seats of cars. She refused to engage in these inglorious dealings. She was aware that the males buzzing around her now like bumblebees were not interested in what was inside her. Their concern stopped at the curve of her breasts, the set of her behind. Dieudonné alone seemed to her to be capable of transforming her days. Why him? He was almost seven years younger than she was. But what does that matter! Age is a convenience, not a bargaining chip anymore. The days when marriages delivered teenage girls up to old men are over. Stubborn, she set off again that very evening for the *Belle Créole*.

At the end of her dock, the boat's silhouette stood wrapped in the fur cape of night. The water was murky and dull. On the left, Le Goulet's lighthouse glowed red like a gouged eye in the middle of a puddle of blood. When she turned on the light in the galley, a rat and some cockroaches scurried off. The sink was overflowing with dirty dishes. The smell of trash assailed her nose. Where was Dieudonné? Where should she look for him?

Tired of waiting, she went back home through the rain. It wasn't prudent for a woman—especially a white woman—to venture through the streets at this hour. *France-Caraïbe* fed their readers on stories of robberies and rapes. The atrociously mutilated bodies of two tourists had been recovered in Trois-Chemins-Dugazon. Ana had no time for those sorts of fears. She was watching her life trudge forward, dragging its feet in its rags. When would love's light transform it?

It was a few days later that the unbelievable happened. New Year's Day had made its entrance. She didn't like this new year, which had no kiss under the mistletoe to bring her, no mandarins for good fortune, nor polka-dot dress for luck. That morning, she was lazing in bed. She had just left her mother in the cool and dark apartment on Joachim-Friedrich-Strasse where, curled up on the old sofa sagging with age, she had turned the pages of a storybook. A brutal pounding on the door had made her jump. Pushing it open, she had found herself face to face with Dieudonné. Unexpected, his silhouette stood out against the milky daylight under the whitish gourd of the sky. In her surprise, she stuttered, "You? It's you?"

"Let me in," he had ordered.

She obeyed and the door closed behind her, locking them both in the bowels of shadow. She had not dared make any move toward the bedside lamp and they stayed still for a long while, without speaking to one another, almost without seeing one another. Then she had asked, "Do you want anything?"

He didn't seem to have heard her, and she added, feeling deep in her heart that it was a stupid question, "Some water? Coke? Coffee?"

Since he still didn't answer, she turned on the light and inspected him from head to toe. Naively, she had imagined his clothes would be in disarray, covered in blood or some sign of a crime. No, he was himself, dressed as usual in some sort of cosmonaut outfit. His face expressed no emotion. His eyes were no more unfathomable, no more secretive than usual. He asked, "Can I stay with you?"

She answered, her voice pitching unsteadily with all the passion he inspired in her and to which he clearly paid no heed, "As long as you want. If you came to me, it's because you trusted me. You only have to tell me what you want to tell me."

He told her nothing.

It was the radio, the television, *France-Caraïbe*, and the excited comments from the *bòbòs* that informed her. The island's entire police force was looking for Loraine Féréol de Brémont's gardener.

And yet Dieudonné stayed with her for four days and four nights without hiding, as if he had nothing to fear. Every morning, a terry towel wrapped around his waist, baring a muscular torso that surprised Ana, who had thought of him as fragile, he walked to the public shower, a hut pieced together with sheet metal under a patch of sky. And she swooned imagining him covered in soapsuds, passing his hand again and again over what she so strongly desired. After which he got dressed and sat all day in front of the television. Anything seemed fine to him: cartoons, documentaries, sitcoms, thrillers, roundtables, news programs, debates over the course of the advancing century. She suspected he was staring at the images blindly, locked in his obsessions. He paid no attention to her and, invisible, she would serve him something to eat before slipping out to buy groceries, feverish, anguished, like the mother of a sick newborn, her heart pounding at the sight of a police cruiser patrolling this shady neighborhood or a harmless traffic cop directing cars. At this development, the *bòbòs,* who had never known her to have male visitors, thought they had picked up the bland scent of sperm, and treated her with respect. They stopped walking in at all hours without knocking to borrow a cup of rice or oil, or a 100-franc bill that she'd never see again. Eudoxia in particular was satisfied—she who held the conviction, after so many years on the job, that men were worthless, but that solitude was even worse for women. The *bòbòs* didn't know that, in reality, Ana was going through torture. Having the one she adored so close, within reach of her caress, smelling his scent, falling asleep not far from him without anything happening.

The fourth night, when she had given up hoping for it, he made love to her.

The next day, she was sleeping in the satisfaction of her finally gratified body when he turned himself in to the Cadenat commissariat. And she realized that this last-minute embrace had been his farewell to freedom, to happiness, to peace, to everything he had wanted so badly and that existence had always denied him.

A month later, she missed her period.

Abruptly, Werner woke with a great cry at the same time he always did. She hurried to carry out the magic movements: open her blouse, give him her breast. Once full, he smiled at her with his toothless grin, wriggled around, and happily creased up his black eyes, so like his father's. She pulled him close and hugged him passionately.

"My little Hindu prince," she murmured, "Papa's come back, Papa's come back."

NIGHT

9

"How did you find me?"

"It wasn't hard. I went to Radio Solèye Lévé. I asked where you were living."

"Did anyone recognize you?"

"I don't know . . . Yes. Maybe."

Boris was bothered and wasn't hiding it well. He inspected the surroundings. Nothing noticeable to report. The dark sky was running low over the rooftops. The Grands Hommes complex was located in a densely populated neighborhood, a mosaic of four-story buildings and modest villas so alike you could mistake one for the other behind their small gardens of hibiscus, bougainvillea, and crotons, where everyone was too busy surviving to spare a glance at what their neighbors were doing. Rather, they had to take advantage of the last remaining hours of electricity before darkness settled in, sovereign and impenetrable. In haste, the women were snatching up what was left in the convenience store. On a makeshift sports field, dodging the piles of trash as best they could, youngsters were kicking balls around. The very rare few who owned generators were rushing home to watch CNN. Just when he was about to make his master stroke, Boris should be avoiding any association with an ex-convict. At the same time, his friendship surged back into his heart like a freshwater tide. He had forgotten how young Dieudonné was, thinner and more vulnerable now after his eighteen months in the shadows. More gently, he said, "Listen, Benjy and I are in a meeting with colleagues. You can wait for me in the guest room . . ."

He added, a little ashamed, "Don't show yourself. It's better that way."

He moved aside, opened the gate he had up to that point kept shut, and with a kick, pushed away Prince, his creole mutt who was skulking around. If Dieudonné had been expecting a warmer welcome, he didn't show his disappointment. Walking one behind the other in the narrow hallway dividing the villa in two, they nearly ran into Benjy's big belly as he was coming out of the toilet zipping up his fly. Recognizing Dieudonné, he scrutinized him with curiosity. But the other paid no more attention to him than he would to a stranger. However, he couldn't have forgotten Benjy, whose traits stuck in your memory once you took a look at him. Picture a black man built like a *pièce d'Inde* of old, a prime slave, with a mask under his shaved skull that would not have looked out of place on a Roman emperor. Journalists scrambling for inspiration called him Caesar Augustus, a nickname that didn't fit his personality at all. He was a gentle man at heart, hesitant and timorous. He elbowed Boris.

"I remember his nice face. You wouldn't know what he is by the way he looks."

Boris replied mockingly, "What is he? Serbulon repeated it plenty, he's a victim."

Then he felt bad for being sarcastic.

Around them, the discussions weren't making much headway. Not without difficulty, Boris had convinced Benjy to undertake a historic action. He should meet the leaders of the PPRP without delay and propose a merger with the PTCR in order to create a new party, the PPSN, which, bolstered by the ranks of the trade unionists, would lead the country toward *lendépendans*. Across the island, from the North to the South, people's minds were ripe and just waiting for that. The PPRP had not rejected the offer to meet. However, from the start of the deliberations, it was clear that its delegation of hardened fifty-somethings, deserters from the Algerian War, ex-tenants of the high-security Fresnes prison, felt only contempt for Benjy and his troops. It was led by one of its founders, Roméo Serrutin, a professor of constitutional law at the university whom everyone called "The Elder" in African fashion. Roméo Serrutin was showing off. He had conveniently forgotten that, two years away from retirement, some cleaning ladies had walked in on him with a female student on the floor of his office, engaged in an act whose nature left no room for doubt. At the time, he had bragged that this attested to his virility. Now, his mouth was frowning strictly: what did these PTCR youngsters have to brag about? Of having organized strikes without any clearly defined goal that, consequently, were ineffective and only served to inconvenience the population! They were so unsure of themselves that they hadn't dared launch a general strike, the wake-up call that management took most seriously. Even if they succeeded in hauling the country out of the muddy rut it was stuck in, no one should forget that it had happened, first of all, thanks to the efforts of the PPRP.

The door opened. In came the Angel Carla, as Boris had nicknamed her because she liked to wear blue and, with her flutter of blonde hair, looked just like the Gabriel in an Annunciation painting whose name, unbeliever that he was, he had forgotten. She brought cans of Coca-Cola, ice cubes, miraculously, and ham-and-cheese sandwiches. Some of the PPRP dinosaurs were tempted to tell her in no uncertain terms that she was making a mockery of them and that she should bring them more manly drinks, some CRSs for example—citrus, rum, and sugar—but something held them back. Carla's movements were so gracious that, in her magician's hands, paper napkins changed into woodpigeons, turtledoves, and white rabbits. Each time Boris looked at this companion that the Good Lord had sent him to transform the desert of his life, he couldn't get over his happiness. He recalled his stupor when he had realized that this talented journalist was in love and, because of him, was thinking of settling in a small, fitful, and remote country. So he still had appeal, then? He who possessed nothing? He who at fifty was practically an old man, with his flabby body and the onset of osteoarthritis? Since he had started living with Carla, her sweetness and constant admiration had brought his heartbeat back to life. She had already translated his poems into Italian and had sent them by FedEx to Lavoro Editions in Milan. The only thing she still needed to do to reach the seventh heaven of perfection was to learn Creole, which would shut the grumblers up. A sign that the Good Lord blessed their union was that a fruit was ripening in her loins and her stomach was growing round as a gourd. Because of all this,

Boris, completely unconcerned about contradicting himself, had disavowed the misogynistic verses he had written in the wake of his conjugal misadventure. Yes, tradition and Joseph Zobel got it right: a woman can take a guy to heaven or plunge him into the depths of hell. The trouble is that modern women, *poto mitan* pillars of old, formerly mothers and servants for their men, tigresses for their brood, had forgotten the ancestral virtues. Liberation had gone to their heads like an adulterated wine. They cared only about their careers now, or financial gain.

When everyone had finished the sandwiches, Roméo Serrutin pointed out that it was almost ten o'clock, which meant that in a few minutes, the electricity fairy was going to take leave of the inhabitants of the Grands Hommes complex. She would fly off to the other end of the city and with a wave of her magic wand she'd light up the Fleurie complex where he lived. He was proposing, then, that everyone meet up there in an hour. In reality, this was just a flimsy pretext for bringing the debate back to the PPRP's territory. When Benjy and Boris were alone again, Boris suggested, "What if we send him to Cuba?"

"To Cuba? What an idea!" grumbled Benjy, whose mind was already on other things.

Boris armed himself with patience and explained, in a tone he would use with a child, "The Cubans always take three of our youths to train them as health workers, and two others for training in agriculture. He was a gardener, that might suit him."

Since Benjy didn't seem too convinced, Boris laid out in detail the merits of such a deal. It wasn't only that this solution would resolve the question of Dieudonné's future. It would be great publicity for the PTCR if it took this boy in hand, a boy who in the public's eyes had just had a brush with perdition, and reformed him into a socialist youth! They would score points with all the unions and rival parties.

Benjy was still hesitating when, without warning, the electricity disappeared.

Boris quickly lit a camping lantern, and, followed by Benjy's shuffling feet, returned to Dieudonné. Motionless, the latter seemed to be floating in the lake of shadows lapping every nook and cranny of the room. Boris took a seat next to him and, with his usual loquacity, set himself the challenge of charming him.

He went through the whole list. The *barbudos,* the Sierra Maestra, the victorious revolution, the friendship between Fidel and
Che, avatars of Achilles and Patroclus, their political differences,
Che's departure, his final battle in the Quebrada del Churo and
La Higuera deep in the south of Bolivia, his elimination. He
waxed sorrowful over the moment when the most illustrious
citizen of the great Latin American homeland fell, under the
barrage of a common sergeant drunk on chicha. Dieudonné did
not really seem interested in this story. When Boris finished, he
declared, "I would rather have gone to Jamaica!"

Boris was undeterred. "No, no, no! Jamaica is like here. Even
worse, violence and drugs. What you need is structure and dis-
cipline, and, especially, to learn a trade."

Dieudonné asked a question, but his flat voice betrayed not
the least bit of enthusiasm. "When do I have to leave?"

Boris looked at Benjy, who wasn't saying anything and
seemed bored, and asserted, "Very soon. We'll take care of your
documents for you."

Without a word of thanks, Dieudonné inquired, "Can I
sleep here?"

Boris reluctantly agreed.

The two men came back to the living room and Benjy repeated, as if he didn't know how to say anything else, "I remember he always seemed like a good guy!"

Deep inside, Benjy was troubled. Once again following Boris's advice, he had not informed the PTCR's executive committee of his meeting with the PPRP and he wondered whether he
wasn't committing an abuse of power. And also, he noticed that
the dinosaurs of the PPRP, despite their fifty years of failures
and setbacks, had not learned humility. They took it upon themselves to lecture everyone and thought they held the truth. They
pretended not to know that *lendépendans* scared everyone in
the country. He himself couldn't shake the question: *lendépendans,* to what end? If they ever reached this Desirada, the sun
would still rise on the same side of the world. The needy and the
well-to-do would still be among us, as would the blessed and
the cursed, the prosperous and the empty-handed. The procession of the destitute would still be lined up outside the door to
happiness, waiting in vain for it to open. Everybody wants to

change the world. The world doesn't change. In disbelief, he heard Boris rehashing his arguments. This merger would be an opportunity. Thanks to it, they would galvanize the patriot side and rekindle the flame of years past.

Boris escorted Benjy back to his car and listened to the grievances of the guards, who were having trouble holding back their watchdogs built like young bulls. Last night, once again, a commando had tried to attack the convenience store, even though its shelves were depleted. What did they think they'd find? Not a single merchant kept any change in the registers anymore. Good Lord, how was this all going to turn out? Around them, the neighborhood had become a gaping hole of darkness, as everyone barricaded themselves from their fears as best they could. In the streets, in the small yards, not a single sign of life. Nothing was moving, apart from the dogs fighting over the sparse tidbits they could find in the trash and the brazen cats running after romance, come what may. Boris considered talking to Dieudonné again, then abandoned the idea. There would be time enough tomorrow to give him a sermon on the meaning of life, the virtues of work, and the future of socialism. First he had to calm Carla down, who was now at term, and persuade her to accept that he wouldn't be back anytime soon. The meeting with the PPRP was of the utmost importance. The Angel Carla wasn't sleeping. She had lit a candle and was sitting on her bed, her hands clasped nervously over her stomach. For a second, he thought her first contractions had started. She shook her head, then asked him in her careful French, "You aren't going to leave me alone with him are you, in the middle of the night?"

He shrugged his shoulders and asked casually, "What are you afraid of?"

Without responding directly to his question, she rebelled. "Why doesn't he stay somewhere else? At his mother's!"

"Serbulon repeated it a million times, he doesn't have a mother."

"At his grandmother's, then!"

To pacify her, he tried to wrap his arms around her, but she resisted, hammering home grandiloquently, "Listen, Boris. It's him or me. If he stays here, I'm the one who's leaving."

He made the mistake of letting out a snort of laughter, teasing despite himself, "And where, may I ask, will you go?"

At that, she burst into loud sobs, pitiful sobs that betrayed her fear but even more so a deeper malaise that was suddenly revealed to him: a feeling of loneliness, of abandonment in this country where no one was like her. He was floored. He had thought she was happy, successfully transplanted, at ease in her surroundings. He understood now that this was just an appearance, a facade. After a minute, her cries got more and more raspy and desperate, leaving him no choice. He got up.

Dieudonné still hadn't moved, motionless in the dark. Boris lifted the lantern high, all the while stammering excuses having to do with the character of women, especially if they were pregnant. Yes, afraid so! That sex is weak, pusillanimous even. At first, Dieudonné stared at him with his bottomless eyes, as if he didn't understand. Then, a flicker of rage set them ablaze and frightened Boris. Could the boy actually be armed? He was mistaken; the flicker went out as fast as it had caught. Dieudonné got up, headed for the living room, and opened the front door. The animal of night swallowed him up in its jaws.

Ashamed, Boris went back to the bedroom where Carla had been listening. Despite her halo of curly hair and her blue eyes, she didn't seem like an angel to him at all anymore. He addressed her sharply. "He's gone. Are you happy now? Because of you, I put him out like a dog. Like a dog."

He slammed the door shut on his way out.

It was their first quarrel.

10

Au clair de la lune, mon ami Pierrot,
Prête-moi ta plume, pour écrire un mot!

The night vomited up its India ink in a great gush. The mangrove is a *jablesse,* a witch with kinky hair steeping and stewing her ouabain poisons. Her hut is hidden in a tangle of tree roots. This is where she plans her heinous crimes. In the foredawn, wearing water serpents for anklets and leeches for earrings, she casts off to cast her spells and the cadaver count swells. In her wake stretches a trail of bones, as white as Hop o' my Thumb's pebbles.

> *Qui veut voir ma lanterne des magies pour*
> *deux noix?*

Dieudonné was afraid and, to muster his courage, was reciting nursery rhymes. One of his earliest memories was of a December 24th, when he was five years old. Marine had sung carols with the chorus of neighbors and had then gone down to the Sainte-Hyacinthe Church to attend midnight Mass, leaving him asleep alone on his *kabann*. About a half hour past midnight, he woke up, startled to find himself adrift on this raft in the darkness, deprived of the protective body that was always stretched out beside him. With great difficulty, he had set foot on the floor and explored the immensity of the cabin. In the other room, Marine had taken care to leave the nightlight lit. Unfortunately, the voracious wick had drunk up all the oil and, rushing in from without, the animal of night had come crawling, crawling under the door. She had gotten in. She had swallowed up the chairs, the table, and the kitchen cart, and devoured the devotional images on the walls. She was circling, threatening from all sides. Terrified, Dieudonné had climbed back up on the bed where Marine had found him an hour later, like a castaway on his island, screaming at the top of his lungs. It had taken her days to get over it, hugging her beloved tight enough to smother him and repeating, "Good Lord, Good Lord, my child could have died of fright! Of fright!"

Not a single car on this stretch of highway. He started running and his footsteps echoed in the silence. He wasn't upset with Boris and wasn't angry at him, having understood right off the bat that this was no longer the man he knew. The poet in rags and dreadlocks had nothing in common with this person, his skull shaved close like Benjy's, his neck trapped in a military pea coat. This new Boris had even grown pot-bellied. How sad to end one's days a politician!

Bitterness, anger. Generally, Dieudonné's heart didn't experience these types of feelings. Only one time had he engaged

in an act of violence, and see where it got him! In the secrecy
of his heart, Dieudonné relived this story he had never confided to anyone. It was the night before Christmas Eve. For
two days, leaving her computer off, Loraine had been scribbling
addresses on envelopes in the old-fashioned way. A thousand
other signs—telephone conversations with caterers, a ballet of
delivery trucks dropping off flowers, table linens, glasses, and
dishes, Amabelle putting in overtime—had heralded Loraine's
intention to hold a sumptuous Christmas Eve dinner. Was it in
Luc's honor that she, who never spent time with anyone, was
breaking out of her routine? One morning while he was filling
the lawn mower with gas, Loraine had approached him. Avoiding his eyes, she had held out a fistful of bills.

"This is for you!"

Not understanding, he had stood up. So, waving the money
around, she had mumbled some quick, incomprehensible words
in her chaotic way. Since he still didn't get it and kept standing there in front of her, she had articulated more clearly, with
exasperation, "Don't give me that goggle-eyed look, like a fried
big-jack. It's Christmas for everyone. I'm giving you a few days
off. Go have fun."

Where? Where did she want him to go? He had stammered
out that she knew he didn't have any relatives who cared about
him, or any friends, and so had nowhere to go. Then she had
started screaming furiously, as if his words, forcing her to take
the measure of her own cruelty, were enraging her. "I don't give
a damn! In any case, get lost. I don't want to see you around
here tomorrow or next week."

The door had slammed shut behind her. Sick with outrage,
Dieudonné wiped his hands and lay down on the bench in the
garage. At two o'clock in the afternoon, the heat was suffocating. Rays of sun danced through the gaps in the sheet metal.
However, he was shaking as if he were cold. This was how she
repaid him. He had made an effort to be discreet. He had kept
his pain and his jealousy buried deep inside him, had never
said one word of reproach to her, and had gone on breaking
his back in the garden as if nothing had happened. The day
before, he had planted purple allamandas for her, so hard to

acclimate. Despite that, she was throwing him out like a dog. Did he deserve such mistreatment from her? Tears rolled down his cheeks. Only Loraine had the talent of making him cry. He hadn't cried at the Cohens' departure, when their Boeing 747 got tinier and tinier in the sky over the sea. Or at Marine's death, when he had become a motherless, fatherless orphan.

Abruptly, Luc had slipped into the garage. The grace of his movements, like a ballet dancer's, was surprising. At the same time, it was worrying, because you could sense that it hid a formidable strength, like the one some judokas have, just waiting for an opportunity to manifest itself. Luc had sat down on the edge of the bed, looking at once tender and amused. With a tissue, he had wiped Dieudonné's cheeks, murmuring, "A big boy like you isn't going to cry over that old whore!"

Dieudonné wasn't sure he had heard right and stayed quiet. Luc dabbed him again with the tissue.

"I would love to have your luck and get my time off. But no! I have to stay here and perform. Perform! You know how that nymphomaniac can never get enough!"

Dieudonné was astounded, petrified. When Luc lay down next to him, he had at first recoiled as at the touch of a reptile. The other clasped his hands behind his head, declaring, "The whites have always owned us, since slavery. Even today, the men steal our sweat and our strength to get rich off of us. The women take our manliness for their gratification. Sometimes, I imagine that I'm finishing her off. I imagine that her cries of pleasure are death rattles and that I'll awake free as the air. But then, the day breaks. I open my eyes and see that she's still there."

There was a silence, and Dieudonné could hear his heart stampeding. Then Luc started talking again in a very different tone. "If you want to join me, you'll find me at Fifth Avenue every evening, after midnight. You know where it is?"

Dieudonné nodded yes.

Luc insisted, with a kind of seriousness, "You'll come? You shouldn't keep to yourself like this. I'll introduce you to friends, young people, people your age. A guy like you deserves better than the life you have. First thing you have to do is let yourself have a little fun."

Dieudonné was overwhelmed. Nobody had ever told him he "deserved" anything at all. While his heart flamed with gratitude, Luc rolled over and placed his lips lightly on Dieudonné's neck. Stupefied, he didn't move. Undoubtedly emboldened by this lack of reaction, which could mean whatever one wanted it to mean, Luc's hand caressed him, ventured further.

During the time they were residing on Morne Lafleur, Marine and Dieudonné lived near a man who behaved effeminately and, during Carnival, dressed up as a dragonfly. For this reason, the neighbors had nicknamed him Mamzel Marie. He was a master cabinetmaker, and, besides his furniture, he carved wooden figurines, horses, zebus, goats, donkeys, that he distributed to certain children. Marine had made Dieudonné swear that never, ever would he go near Mamzel Marie or take anything from his hands. One day, he was playing in the culvert when Mamzel Marie came toward him, honey-sweet and smiling:

"Bel, bel ti moun! Vini vwè sa an ni pou-w." (Beautiful, beautiful child! Come see what I've got for you.)

Without hesitation, Dieudonné followed him, close on his heels.

Mamzel Marie's workshop smelled good, like a bakery when the bread comes out of the oven hot and crusty. The floor was littered with springy wood shavings fallen from his plane, blonde, curly, and bouncy. They went into the house, furnished elegantly and divided into two rooms by a curtain of floral Indienne with yellow blossoms. On the table, on the kitchen cart, and everywhere, tons of animals were arranged, forming entire menageries. And also airplanes rolling on their landing gear, two-wheeled carts, racing bikes with curved handlebars, automobiles equipped with rearview mirrors. Some of the miniatures were painted, others only polished or varnished. Charmed, Dieudonné stretched his little hand out toward a plane. Mamzel Marie shook his head and whispered, "No, no, no! It's give-give. I give what you want. You give what I want."

Dieudonné had gone along with it. Two days later, he had come back for another airplane. Then, another time, a racing bike. Some time after that, the neighborhood was in a frenzy: the police had locked Mamzel Marie up in jail because he was sodomizing little boys. Which little boys? Who had denounced him? From then on, Dieudonné had lived in terror of being arrested by the police himself.

Luc's hand, insidious and bold, stirred up all these memories stuffed down deep in shame and secrecy, these memories he never, ever brought back up to the light: his disobedience, those unspeakable acts, the pleasure he had taken in them. A surge of blood went to his head, blurred his vision, set his body on fire. He seized Luc by the throat, fell to the ground with him, and set to smashing his skull on the concrete. And it was as if, years late, he was defending himself as he should have defended himself against Mamzel Marie, destroying the horror of what had been. Hearing the racket, Amabelle and Loraine ran outside, the one from the kitchen where she was finishing the dishes, the other from the bedroom where she was just lying down for her nap. Loraine didn't think twice. She grabbed a gardening tool, a spading fork lying in a corner of the garage, and screamed, pulling out her Creole:

"Lagéye, lagéye! Si ou pa lagéye, an kaï tchyoué-w!" (Let go, let go! If you don't let go, I'll kill you!)

Like a dog restrained by the voice of his master, Dieudonné obeyed. He released Luc. The two boys jumped up, Luc in no way bothered, rubbing his neck with his hands, and on his lips an imperceptible smile that dared Dieudonné to reveal the agreement concluded between them, despite appearances. Loraine brandished the fork dangerously. She was beside herself. Her face had become a savage mask in which her eyes burned black with rage.

"Get the hell out of here. Don't ever set foot here again. If I ever see you in the vicinity, I'm calling the police, do you hear me?"

He wanted to protest. But the only thing that came out of his mouth was a cry, more like a plaintive moan, ridiculous and pathetic. He hurried outside. A red Mercedes tearing down the street almost hit him.

11

Before going to Roméo Serrutin's, Benjy decided to walk to his house through the obscure darkness, which was blissfully cooler after the recent showers. He couldn't stop thinking about Dieudonné. Back when he was visiting Boris's bus stop, he hadn't paid much attention to this taciturn youth, who, moreover, turned tail the minute he showed up. Yet, curiously, when his face had appeared on the front page, looking secretive and naive at the same time, Benjy had felt implicated. What was the point of his grandiloquent speeches, his often-violent tactics? While he and Boris boasted of regenerating the country, a human being he was in contact with every day was wasting away. Not only had he not offered him a helping hand when he should have, but, even more seriously, he had also been insensitive, indifferent to the passion he was suffering. As the weeks passed, he had ended up relegating these inconvenient feelings of guilt to a nook deep in his memory. And yet now, tonight, at the sight of Dieudonné here they were surging back up again and taking possession of him entirely. He understood that this acquittal was no solution. Far from it. It only opened the door to an anguishing future. Who would help Dieudonné get his life back together? Boris's proposal to send him to Cuba on the PTCR's account shocked him, for he saw cynicism and opportunism in it.

Benjy's villa was a stone's throw from Boris's, at the corner of a street that had recently been rechristened Cheikh-Anta-Diop. It stood out because a Caribbean pine towered tall in its garden, and because it was guarded by a couple of Dobermans with ominously silky coats. And especially because it alone in the neighborhood shone like the Sun. To be completely honest with you, Benjy was among the fortunate ones who owned a generator. That set a lot of tongues wagging in the Grands Hommes complex. What! The secretary-general of the union organizing the power company strikes was keeping himself and his family sheltered from the dark! His dogs weren't ordinary local mutts, born of who knows what couplings, but looked like the ones the bourgeoisie ordered out of catalogues from kennels in countries in the North. These were clear signs to be heeded. If, God forbid, the people gave power to this man and those of his kind, they would be worse than the whites. They'd breed a thousand Papa Docs, Baby Docs, and Titides, and things would be worse than in Haiti! In reality, apart from the three characteristics we've mentioned, Benjy's villa was as small and banal as the others, its interior just as modest. In the minuscule kitchen, Inis, his wife, was finishing up dinner with their three boys.

"Already?" she exclaimed when he pushed open the door.

Benjy kissed his three children whom he hadn't seen since the night before, or the night before that, or maybe the night before the night before that, and who received him sulkily, as though he were an intruder come to disturb their tête-a-tête with their mother, then corrected her listlessly. "No, the meeting was interrupted by the blackouts. Now we're going over to the Elder's place. We'll most likely spend the whole night there."

She didn't say anything. He knew what her silence meant. Inis was a good friend of Ixaura, Boris's former wife, who held her ex in low esteem. Not because of the quality of his verses; she had never really read them and didn't know anything about poetry. But because she accused him of being a megalomaniac with a huge taste for power. His advice was deadly. Under his influence, Benjy was going too far. This meeting held at Boris's without the knowledge of the PTCR's executive committee smacked of a power play and should never have happened. Inis made as if to add a place setting for him and he made a gesture signaling that there was no point, thinking to himself that she was still really beautiful at her mature age of forty-two, that they hadn't made love for months, they who, way back when, made love three times a day, plus at night as a bonus. When all this was over, he'd take her to spend a week among the flowers and fragrances of Margarita Island off the coast of Venezuela, without the children; *luxe, calme et volupté*—luxury, peace, and exquisite delight. Just the two of them, like old times. But when would it be over? And besides, what exactly did the word "over" mean? Should he think of himself as a revolutionary hoping for the ultimate tabula rasa of revolution?

"Papa!"

The tiny voice of Kevin, his youngest son, who, he sensed, always harbored a secret hostility toward him, pulled him out of his reflections. The child fixed him in the eyes.

"Is it true you're going to roast in hell among the damned?"

Badly hiding their glee at this insolence, the other children held their breath. Benjy asked only, "Who told you that nonsense?"

Kevin protested, "It's not nonsense. The teacher said it in class."

At first, Benjy was speechless, and Kevin took advantage of his silence to embellish his story. According to the teacher, Benjy was doing so much harm to the country, to its inhabitants, to the children who didn't have milk because of him, and to their mamas, that the Good Lord was sure to punish him. Benjy knew that he was the devil incarnate in the eyes of the bourgeoisie and petite bourgeoisie, who didn't understand the government's indulgence toward him. However, he never thought people would slander him in front of his own child. Even so, he forced a smile. "First of all, hell isn't real."

The older children, abandoning their role as spectators, took Kevin's side. Together, the three boys protested vigorously. "Of course it's real!"

Raised by their mother, pupils at a religious school she had chosen, they believed all that Catholic mishmash—saints, angels, purgatory, eternal fire—that Benjy professed to scorn. If any religion appealed to him, it was Islam, which he pictured as austere, pared-down, with its flowing boubous, its five prayers punctuating the day, its fasting, its pilgrimage to Mecca.

A ring of the telephone interrupted their exchange, which was more like a dialogue of the deaf. It was José Merlot, the deputy secretary-general of the PTCR. For years José Merlot had suffered from migraines and chronic toothaches, and had vainly made the rounds to hospitals and *doktè fèye* healers in search of treatment. It didn't do much for his character. On the phone, his voice was edgier than ever. Was it true, what he had heard? That Benjy had entered into an agreement with the PPRP? In whose name? By what right? Benjy tried to explain himself. But José, shouting, wasn't listening. He concluded by announcing he was coming over on the spot along with the full membership of the executive committee.

"At this hour?" exclaimed Benjy, astonished.

"The situation requires it," José responded melodramatically.

He hung up. Forcing himself to make light of it, Benjy turned to Inis.

"Well, that's promising. They're all about to show up here. I'm going to make myself some coffee. I predict I will soon be very much in need of it."

By way of response, Inis gave him her cheek to kiss and left the room, ushering out the kids, who were thrilled to have bested their father. Actually, foreseeing what was about to follow, she had a hard time hiding her satisfaction. The man she had married some fifteen years ago had been a stay-at-home kind of guy, hiding his fire under the outward appearance of a placid father but fornicating with her in bed as soon as the clock struck ten. Then, abetted by Boris, he had been bitten by the trade unionism bug. His guru had passed his great ideas on to him: the European confederations understand nothing whatsoever about the problems of the colonized. Thus, he got it into his head to create a unified local syndicate. From that moment on, the placid father had morphed into a blazing star. He never stood still anymore. Inis never saw him at night anymore. He was traveling all over the country from north to south, from east to west, including the remotest corners and hamlets, to sow the seeds of contestation everywhere. His sons were coming into the world and growing up, his wife was fading, his father dying, and his mother confined to a wheelchair, but he never noticed. Only the PTCR counted. Around her, families were taking their kids to Orlando and couples were going off to Havana to sip mojitos. Still others were embarking on cruises in the Caribbean. Would all this happen for her anytime soon? When she had finally gotten her boys to bed— they kept begging to stay up and play with their PlayStation— she retreated to the marital bedroom where she spent most of her nights single. To fight against a feeling of loneliness, she left the television permanently turned on, and, at the moment, an anchorman, a former *négropolitain,* judging by the way he rolled his *r*'s, was reporting the latest news. That was how she learned of Dieudonné's acquittal. At first, she didn't know what to think. Like the rest of the country, she had taken a passionate interest in this story, devouring her *France-Caraïbe* every day. One morning, she had even gone to the courthouse. But the large crowds had made her retreat. Without espousing Serbulon's Manichean formula, her sympathies obviously leaned toward Dieudonné. He might have been one of her little brothers or, God forbid, one of her sons who had gone astray. At the same time, Loraine was a woman, and even though she was a *békée*, this put her in the interminable list of victims of almighty male power. Women beaten, women raped, women deceived. So you could put a woman to death and go on with your life, with free rein. The extent of the injustice stupefied her. Despite everything, her intuition told her that the life that was being handed back to Dieudonné might not be worth the trouble of living and before long, people would be hearing of him again.

During this time, left to himself, Benjy had been melancholically downing cup after cup of bull's blood, as people called this coffee so strong that it left an indelible, mournful border on the earthenware. Then he went out on the veranda to wait for his colleagues. No fiery downstrokes blazed their writing in the sky, just a dotted line of harmless rainclouds that would soon burst open and finally refresh Port-Mahault. No comet was crossing the air. In short, no manifest signs. The Good Lord wasn't speaking up on this very ordinary night, identical to any other. However, Benjy knew that everything was about to change. For some time now, complaint after complaint had been coming from their base. In good faith, they had fought with tenacity for salary increases and improvements to their circumstances. At present, they could no longer understand where their helmsman wanted to steer them. If it weren't for the handful of raging picketers still surrounding the firms, the employees would have gone back to work a long time ago. This unusual meeting, through an unusual vote, was going to remove him from office. In the small hours, Port-Mahault, and all the rest of the country's inhabitants, their breath sour, only half-awakened from their night sweats and fears, would learn the name of the new secretary-general. Little by little, the strike orders would be lifted, the road barricades would be removed, the sequestered bosses would be set free again, and the well-to-do would heave a great "Phew!": "A waste of effort. We got away by the skin of our teeth. *Lendépendans* is not yet to be."

In truth, deep inside he felt relieved. He had never been able to break the hold Boris had had over him ever since childhood. But he'd had enough and was tired of being pushed down this bumpy road to nowhere.

Benjy had begun his career as a substitute teacher with some of the poorest scores. In Fauconier, an underprivileged town in Haute-Terre not far from the hot springs of Bains-Jaunes, whose sulfur odor wafted down all day, he was responsible for a one-room school. His pupils, too poor to afford the luxury of a lunch at the school cafeteria, filled their stomachs with mangoes. From trudging under the sun so long, the cap of wool covering their heads turned reddish while their cheeks took on a blue sheen. Benjy didn't dare bore them by making them recite La Fontaine's fables or find the square of the hypotenuse. He preferred to distract them with the seafaring adventures of comic book captain Corto Maltese. And so it was that the primary certificate exams produced so few successful results in Fauconier that one year a representative from the Ministry of National Education had made the trek up to this tormented mountain town to check out what was happening there. This civil servant with his blue-eyed gaze, red cheeks, and eyelids bordered with the same color had looked down on this *bitako,* who was barely more presentable than his students. He had asked him a few questions, and, at his muddled, embarrassed answers, had penned such a report that Benjy was transferred to Marjane. Marjane was a rocky cay a stone's throw from the country's northern coast, to which everyone dreaded being assigned. There, the goats were more studious than the children. Tired of waiting vainly for pupils to show up in his empty classroom, Benjy had taken refuge in the office of Gaston Ferbois, who manufactured all the pipes and bathroom fixtures needed in Marjane. In a snap, he had started learning a new trade: plumbing. In our modern societies, plumbers are in high demand. Much more so than poets or novelists. On his return to Port-Mahault, he was tasked with fitting all the HLM and LTS housing projects that the municipality was churning out. His ascent had begun.

People say that the mayor was particularly galled when Benjy organized the city services strike that hit the capital so hard and put his reelection in jeopardy. He liked this hardworking and courageous young man, who had gone from white-collar teacher to worker with no collar at all, a trajectory which warmed his communist heart, for he was a rightful member of the Communist Party and a regular at the annual Fête de l'Humanité festival in France. In addition, the mayor had long favored him because for a time Benjy had been hanging around one of his daughters, and he could already picture himself as father-in-law to this model proletarian. That had happened before Benjy met Inis at a wedding and fell in love with her while dancing the Java.

Around ten thirty, the PTCR executive committee members pushed open the villa's gate. Prudently, Benjy had chained up his dogs. However, he couldn't prevent the unruly creatures from barking like furies and arcing up on their hind legs, making, in other words, an infernal racket and further inconveniencing the newcomers. Led by José Merlot, his tortured face stern as justice, the eight members of the PTCR approached single file, given the walkway's narrowness, all of them looking serious and determined, as if it were Judgment Day.

Very little transpired at this meeting.

What is certain is that the board forced Benjy to call the mayor of Port-Mahault, the CEO of the electric company, and the chief officers of a thousand other services and firms to inform them himself that the PTCR accepted their most recent proposals and that, in the morning, memoranda of understanding would be signed. He choked on the name of his successor as it came out of his mouth: José Merlot, who had been his loyal second-in-command for years.

Once all this was done, Benjy and José Merlot, who, to tell the truth, didn't hate each other, talked as usual about José's migraines and toothaches before sipping two cups of bull's blood. José went so far as to compliment Benjy on the quality of his brew.

"I can never get anything good out of their infernal electric coffeemakers!" he complained.

"It's because I use an old grinder that my mother handed down to me," explained Benjy.

Ah, the good old days! And these two men purporting to pilot the country toward the future joined together in singing the praises of the past and its traditions.

12

For some time, dogs had been chasing him yapping. Where had they come from? Most likely from the depths of the mangrove. Dieudonné, hearing their galloping and their panting breath behind him, knew that they were Spirits come straight from hell. He could already see himself ripped to shreds, his body mangled, when a sports car's headlights scared them and made them scatter in the shadows. Forced to run like mad, Dieudonné had got all the way back to Port-Mahault and the all-pervading reek of rubbish. You would have thought a cemetery had opened up and spit out its rotting carcasses. This stench combined with the more far-off scent of the sea to create an acrid, unhealthy atmosphere that choked your throat. On the right, as you entered the city, there was a stretch of land where bands had put on zouk and compas concerts back in the good old days, when people still had love on their minds and wings on their feet. The Guadeloupean group Kassav had got people dancing there, as had the Haitian band Tabou Combo. At present, the space was given over to the whims of the seasons. The rainy season transformed it into a swamp. The dry season made pipe-organ cactuses grow as tall as teenagers. In every season dogs pooped in it, and their droppings, baked to a crisp by the sun, emitted a distinctive odor. Dieudonné entered it blindly without really knowing where he was heading. After a few minutes, his feet stumbled over something in the shadows and he fell flat on his face on the hard, stony ground. At that point, silent, ferocious shapes surged out of every corner. Dogs? No, this time more like hyenas, recognizable by their jeering laughter. They lunged at him; up close they transformed, and he could make out human shapes. Expert hands felt him over and plucked him in no time of all his poor possessions. Menthol cigarettes, a box of matches, a pocket knife, a wallet containing a few photos in lieu of money. At the conclusion of this search, a youthful voice exclaimed, miffed, "*Hak!* The bastard doesn't have *hak* on him!"

To punish him for this, someone kicked him. A searing pain. Another hit him smack in the face. A pain even more violent. He moaned, "Guys, leave me alone! I got out of jail this morning. I'm as poor as Job. I have absolutely nothing."

Another shape came closer and shoved a flashlight under his nose. At first, blinded, he blinked hard. Then, in the circle of light, the profile of a childlike but brutal face came into view, with a forehead swallowed up by a baseball cap. The stranger snickered.

"You just got out of jail? We haven't been in yet. Let us in on it. What's it like in there? People say it's a real den of *makoumè*. But who are you, for starters?"

Dieudonné, for the first time, felt something akin to pride in giving his name: this gang of kids mugging and beating up reckless people passing by at night, could they really compare to him? He declared, unintentionally emphatically, "I'm Dieudonné Sabrina."

What did he expect? Unruffled, the kid smacked him right across the face before winding up and planting his foot in his stomach. Dieudonné fell over backwards and the hyenas attacked him noisily, like the cadaver of a fallen impala in the bush. He lost consciousness.

Time passed.

When he opened his eyes again, everything around him was spinning and he thought he was on a carousel. Merry-go-round music danced in his ears. Then the world regained its silence, its solid foundation. The hyenas had scampered off. Above his head, the moon and the stars were adorning the gloom with pinchbeck jewelry. The bell in the Saint-Jean-de-Obispo Cathedral rang out ten o'clock. That's when Dieudonné realized he wasn't alone. A shape was seated next to him. A tiny voice inquired, "Can you walk?"

A taste of blood in his mouth. He checked his body: bruises everywhere. Wincing, he forced out the words, "I can try."

Nearly crying out in pain, he stood up, wobbled, but held fast. Yes. He was right, it was a girl. She had turned on her flashlight and in its glow she appeared, a tomboy rigged out in jeans and a baseball jersey reading "Yankees" across the chest, with a pair of splendid Doc Martens on her feet. Under the tiara of wild hair, her cheeks had the roundness of sweet cups. She couldn't be more than fourteen or fifteen. She introduced herself:

"My name's Dorisca. I'm not from here. I'm Haitian. My family comes from Jérémie."

Ever since he had lost Rebecca Cohen, Dieudonné had dreamed of having a little sister. As a child, he kept a close eye on Marine's stomach. Hopelessly flat, and for good reason. His mother, as he knew, didn't make love. However, instead of appreciating this chastity, he wished she were constantly pregnant by some man or another, like all the mamas. Unexpectedly, Dorisca revived all the nostalgia in him and he got irritated. "You're crazy to be outside all alone at this hour!"

She shrugged her shoulders. "I love nighttime. I've always loved nighttime. It's because I was born at eleven o'clock at night. When I was a baby, I mixed up day and night. I would sleep and sleep. I'd wake up around eight in the evening and start crying for my mother's breast. Plus, I'm not in any danger. Around here, everyone knows me. No one will lay a finger on me. You know, the guys who attacked you aren't so bad. They're the Leopards, a gang from the Droits-de-l'Homme junior high. They don't have good parents, that's all."

She added quickly, "Like you. You don't have good parents. Why did you do it?"

At least she knew who he was. He fell prey to that feeling that made him close up on himself every time and murmured, "Don't ask me."

She didn't press. She offered him her arm and he took small steps forward, leaning heavily on her slender body. As they got closer to the docks, the stench began to dissipate. Soon, they heard the throaty laugh of the sea, her voice the voice of a female giving herself over to pleasure with exaggerated abandon, and the crack of the bawdy, dominating wind whipping her. The night's jailer was dismissing his security detail. The depths of the sky were poking through the clouds, and the color of the air was growing brighter. On the other side of the bay, you could make out Petite-Anse, crouching, with its houses and its steeple, like a wild animal about to leap. You would have thought it was a life-size painting. An artist had delighted in the variations of a single hue. Sequined black for the rare stars in the sky. Opaque black for Haute-Terre's mountain chain. A more muted black for the expanse of the ocean. They sat down on a bench on the Victor Hugo promenade, between the allamanda bushes and the royal palms, and the sea breeze clung to their faces. The scent of open water flooded Dieudonné with nostalgia.

"In the past," he murmured, "I used to live on a boat."

"I know," she said, "The *Belle Créole*. They said it in *France-Caraïbe*. There was even a photo of it."

He realized once again that his life no longer belonged to him. It was floating around in the media. He reflected that he hadn't thought to go say hello to the monohull, his refuge in bad times, in times of loneliness, and his ingratitude hurt him. To redeem himself, he turned to Dorisca.

"One day, I'll take you to go see it. Once, it was a magnificent sailboat. Almost every weekend we used to go out to sea. Papa Cohen made me his skipper and used to leave me at the helm for hours on end. Sometimes even at night. I used to guide myself by the stars. I knew them all by their names. The Great Bear, the Little Dog . . ."

She made a face. "For me, the sea is a traitor. It's sunk so many Haitians fleeing the country in all manner of canoes and rafts to go to the United States of America. In 1985, before I was born, my papa's brother died off the coast of Florida with his wife and three children. The Americans forced them to jump into the water and drown."

Dieudonné repeated, floored, "Forced people to drown? How is that possible?"

"You don't know Americans," she said authoritatively. "They're the worst of all the whites."

So why did people risk death to go live in their country? Dieudonné held back this question. What's more, any conversation on the topic of "whites" made him uneasy, putting into question his attachment as a child to "whites," the Cohens, and above all his love for a "white woman," Loraine. Maybe you had to hate them collectively, but individually you had the right to cherish them? Maybe, collectively, they formed an army of predators, relentlessly trampling and devouring those who were unlucky enough to cross their path while, individually, they allowed their hearts to blossom with the simple, human feelings of love, pity, and respect? In one of those about-faces characteristic of the weather, huge gusts of wind, laden with humidity, suddenly began to blow. The darkness of the night grew thicker. Dorisca stood up quickly.

"Let's go to my place," she ordered. "The rain is coming, and also you need to get your wounds treated."

He hesitated and she added, reassuringly, "It's just my godmother and me at home. The Tontons Macoutes killed my papa and my mama when I was very little. So my *ninnaine* took me in with her. We came here when I was six. My *ninnaine*'s husband died three Christmases ago. He was poisoned remotely."

Can you poison someone remotely? Dorisca lowered her voice and said with sadness, "Since he's been gone my *ninnaine* spends the days waiting for him and praying. He comes to see her every midnight. She won't even notice you in the house."

He stood up again with difficulty. They walked the interminable length of the blind facades of the HLM projects and went back up Boulevard de la Victoire. Suddenly, lights shone in the windows. At top volume, with no regard for the neighbors, someone in the throes of nostalgia was listening to that Isolina Carillo tune that always worked its way deep into your gut, each time just as moving as the last, stirring up snuffed-out dreams and desires:

> *Dos gardenias para ti*
> *Con ellas quiero decir:*
> *Te quiero, te adoro, mi vida*
> *Ponle toda tu atención*
> *Porque son tu corazón y el mío*

At one corner, a bar was open, filled with daring souls more concerned about the good taste of their rhum agricole than their safety. Nevertheless, once you passed this little island shining like a diamond, you were wading knee-deep in darkness again.

Dorisca lived in a renovated neighborhood nicknamed Little Paradise, an ex–Hell's Kitchen slum that had long been the shame of Port-Mahault. The municipality was very proud of its piazzas, its balconies, its loggias—of all this flashy architecture designed by a Puerto Rican who had done his training in New York, and on the morning of its inauguration, the mayor had given a beguiling speech vaunting the unity of the Caribbean Region. No one could predict that, in less than two years, this much-touted achievement would become one of the top havens for coke and crime. The young women attending high school next door at the Alexandre-Dumas campus would commend their souls—and, on the rare occasions they had to, their virginity—to the Good Lord. Dorisca held a finger up to her lips and showed a key tied to a string around her waist.

"My *ninnaine* never sleeps. Like I told you, it's at night that she sees her husband. Because of that, she can't go back to Haiti, because that would mean leaving him all alone here."

They went inside. In the living room, which smelled of incense, a nightlight kept the heavy shadow in check. The already narrow room was congested with oversized furniture: rockers, high-backed chairs, low-backed chairs, bar tables, and coffee tables decorated with vases of artificial flowers displayed on crocheted doilies. The walls were just as cluttered, covered with prints and photographs: photos of two identical children, though of different sexes, a boy and a girl, naked on a blanket; older, seated side by side in little armchairs; bigger still, the little boy in a suit and tie, the little girl with ribbons in her hair. Some half-extinguished candles were puffing out spirals of smoke in front of one showing a mustached man with big eyes who looked utterly harmless. The *ninnaine*'s husband? Dorisca and Dieudonné were trying to forge a path through the room without knocking anything over when a voice called out from above. "Is that you, Dorisca?"

"Yes, it's me, Ninnaine!"

They started up the stairway. A large woman was standing on the landing, illuminated by the oil lamp she was holding high. Wearing her hair in buns, she had a pleasant face, eyes that looked a little scattered, and breasts bobbing in a white cotton nightgown with a crocheted yoke. She said softly, "Tonight, he's late getting here."

Then she considered Dorisca pensively and, frowning, she asked her goddaughter, "Doudou, who is this person? I don't like the look of him."

Dorisca seized Dieudonné's hand and declared firmly, "He's my boyfriend, Ninnaine!"

With that, she pushed him from the other side of the landing into a bedroom, a mouth of shadow, hardly bigger than one of the cabins on the *Belle Créole* and just as suffocating, and shut the door. Through the panels, the godmother persisted, "Chérie, darling, be careful with your body!"

Dorisca shrugged. In the bedroom, she lit some candles, and a startling image floated to the surface of the shadows. Against a backdrop studded with stars shone a heart, extended by a sort of sword ending in three handles.

"It's the veve of Erzulie Dantor," explained Dorisca.

Grimacing, she kicked off her Doc Martens, revealing frail childlike feet, her toenails daubed with a red nail polish that had nearly worn off. "They're tight. The size is too small. You know what it's like, I had to buy them secondhand."

On the other side of the landing, a door closed and the bed springs creaked. The godmother was going back to bed. Dorisca ordered, "Get undressed and get on the bed."

He thought he had misheard. She started laughing. "I haven't done it with anyone yet, you know. And you're not going to be my first. Ninnaine says that virginity is a woman's treasure. I'm only going to give it to the man who puts a ring on my finger and walks me up the steps of the church in my veil, all dressed in white. Have you ever heard of Vodou?"

Dieudonné shook his head no. She got serious. "Some people are Catholic and believe that the Good Lord made everything on earth. Others are Protestants. Or Buddhists. For us, Vodou is our religion, that we brought with us from Africa in the old days. Our holy spirits are called loa. There are male loa and female loa. The most beautiful of the female loa is Erzulie. Sometimes we call her Dantor, sometimes Freda.

Dahomey sometimes too. I'm going to massage you like the *mambos* do back home."

Dieudonné gave up trying to understand this gobbledygook. He took off his clothes, holding back cries of pain, for the fabric stuck to his wounds, which reopened and started bleeding again. He was ashamed of his body's lack of desire, his limp organ, whereas he would have liked to boast a powerful erection. But he only got hard for Loraine. She would laugh and fondle him.

"Is all that for me? It's like giving candy to a pig!"

He didn't like it when she demeaned herself that way.

Only once had he gotten hard for someone else. Ana, the American. Boris claimed these foreigners were all *bòbòs*. According to him, despite her holier-than-thou attitude, this one was making eyes at him and was always holed up at the *Belle Créole* because of him. In reality, Boris was only bragging and he knew it. From their very first encounter at the Sphinx, Dieudonné had sensed Ana's desire buzzing around him annoyingly, like a mosquito circling over someone trying to sleep. Back then, he didn't have time for her. If he had given her what she wanted a few weeks later, it was against his will, so to speak. When the moment came to turn his back on the world, the life instinct had won out.

During this time, Dorisca was rifling through her dresser drawers. From the top one, she pulled out a chipped plate. From the next, three vials whose contents she poured carefully into it. Then she struck a match. The mixture ignited at once. Small blue flames started rippling. Remembering the arsenal of those *kimbwazè* and *gadèdzafè* that he had gone to see with Marine so many times, Dieudonné made fun. "You do magic?"

She retorted gravely, "Vodou isn't magic!"

With that, she dipped her hands in a jar of Vaseline, came over to him, and, after crossing herself vigorously, traced a series of crosses over his shoulders, his navel, his genitals, the top of his thighs. Next she went to work. As her expert hands came and went, rose and fell, pressured and kneaded, her face absorbed in concentration, he started to understand that she was accomplishing a mystical operation that was directed not only at his body, but also at his spirit, his soul. Knots came undone deep down inside him. Moorings came unmoored. Stoppers came unstopped. And he began to cry as he had never cried before. Over the one he had lost, through his own fault. Over himself, who, as supreme punishment, would have to lug his life around without her. Over the solitary existence, as miserable and painful as Calvary, that was to be his lot.

"Tell me about it!" she suggested affectionately.

Usually he kept everything inside himself. He had let Mr. Serbulon construct that terrible story line—such a profitable one at the end of the day, since it had won him his freedom, a freedom he didn't know what to do with. Now, he couldn't stand it anymore.

"What is there to tell? You tell stories about bad luck, about tragedy. You don't tell stories about happiness. I was happy. Sometimes, when she'd had too much to drink, around midnight or one o'clock in the morning, she'd get a little boring. She'd ramble on about a ton of people I didn't know and things I didn't understand, and then she'd get irritated: 'You're so stupid! Dumb as a donkey! Why am I wasting my time with a stupid guy like you?'

"But apart from those times, she was always nice. She liked to make fun of herself. She'd say, 'I could become a great writer, another Marguerite Duras. I've got as much talent as she does. More, even. Only, it's my bad luck to be a *békée*. The *békés* are a cursed race. We did the dirty work for the whites in France: putting the blacks from Africa to work, cultivating sugarcane, trying to save the plantations after emancipation. But they were never grateful. Not a word of thanks! They even went so far as to scorn us because the masters slept with their slaves. As for the blacks, they hate us. Even today they accuse us of all the sins of Israel. They only want to remember the punishments and humiliations of the bad masters. At the same time, according to them the good masters were even worse than the others—hypocrites and paternalists. All in all, we lose across the board.'

"I think what screwed up her life was the death of her sister, Florelle. She couldn't forget her for a single second. She'd show me photos, saying, 'She was pretty, wasn't she?' I saw a girl who was a little stocky, too pudgy, not at all my type. She'd be crying, 'We were as alike as two drops of water. The only difference was that she was a brunette. I was blonde. Also, she was smart. She was good at school, whereas in that area, I couldn't do much of anything. That's why my parents never loved me. Parents want to be proud of their children, it's natural. My mother, who had been thwarted by forty years of marriage to a despot, dreamed of taking her vengeance through me. For his part my father, who had been christened Jean-Eustache, but who everybody called Jean the Moron behind his back, dreamed of a daughter who'd be a doctor, a lawyer, or who'd marry well. But I got married three times. With three good-for-nothings who would have finished off my money if I'd let them. The best one was the first, Antoine, a painter who only painted the sea. Blue squares and rectangles. Nobody would buy them. To console him, I'd say, "What do you expect? You can't paint the sea." He'd answer back, "So you can't paint life, then." The worst one was the third, Paol, a guy from Brittany who only wanted to write poems in his language and kept yammering, "Your country, my country: same fight." I left him so I wouldn't have to hear any more of those crazy theories.'"

Dorisca dipped her hands in the Vaseline again and protested, "That's not what they wrote in *France-Caraïbe*. They wrote that she treated you worse than a dog and that one day, at long last, you rose up in revolt."

Yes, yes! That was Serbulon's version. But she only got angry and lashed out at him because of Luc. It was when Luc arrived that she changed. It was because of him that she had trampled on his tenderness, his love. Because of him that she had mortally wounded him. That she had wanted to kill him.

After she had ordered him to get out of her house, he hadn't dared venture near the villa. He had holed himself up in the *Belle Créole*, putting up with Boris's tirades, Ana's visits, and her silent advances. In the end, one afternoon when his suffering got to be too much, he couldn't help but go prowl around the Allée des Amériques. On the surface, nothing had changed. The neighborhood was dozing in luxury. At that hour, tongues lolling, the dogs in their kennels were dying of heat. Thirsty, the wilted flowers in the garden were hanging their heads. Above the veranda, the green-and-white striped blinds gave shade. From afar, he was contemplating the paradise he had lost when Amabelle came out the door, quickly opening her parasol. According to all her depositions, her heart was torn between sympathy, pity, and sorrow. She put up with things for Dieudonné's sake. The reality, though, was a different matter. That day, her silhouette flat as a breadboard in her green dress, the *zindienne* had quickened her step in order to put distance between herself and such an undesirable person. Her short responses had fallen curtly from her mouth. Yes, the Christmas Eve dinner had been a success. Nearly a hundred guests. It seemed that Luc had sold all his paintings. Yes, he was still there, but from what she had heard, he was supposed to be leaving soon for New York.

Indeed, the day after New Year's, Luc had left. He hadn't even come back to Guadeloupe for Loraine's burial, which very few people had attended anyway. Only relatives. None of all those people she had helped out. Luc was in New York. That meant the guilty man was still free. He was coming and going as he pleased. He was sitting in Central Park. Autumn was over. Around him, the trees were stretching out dark charcoal-penciled branches and his painter's eye was eating up those tortured shapes. At night, he stretched out next to whomever he liked. When would people see that they had mistaken the executioner for the victim?

There's no shortage of stories of this kind. A man is locked up for a crime he didn't commit. His hair turns white. His eyes cloud over in the dark of his cell. One day, the unspeakable error is discovered. The man is freed, but he no longer has any desire for anything. No one can give back that elusive something he has lost.

At that moment, Dieudonné heard a cry of joy, followed by the murmur of a conversation. Dorisca looked up and said, pleased, "He's here. In a little while, the bed springs will be creaking. They'll make love."

"How can you make love to a dead person?" Dieudonné ventured to ask.

"In Haiti it happens all the time," Dorisca said calmly. "All the women whose husbands were killed by the Tontons Macoutes see them again at night. The only thing is, they can't have children with them anymore."

Once again, Dieudonné gave up trying to understand. Dorisca continued to massage him expertly with her small, burning hands. Suddenly, the joyful and rhythmic sounds of pleasure stopped coming through the walls; the door opened. The godmother stormed in, brandishing her oil lamp. She had lost her calm, dreamy demeanor and seemed to have transformed into some kind of dangerous animal, like a tigress. She was trembling, pointing an accusing finger at Dieudonné, who had sat up hastily, trying to hide his private parts, and she stuttered, "Doudou, he recognized him. He smelled his stink as soon as he came in the house. He's the one who . . . He's the one who . . ."

In her mouth, the words mushed together in an inaudible muddle. Furiously, she gathered up the scattered clothes, threw them into the stairwell, and with a single shove sent Dieudonné rolling down behind them, shouting, "Murderer! Devil! Get away from my child! Get the hell out! Murderer! Devil!"

Dieudonné picked himself up at the foot of the stairs, groped his way across the living room, and finished getting dressed on the sidewalk. He got his clothes on somehow, wedged his feet into his old Reeboks, and left limping.

A few yards away, in the glow of a burning car tire, a group of boys was playing cards in the most perfect silence. The light sculpted their features, formed a halo around their dreadlocks, and gave the whole scene an unreal quality. Absorbed in their game, they didn't look around at Dieudonné, who slipped into the shadows, which, for the time being, were beneficent. He was in more and more pain, Dorisca's massage having only served to reawaken his bruises, and he was thirsty and hungry. Nothing in his stomach since the infamous colombo at lunch. Where could he go? He remembered that Fanniéta lived downtown. She wasn't very generous, this woman who had held him at the baptismal font. Just as she hadn't really treasured her sister, she didn't really treasure her sister's son. Neither at Christmas nor at New Year's had she ever given him a gift. Not a kiss. Not a smile. However, the proverb assures that blood, that salty red liquid flush with hemoglobin, is thicker than water, which, as we know, has no scent or color or taste. On a day like this, she'd make an exception and make a little space in her house for him to sleep.

He headed in the direction of Rue de Lesseps.

13

After years of hell, living with womanizers who played the field, lonely pregnancies, children whose fathers refused to acknowledge paternity, unemployment, RMI welfare checks, and the torments of making it to the end of each month, Fanniéta had finally found Magloire.

Magloire never worried about finding out which men had given Fanniéta her two boys and her daughter, who, at fourteen, was already the mother of a little girl herself. He hadn't insisted on knowing the date and year of her birth, and he hadn't been put off by her false teeth or the wrinkles that age was already starting to burrow around her eyes and mouth. No! He hadn't asked anything of her and had simply moved in with her, to the astonishment of the bad-mouthers and the envious. It's because Magloire wasn't a born-and-bred native, an ordinary Guadeloupean. His placenta wasn't buried at the foot of a sandbox tree. He didn't speak Creole and his French *r*'s rolled like the *métros*' did. His father's side of the family had emigrated to France after the war and, a second-generation child, he had seen the light of day a few yards away from the Renault automotive factories in Boulogne-Billancourt where his father was a semiskilled worker. However, we owe it to the truth to say that Magloire was the black sheep in the flock. While his six brothers and sisters all studied hard in school to make their parents proud, by the age of sixteen he had gotten himself expelled for some sordid business. From then on, he had hung out with no one but bad influences, barely escaped prison, and bounced from pathetic job to pathetic job. He had made a bad marriage and split up with his wife, leaving her with a pair of twins as a souvenir. At the age of forty-five, he had come back to the country of his ancestors, obsessed by the glossy images that had trailed him from summer camps to school skiing trips to language-study vacations in the remote corners of Kent. Royal palm trees. Bubbling springs. All around, the sea. He had been naively convinced that the baking sun would reshape him, like the man in the tale his grandmother had told him, and that he would be baptized anew by the rivers' waters. With reality turning out to be far inferior to his dreams, he was getting ready to return by chartered plane when, at a cousin's wedding, he had met Fanniéta. Dressed in red and carrying a tray, she was serving the crab pâtés and blood pudding.

O, giddiness of love!

For her, he had repaired and repainted with his own two hands a house on Rue de Lesseps that had once belonged to his family, with a yard in the front and a garden in the back. For her, he had looked for work, a quest as arduous as finding a needle in a haystack. Luckily, it happened that, fed up with the thefts, the robberies, and the murders of the guards they were paying a fortune to post on the sidewalks of Port-Mahault, the shopkeepers had raised a private militia, a formidable contingent of tough guys who could be seen practicing shooting and martial arts in the field of *razyé* behind the hospital. Magloire had been hired because of his uncommonly large frame and the familiarity with firearms he had built up during his troubled youth. Now, five nights out of every seven, in exchange for a good paycheck, he put on his khaki fatigues and a cap of the same color, and took up his place in the patrol. It is impossible to describe the change this job brought about in him. He went from nonchalant dreamer to energetic. From laughing and joking to focused concentration. Whenever he had the chance, he would oil his Smith and Wesson 686 six-shot revolver, the symbol of the new man he had become. Before too long he had earned his stripes and was taking command of his division. Thanks to them, more crooks than you could count had seen their machinations disrupted, more dealers had been caught trafficking, and more addicts saved from overdosing in the nick of time. Their vigilance had led to the arrest of a masked gang that had been attacking jewelry stores in broad daylight, and of a rapist who, on top of everything, was robbing his victims.

That night, his revolver by his side like a mistress you can't bear to leave, Magloire was savoring a well-earned rest. By the light of a camping lantern, he had eaten dinner with Fanniéta, Hélène, and the two teenage boys. It had been a long, tumultuous day. The conversation had revolved around Dieudonné's spectacular acquittal and his seeming indifference to this outcome beyond hope. He had barely even opened his mouth to thank Mr. Serbulon for his fine work. Even so, they should give praise to the Good Lord and rejoice over it for the sake of poor Marine, who, from where she was now, had witnessed the whole thing and who must be in seventh heaven, she who had idolized her boy. While the two sons were only half-interested in the whole business, Fanniéta and Hélène were all keyed up. In less than three months, they predicted, that scoundrel Dieudonné would be taking up residence in the Basse-Pointe prison again. They didn't believe a word of the lawyer's hogwash. His theory that Loraine had in a way provoked her own death by transforming someone weak, tender, and completely devoted to her into a killer. Nonsense! Some people are born to do evil, and Dieudonné was among them. Fanniéta and Hélène arrived at this conclusion by different paths. Fanniéta had never held Dieudonné close to her heart. When he was a baby, Marine had her watch him sometimes and he would scream nonstop, a deafening scream, until his mama came back. When she had done him the great kindness of taking him in, not only had he tried to dishonor her house by bringing those *kokdjèm* into it, those hellish creatures, but also, she hadn't forgotten his silences. Hardly ever a hello or a goodnight. Seated at the table, stuffing himself with food, he wouldn't say a single word. He had a way of getting up and wiping his mouth with the back of his hand that seemed to say he had heard enough foolishness. Hélène's grievances were even more serious. To each their own memories! So many years later, Hugo seemed to everyone in the country to have been a kind of magical time when they had experienced the violence of nature. For her, that night marked the bloody end of her childhood. OK, so it wasn't the first time!

At fourteen, she had already let more than a few scamps mount her. But three hot-blooded guys one after the other? Despite her cries and protests? Shouldn't those kinds of abuses be called rape? Didn't people go to jail for that? Strangely, she particularly hated Dieudonné, who hadn't done anything to her. If he didn't want to follow the others, why hadn't he defended her? He had stood there mute and motionless, like a piece of wood, crying as if he were the victim. The worst part was that he didn't seem to remember anything about it. He treated her with utmost indifference and was impatient with little Huguette. He refused to drive the child to school, to hear her recite her lessons, and, once, when she had rifled through his dresser, he had taken the liberty of raising a hand to her. Magloire thought otherwise. He barely knew Dieudonné, who seemed to avoid weddings, baptisms, and funeral wakes. The family considered him an addict and a good-for-nothing, and never stopped going on and on about those *kokdjèm*. The way they told it, he had as many as twenty of them, veritable beasts of prey that he raised in wicker cages and gave fearsome names—Beelzebub, Lucifer—that betrayed his true nature. Magloire, who still remembered his own troubled youth, was more indulgent. Above all, he told himself, people never stop surprising you. At the age of twenty-two, everyone is perfectible, and this young man that everyone kept dumping on still had time to get himself together and end up an honest papa. However, work is the key to a good life. If the country was producing so many sick and rebellious minds, it was because it was incapable of providing for its children.

Well before ten o'clock, everyone said goodnight since they could no longer gather around the small TV in the living room. Fanniéta was especially proud that Magloire had done such good work on the addition that everyone now had their own bedroom. Even Huguette, who no longer spent her nights in her mama's warm *kabann*. Magloire and Fanniéta retired to their room, which had a view of the small garden and the row of dragon's blood trees separating it from the street, which, for the moment, formed a dark trench in which not even a cat stirred. Ensconced in his pillows, Magloire began chatting. Each time, it was the same ritual. In the evenings, he'd rehash his memories of adolescence, his youthful mistakes, the nighttime dangers, the encounters with the police, the mad scrambles to escape, the unhoped-for getaways. Listening to him, a little weary, Fanniéta wondered whether the times spent living on the fringes of accepted canons were the only ones worth the trouble of remembering and recounting. By contrast, she had nothing at all to offer, she who had never done anything but pray to God and suffer his Holy will.

On her conscience there was only one stain.

She must have been about ten years old. Her knapsack on her back, she was on her way home from school, walking past the Alhambra Cinema Theater, when a lady had come out of one of the upstairs-downstairs houses lining the Place des Écarts. One of those ladies with light skin and good hair who press forward in a rustle of fine frocks and leave a cloud of perfume behind them. Fanniéta was standing there gaping in admiration when the lady rummaged through her bag for her sunglasses, which she perched gracefully on her nose. Elegant, movie-star glasses, with very dark lenses rimmed by a wide white frame. Just then, something fell to the ground without her realizing it: an elegant wallet, in brown Moroccan leather. Fanniéta would have had plenty of time to retrieve the object, which was rolling in the dust, to run and return it to its owner who was settling unhurriedly behind the wheel of her car, and perhaps to be graced with a smile by way of thanks. But instead, she was held back by invisible strings. She felt as though she was stuck to the spot, like Brer Rabbit, while the car started up, moved off, and turned the corner. Only then did Fanniéta rush forward. She didn't open the wallet until she got home, in the room she shared with her mother and her two sisters. It had some coins in it, and, folded up small, a 500-franc bill. Fanniéta felt dizzy. Never in all her life had she possessed so much money. Where should she hide this treasure? Her heart beating, she slipped it under the mattress. She spent the evening on cloud nine, calculating the number of marvels she could buy herself: spiral-bound notebooks, ballpoint pens. But also Chicklets, and strawberry-flavored yogurt drinks. She went to bed before everyone, the better to keep watch over her hiding place. She got up last for the same reason. At lunchtime, the wallet was still there. At five o'clock, when she got home from school, it was gone.

At first she thought it was a miracle from the Almighty, who sees all. The Good Lord, spiriting away the object of her crime, had punished her for her sin, and, in tears, she fell to her knees, repentant. Then, she started to suspect her sisters, especially Marine, whom she had never held dear to her heart. Then, noticing Arbella's unnatural expression, she was seized by the thought that it might have been her mother who had stolen from her, her own mother, the mother she adored, the mother who in her mind was on the same level as La Vierge du Grand Retour, Our Lady of Boulogne, on the same level as the Virgin Mary, Queen of all virtues. Fanniéta observed her feverishly in an attempt to find certainty. She was unable to, while the enormity of her suspicions made her ashamed of herself. How could she admit all this at confession? Three Thursdays in a row, she skipped Catechism.

Reminiscing about old times seemed to help Magloire get back up on the wild stallion of his youth. Afterwards he would wrap Fanniéta in his arms and make love to her as if he were twenty. That night, he was preparing to plunge into her generous and consenting flesh when a racket kicked up: it was the dogs. The dogs had started barking. Previously, Rue de Lesseps, which cut across the Orban dock and sank into the sea, had been an eccentric little artery, a jumble of sheet-metal shacks populated by needy folks. Then the city had gotten larger. It had eaten away at the surrounding towns, and constructed apartment buildings. Rue de Lesseps had become gentrified with coquettish houses. Behind the gates, like everywhere else, dogs kept watch, creole mutts or foreign breeds according to preference, set loose the moment the daylight started to dim. Magloire jumped up, ran to the window, and opened the shutters. The street stretched ahead, opaque. It was darker than a black guy's asshole. But as his eyes grew accustomed to the dark he thought he could make out a silhouette, a shape moving on the sidewalk, beyond the hedge. It was coming closer to the gate, trying to open it to get into the yard. Quickly he went back, grabbed his

Smith and Wesson, and fired in the direction of the phantom. Once. Twice. As a precaution.

Ripples of tumult swirled in concentric circles through the lake of darkness surrounding the house. Magloire's sharp ears caught the sound of someone rushing away. Satisfied, he came back to the bed, set the revolver on the nightstand, blew out the candle, and lay down.

"I don't like those things," Fanniéta commented in the shadow. "The noise makes my head all jumbled."

Then the couple embraced to make love.

Dieudonné—people will have already guessed that it was him, the unknown prowler—took to his heels. The night was roiling. This was the second time that bullets had whistled so closely past his ears. The first time, they had gotten lodged somewhere in the wall behind his back. Running straight ahead, he found himself face to face with the soothing silhouette of the Saint-Jean-de-Obispo Cathedral. Reassured, he flew up the steps. Unfortunately, as he drew closer to the facade carved with niches sheltering stone saints and nestless birds, he realized that the tall hobnailed wooden doors were closed. Why do people close churches? Shouldn't they be there to give refuge to every distress? To give a roof to those in need? Aren't they failing at their primary purpose otherwise?

Unhappy, as if, once again, a friend had turned him out, he went back down the stairs. That's when he saw them. Lined up like soldiers all along the gutter. Calm. Hardly menacing. Some of them were busy with other things altogether: sniffing each other, licking each other. Ten or so dogs, tall and emaciated, with patchy, mangy fur. They had to have come from their rendezvous spot, the Place des Écarts, right nearby. But in his terror, it seemed to Dieudonné they were the very same dogs who had chased him miles away, on the highway, and who were expecting him, against all expectation, barring his way. Distances mean nothing to Spirits. Invisible, they fly through the air as swift as frigate birds and you only hear the rustle of their wings. A plea rose in his heart. "Dog friends! I've never done anything to you! Have pity, let me pass!"

As if they heard him, cocking their ears, the animals turned their heads toward him. Drilling him with their living-dead gaze, they seemed to be weighing the pros and cons. Under their curled lips he saw their teeth gleaming and expected an attack. Suddenly, a miracle happened. One by one, the beasts of hell turned their backs on him, exposing their crooked legs and their bony bottoms pierced by filthy anuses. Lifting a leg, one of them peed loudly. Then, abruptly, the pack started running in the opposite direction, toward some prey their eyes alone could see.

In his relief, Dieudonné sank down onto the stone, rough and cold under his behind.

14

Where was he?

For the tenth time, Arbella went out on the balcony and inspected the courtyard, which was lit up like a concentration camp or a South African township. Deserted. Only the militia volunteers, who had doubled their patrols, could be seen walking there. In this neighborhood, the electricity showed up around eight o'clock and didn't leave again till midnight. So you could almost forget the strikes. The evenings unfolded at the same pace as before. For her seventieth birthday, her daughter Fanniéta had bought her cable, and Arbella gorged herself on American shows. With her four good children who hadn't forgotten her sacrifices and lavished her with treats, she could have thought herself happy. Her last daughter had invited her to Toronto. But Arbella was balking because people say it's cold in Canada.

Unfortunately, there was Dieudonné to think about! Where was he? What could he be up to again? All he had to do was try, and he'd be back on the right foot! So many people had shown they were rooting for him. When he was acquitted, strangers had called to share their joy. A merchant wanted to offer him a job in his shop.

Arbella remembered how happy and proud she'd been when her youngest, Marine, got pregnant, after years of bad luck despite being the prettiest of her daughters. By Émile Vertueux. She would have loved to gloat, proclaiming far and wide who was responsible for her child's belly. Émile Vertueux, known by the nickname Milo, was the one who, out of concern for diversification, had introduced the Cavaillon melon into the country, and, for years, had been the president of the Food-Crop Producers Association. You would see his powerful mug on television demanding indemnities whenever the tiniest gust of wind had flattened the banana trees, whenever the least bit of drought had scorched the melons. He got everything he wanted out of the state, for he was on a first-name basis with everyone in the administration, and *Paris-Match* magazine had even shown him dancing the beguine with the widow of the former president of the Republic. Unfortunately Marine, in her arrogant way, had gotten ideas in her head. She wouldn't take advice and kept raising quibbling objections:

"Why doesn't he want to marry me, then? Because I'm too black? Because my mother is poor? If he loves me, he shouldn't be ashamed!"

So much so that Milo had abandoned her in her fifth month, leaving her with nothing but her mountain of truth and her two eyes for crying. Dieudonné was born one April 14th, right in the middle of Holy Week, and you would have thought that Marine was mimicking the passion of Our Lord Jesus Christ. After Milo, she never opened her bed to any man again, all the while her beauty was fading and her personality, which had never been easygoing, got even more abominable. Not only had Milo failed to lift a finger after her accident, but also Arbella had waited in vain for a check for the orphan. And yet, if he was to be believed, the drama this same child had just experienced had deeply affected him. He claimed to have repented. At present, he asked only to help the one he had too long neglected. His unexpected visit at the end of the afternoon was proof. He had turned up without warning. Seeing him there, this upper-class man with his ringing voice, well dressed, confident, so out of place in the modest decor, Fanniéta (who was never at a loss for words), Magloire, and the other relatives fell speechless. Sensing that they were in the way, they had quickly taken their leave, tripping over one another to get out the door. A real stampede. Milo still looked good despite the sorry gifts bestowed by age: graying, thinning hair, sagging neck, teeth that were too even to be real, wrinkles everywhere. Because of these changes, she hadn't recognized him right away. Plus, the media had turned its back on him ever since he had ceded his position to Julius Rangoon, a young planter from Salines and—a sign of the times—a *zindien* whose first cousin was a member of parliament. Taking a seat at Arbella's side, he had inquired with that characteristic kindness he had shown back when he was courting Marine, when, unashamed, he used to park his luxury Citroën in front of the hovel she shared with her mother, her sisters, and her brothers, "Arbella, how's your health?"

Sighing, she spared him no detail: her blood pressure, her sciatica, the arthritis pain in her shoulders, arms, and knees. In the mornings, her bones grated like rusted metal. Sometimes she couldn't even stand up or move. He had listened to this long tirade without showing any sign of impatience, then came to the heart of the matter, asking abruptly, "Where is he?"

She was forced to admit she had no idea. He had dashed off right after his last bite of lunch, several hours ago. Milo sighed.

"Let's hope he's not up to anything stupid! See, what was missing in his life was my guiding hand. A woman can't raise a man all by herself. I kept trying to tell Marine that in all my letters."

His letters? He bowed his head.

"Yes! I can't tell you how many letters I sent her. But she was a stubborn woman and never even answered me. You see, the Good Lord has punished me. With Arielle, my lawful wife, a Martinican, I've only had girls. Four girls. He's my only boy. Whenever I'd see him on television, I'd blubber like a baby because he's my spitting image, only darker obviously. I'd summon my daughters and say to them, 'Take a good look. The person you see here is your brother. He is innocent. The guilty one is the man you call papa. I'm the one who should be in jail, in his place.'"

Then, theatrically, he took his head in his hands.

"I tell you, Arbella, not a day has gone by since she died that she hasn't been in my thoughts! If there is any woman

I have loved, it is Marine. Unfortunately, when you're young, you don't know your own heart well. I wanted to be successful. That's why I married money. Arielle is from the Bavarois family, of Bavarois Rums."

Arbella listened to him dumbstruck. She was surprised, but not for a moment did she think to doubt his sincerity. She never had any doubts about men, especially when they had friendly faces. Hence her five children, all from different fathers. Milo's statements confirmed her opinion that everything that was happening to Dieudonné was really Marine's fault. Marine had poisoned her son's life just like her mother's, her brothers', and her sisters'. You need to know your place on this earth and not ask too much from life, and that was one thing she had never understood. Even when she was little she would fill Arbella's head with odd questions:

"Who's my papa? Why doesn't he ever come over?"

"Why don't all of us kids have the same papa?"

"How come we don't have a car?"

"How come we live in this old shack?"

As a teenager, she had unrealizable dreams:

"I want to be a doctor."

". . . Or an ethnologist, so I can go to Africa."

An ethnologist, can you believe that! At the end of the day, she had died destitute and her son's sorry behavior was making front-page news.

Before they noticed it, night had climbed in through the windows and doors and they found themselves sitting face to face immersed in its ink, prisoners of thoughts circling round and round a sole common object. At the stroke of eight, the lamps overhead had flooded them with light, brutally hounding them back into reality. The woman they were thinking about was no more. Milo got up, embraced the old lady, and repeated his advice emphatically, still mustering his showmanship: "No matter the hour, when he comes back tell him his papa is waiting for him. Tell him to call me: here's my number. Or, even easier, he can stop by. I live just up the road, in Doria."

Once Milo was in the stairwell, Arbella got up to turn on the television. Yet that night she didn't watch *The Jeffersons,* which was her favorite series because it was about the ups and downs of a black family, whose husband and wife resembled her late brother Siméon and her sister-in-law Jeanine. Her thoughts were rambling, taking unexpected turns. She was pondering things over, which wasn't something she did very often. When a bastard child who grew up in hardship suddenly finds out that his papa is part of the country's elite, how might he react? Will he be able to grasp that his misfortune was caused by his mother's stubbornness? Dieudonné had adored Marine. All through her long tribulation, he had been an irreproachable son, spoon-feeding her meals to her, bathing her, rubbing her down, dressing her, getting her to do her business without disgust. When she died, which had been a relief for the whole family, they thought he might go crazy. He had disappeared right in the middle of the wake. They had noticed his absence while Fanniéta, wiping away her crocodile tears, was launching into Psalm 13:

> How long, O Lord? Wilt thou forget me for ever?
> How long wilt thou hide thy face from me?

Right away the men had interrupted their boozing and gone searching for him. Hours later, they had found him wandering over some boulders at the edge of the sea. They had brought him back to Morne Lafleur, but he was too weak, too wobbly to walk behind the casket during the procession, which meant that at his own mother's burial, he had not observed mourning rites. They had to have Fanniéta's boys take his place.

Tired out by waiting so long, Arbella fell asleep in front of the television. She had a dream. She dreamed that, shedding her wrinkles and her aches and pains, she was once again in the matador dress she had worn in her twenties. Sneaking out behind her mother's back, she had met up with Lucien at the *titane* ball, the Lucien who was Fanniéta's papa, the second of her men and her favorite one of all, but also the most restless, the biggest womanizer, the biggest liar. That shameless sinner had made her cry tears of blood. But that made no difference. Even though he had been sleeping under the causarina trees at the Bonne-Veine Cemetery for ten years, the mere sound of his name still put a stir into her flesh, making her young and quivering again. They were twirling round, square-dancing to the caller's cues under the spying eyes of jealous women, when Dieudonné suddenly made his noisy entrance. True, she had never noticed as much as she did now that he was the very portrait of his father, only darker of course. However, she didn't have time to rhapsodize about this resemblance because he was covered in blood and his clothes were torn, as if he had been in a fight. A shiver went through her and she asked, "Where are you coming from looking like that?"

"It's nothing," he said. "A gang attacked me in Port-Mahault."

"What were you doing down in Port-Mahault?" she grumbled. "You know very well that it's a place for crooks at this time of night."

Without answering, he dove into the bathroom. While he was in there, Arbella prepared a little speech that she treated him to without much preamble as soon as he emerged. She had never been good with words, either in French or in Creole. He stared at her as if she had gone crazy and repeated, in disbelief:

"Milo Vertueux? You mean Mr. Émile Vertueux?"

"That's the one. He's waiting for you. He wants to see you," Arbella said in a rush. "It's never too late for people to make amends for the bad things they've done. Now, making amends is what he wants."

Dieudonné stayed motionless a long while, his head between his hands, as if struck down by a blow, then headed for the exit, slamming the door. She heard him gallop down the stairs. Hurrying out onto the balcony as fast as her aches and her legs would allow, she saw him flying across the courtyard as if he had wings. Where was he going? She burst into tears.

See? He was just too stubborn, that child!

Dieudonné was running like mad, without knowing where he was going, straight ahead, and the waspy wind whirred around him, mercilessly stinging his ears. His thoughts were spinning like a merry-go-round. The blackness of the night blindfolded him.

"I want to die.

"But before, I have to finish him off. I've already killed once. I'm already a murderer. I can kill twice. Only this time, no Serbulon can save me. Prison for life. Her, I never meant to kill. How could I have killed the woman who was my life? The gun went off, that's all. Him, on the other hand, I'll hack him to pieces, unh-unh-unh, like the rotten animal he is. Twenty-two blows of the knife. One for each year of my life. Plus forty-six, for the forty-six years of my mama's life. Because he's the one who killed her. While her stomach was growling, full of air, his was filled with all the good things of this earth. While she was chewing on misery, he lived in the lap of luxury. While she went barefoot, he was parading around in patent leather shoes.

"What does that mean, make amends?

"I'll bleed him like a pig who's met his Saturday. I'll bathe my chops in it. Then I'll light a bonfire. I'll cut up branches and pile them crisscross. And I'll put his body on to roast it. The scent of the smoke will tickle the Good Lord's nose, He who wants justice to reign in the world, who wants the wicked to be punished, and He will be pleased.

"Her, too, he's the one who killed her. Because he's the one who made me what I am. In a way, he's the one who made me say what I said to her so she'd stop crying and quit saying all those mean things that kept coming out of her mouth because of Luc. Because of Luc alone. If I'm 'black trash full of bitterness and spite' like she branded me, 'a common nobody' that everyone has always overlooked, it's because of him. It wasn't written that I would become what I became. If I never saw a smile on Marine's lips, it's because of him. If her kisses tasted like ashes, if the milk I sucked from her breast smelled sour, it's because of him.

"No! No one has ever bothered to see what I'm made of.

"Of course I knew that I wasn't cut out for a woman like her. So beautiful and rich and educated. Even so, I thought I had a niche in her life, like a dog has a doghouse in the yard. I thought she needed me, that she appreciated what I could give her. Someone to play Belote with. Someone to go get whiskey, Glenfiddich or Oban, her favorite. Someone to help her wash up and get dressed. Someone to pleasure her when she wasn't too drunk. On that point, too, Luc lied. She wasn't a nympho-maniac. Often, as early as nine o'clock she'd be snoring in front of the television like a baby. I'd carry her to bed and stay to watch her sleep. Sometimes she was calm. Other times she'd be agitated and complaining. Tears would run down her cheeks. What counted for her was to have company, day and night, to not be alone all the time, rehashing those interminable stories of her miseries, her mama, her papa, Florelle, her three husbands and the children her womb wasn't able to carry. She would have liked to have had a houseful. Girls, boys. Her dream was to have twins. So alike that people would confuse them, like people confused her with her sister. Instead of that, she got an abortion at sixteen, a baby from a friend of her father's three times her age, and after that, it was over. She had nothing at all. Like me. Because we were alike, I thought she cared about me at least a little, but then she made it clear that I was wrong all down the line, that the only person who counted for her was him, the former student she had trained. The same one who kept disrespecting her behind her back, calling her every name in the book, the one who, at the end of the day, was no better than 'Mamzel Marie.'

"What does that mean, make amends? You can't undo what's done. Change what has already taken shape."

Abruptly, the salty wind suffocated him and made his eyes water. Pebbles rolled under his feet, some as polished and round as marbles, others rough and sharp. He realized that, quite nat-urally, he had come back to the sea again. The only friend he had left. The one who had always stayed faithful to him. The sea! The man who has known her embrace can no longer do without her. Neither men nor women are enough for him any-more. He must have her salty mouth and the fresh scent of her body at any price. He must cling to her loose, streaming hair to climax. Seeing Dieudonné's distress, the sea had rushed to the rescue. Now she was there offering him the caress of her belly, opening for him the sticky depths of her pubis, crowned with kelp. He could possess her and lose himself in her, if he wanted.

Taking his bearings, he guessed that he was in the Cadenat neighborhood, not far from Lakou Ferraille.

15

Unhappy with himself, Boris directed a kick at Prince, slammed the gate shut, and got behind the wheel of his used Toyota.

At breakneck speed, he headed toward the Fleurie complex, but he wasn't seeing the road in front of him, or the mangrove left and right. He was unhappy with Carla's petit bourgeois reactions; unhappy, too, to have left her alone when, at any minute now, the little stranger that she was carrying could make his entrance into the world; unhappy, above all, with his behavior toward Dieudonné.

"I didn't even offer him a glass of water," he kept repeating to himself.

Shame and remorse engulfed him at the thought of all his misdeeds. First of all, he had barely visited him at Basse-Pointe. Of course, he could chalk that up to the hurricane ravaging his life at that time. He had just met Carla. He had needed to get used to love again, to the customs and manners of society. Yet that didn't fully explain his behavior. Conversing with his younger friend in a shellacked white visitation room, through protective glass, seeing him sheathed in a prisoner's jumpsuit, tight around the shoulders, too small for his build, with a matriculation number on his chest, he felt guilty. Guilty for not having been able to show him how to live life. It was this feeling of guilt that had dwelt with him all through the trial. Day after day, he would sit in the back rows at the courthouse, between the gawkers and the curious. How he had admired the intelligence and mastery of this Serbulon kid he remembered as a child in khaki shorts buying his schoolbooks! He had known how to raise this sensational news item, this individual story, to the level of a collective drama, turning it into a remake of the primal scene. While this stranger was saving Dieudonné, he, the friend and brother, was wading deeper and deeper into abjection. And now he had cast him out when he came looking for refuge. With tenderness belatedly flooding his heart, he remembered the first time he saw him, this withdrawn teenager who never talked or laughed or smiled, who had no mama or papa or family or roof over his head. At first glance, their relationship seemed odd. They had absolutely nothing in common. Although he was self-taught, Boris, for his part, wanted to be a great man of letters, an adept of Marx and Gramsci, not to mention Frantz Fanon and Cheikh Anta Diop. Dieudonné, having grown up all by himself like a tuft of guinea grass, hadn't read anything. He never even glanced at a newspaper, didn't listen to music, and indiscriminately ingested television shows without retaining anything. Boris had quickly abandoned the idea of giving him a political education, since he didn't understand anything about the major social categories. Proletariat, bourgeoisie, comprador—*ki sa yé sa?* What's that? Yet, at present, Boris was convinced that the years he had spent by his side, homeless, sometimes taking refuge in a bus stop, sometimes on the *Belle Créole,* were the light of his life. Back then, there were no interminable meetings attempting to invent a "new status" for the country. No harangues in Creole on the radio to "raise the consciousness of the people." No contradictory debates in front of city halls, no stormy assemblies. His life recognized no other master than his imagination, his freedom. A ballpoint pen and a notebook were all he needed to be happy. For entire days, forgetting to eat and drink, he would compose his poems. He counted it a good day if he found inspiration. Ever since he had been assisting Benjy, he had written nothing but tedious commentaries on land occupation in Haut-Marigot or diatribes against town councils. Politics and poetry don't make a good pair. The latter was deserting him.

He turned onto the corniche road.

To his mind, having no other choice Dieudonné would have to stay the night at Arbella's. He could almost hear the recommendations and wise advice that the old lady would deluge Dieudonné with, taking her turn after the godmother, the uncle, and all the other members of the family.

"Look for a job! At least enroll in RMI welfare."

"Get yourself a nice little companion!"

"Get out of that boat. Men aren't fish made to stay in the water. Put in a request for a rent-controlled apartment down at Port-Mahault's City Hall."

And himself? What would he say to Dieudonné when he faced him again?

OK, so Dieudonné was blind, naive! You didn't have to be a *grand grek* to understand that nothing good could come from associating with Loraine. Serbulon had shown what kind of a person she was: a neurotic alcoholic, taking pleasure in torturing and humiliating those who carelessly let themselves get scorched by her beauty. However, he wouldn't remind him of his stupidity, which was excusable because he was so young. Besides, he had already been punished enough. Marked for life. He had been acquitted, not absolved. In the future, what woman would have a memory short enough to go to bed with him and share his *kabann?* What man would trust him and call him a friend? What boss would agree to hire him for a position of responsibility? Forever, the memory of his crime would glow red in people's minds. Just as people say, "It was in Governor Sorin's time," or "It was the month Hugo happened," so would they mark that year with words mixing condemnation and pride: "It was the year the *Petit Nègre* killed the *Grande Békée.*"

No! Boris wouldn't bring up the past again but would focus solely on the future. So, would he maintain his offer to spend a year in Cuba? The PTCR recruits who went there would send tearful letters home to their parents and were constantly protesting and criticizing. Right off the bat, they were taken in hand by young *brigadistas* and housed in barracks far from the city centers. No movie theaters, no bars, no nightclubs—no places where people go to chat and have fun. The only neighbors around were the *bohíos,* a bunch of humble cottages with thatched palm frond roofs. Frugal daily living: boiled manioc, honey, and on lucky days, rice and beans. Sometimes, they would send them to cut cane alongside the *guajiros,* with machetes, as in the olden days. In order to find any meaning in this life of deprivation, you had to be convinced that men were hardening themselves for the revolution. And yet, did Dieudonné have any idea what revolution was? Who still believed in it anymore? The word had disappeared from the dictionary, both the Larousse and the Robert editions, and

Fidel, with his white goatee, was now nothing but a Santa Claus without a sack of gifts. For the first time, Boris looked himself deep in the eyes and had to admit that his faith of yesteryear was no longer alive. All that was left of it was a heap of clichés, a pile of ashes without any warm coals to strike it up again. He hadn't noticed its death and had kept on holding forth on the radio, in Benjy's ear, in Carla's ear, in the ear of anyone who had the patience to listen to him. Doubtless, it hadn't held up under all these years of stalls, failures, and about-faces, and had given its last breath before Boris had ever realized it, softly, like a sick person whose organism is worn out. Finally.

What would he propose to Dieudonné, then?

The question so alarmed him that he swerved, hit a small hill, and found himself in a savanna, nose to nose with a cow grazing in the area. Tourists crave these types of contrasts. Cows alongside highways.

The Toyota, which had more than a few years on it, refused to start up again and he had to set out on foot in the grass moist with night dew. Where was he? Somewhere around Bel-Air? He set off walking, a little randomly. A wet coolness fell on his shoulders. Up above, opaque and swollen with rain, the clouds were scurrying to a corner of the sky. He felt very, very small and lost. But strangely, illogically, a feeling of well-being suddenly engulfed him. It was as if he had gone back to the good old days when he was free as the air. Not a penny that called him master. No Carla. No unborn child. No PTCR. Absolutely nothing. In his bus stop, after nightfall, he'd prop his piece of foam on the bench, curl up, and cover himself with a fleece to ward against the cool early-morning wind. All the sounds and scents that the shadows set free would mingle together in his ears, in his nostrils, and he would drift off to the fragrance of jasmine and the clamor of frogs and giant toads begging for water, always more water. When the Good Lord granted their prayers and satisfied them with downpours, he would wade over to the *Belle Créole*. If Rodrigue and his beauties were in the cabins, he'd sleep in the dinette. He was dry, while, outside, the wind whistled its demented song. One stormy night, the *Belle Créole* had broken from its moorings and drifted all the way to the middle of Saint-Christophe Bay. In the morning, when the sky cleared and he went up on the bridge, her prow was turned toward the open sea, as if she had been languishing too long at the docks. As if her nostalgia for departures, the desire to run for the horizon and melt into it, was tormenting her. Abruptly, lights appeared in the *razyé*. Dozens of candles placed right on the ground were burning like a rug of fire. In its middle, a house that seemed to come down from the sky was landing, spinning like a top. Little by little, its shape emerged from the shadows. It was floating, rocking like an astral boat, then landing, shining in the darkness like a diamond in a black velvet case. Its veranda was already full of men circled around a storyteller frolicking and reeling off his tomfooleries. Its courtyard was full of women, darting back and forth with trays heavy with food balanced on their shoulders. The young folks were circled around the drummers seated astride their *kas,* as massive and tall as *pié-bwa,* etching their beats into the heart of the night. Yet the crowd kept thronging in, larger and larger, from thousands of invisible paths, blackening the savanna. The last time so many people had squeezed into a wake was after the death of the musician Vélocité. Whole columns of ants had marched from the sidewalks of Morne Prudent, where he lived, to the Place des Écarts. Boris wondered what important figure had taken his leave from this earth. He hadn't heard any name worthy of attention in the death notices the announcers read every morning, noon, and night on all the radio stations and that he followed religiously like everyone in the country. He fell in with the new arrivals, listening keenly to their reflections.

"So sad, isn't it?" said an old man wearing a *bakoua* hat and bright-white tennis shoes, taking him as his witness. "No one wishes death for the sinner. He had been acquitted. Now, a new life is waiting for him!"

"Who? Who exactly? Who are you talking about?"

Unhappy with these questions, the old man did not answer. On the contrary, he distanced himself hurriedly and danced away. Boris drew nearer to the house and accepted a bowl of meat soup from one of the women's hands. A marrow bone was swimming among the carrots and turnips and it seemed to him it was the best meat soup he had ever eaten. Licking his lips, he thanked her and repeated his question:

"But come on, tell me, who died? Whose vigil are we keeping?"

The woman didn't respond either and, at that, pulled sharply away from him as if he had the plague. Now, Boris was convinced that he should have known whose wake it was, that it went without saying. He went into the living room, barely as big as a postage stamp, and apparently furnished in a manner unworthy of the important figure people were mourning, with some cheap rockers bought on sale at Conforama, "Where life is less expensive." Given the crowd, he had to fight to make his way into the second room, the bedroom. Coiffed with mourning madras in violet and black plaid, women, all identical in their black dresses, were blocking the doorway, chanting the familiar words: "To every thing there is a season, and a time for every purpose under heaven: a time to be born, and a time to die, a time to plant, and a time to pluck up that which is planted . . ." When he finally got where he was going, Boris noticed that the bedroom wasn't very big either, and it was suffocating, lit up starkly by candles. On the bed that essentially took up all the space, a young man, almost a child, was resting. He was wearing a very modern tracksuit, cut from orange nylon, that stood out sharply against the white sheets and the somber colors all around. It was this unusual clothing that attracted Boris's attention. He pushed away people left and right, and arrived at the bed where the body was laid out: Dieudonné.

An arrow of such violent pain pierced his heart that he regained consciousness, his nose on the steering wheel of his Toyota, soaked and numb, because the windows were down and the falling rain had drenched him. A dream. It was a dream whose images clung to his mind, tenacious and terrifying. He shivered. Dreams, older people say, are just messages the Good Lord dispatches to the living to announce reality. That meant that Dieudonné was in great danger. In danger of losing hope once and for all and turning his back on a life he thought was barred to him.

The Toyota, valiantly, started right up again. Boris found his way back to the sinuous spirals of the corniche road. Unfortunately, when he turned off his engine on Morne Julien, the volunteer militiamen, interrupting their patrol, shook their heads. Yes, Dieudonné had come home. But, almost immediately, he had come back out, running as if all of hell's demons were on his heels. Arbella? The apartment was plunged in darkness. She must be sleeping, now that Milo Vertueux had left. Milo Vertueux? And what else, as if that weren't enough? What did he have to do with any of this, anyway? Boris kept these unpleasant questions to himself and restricted himself to inquiring about the other family members. Were they still up there? The volunteers assured him that they had gone home ages ago.

Where should he head? Where should he look?

Mournfully, Boris was about to get back into his car when the volunteers, who were sticking close behind him, pressed him with questions. Since he was in the know, what did he think? People had had it up to here with the filthy condition of the city, with these never-ending strikes, with this violence, this insecurity! Was it true that Benjy had met with the PPRP and that he intended to form a new party with them, the PPSN? Was it true that because of that, departmentalization's days were numbered? Was it true they were soon going to reach *lendépendans?* Boris was speechless, for he and Benjy had thought these clandestine meetings between the PTCR and the PPRP had been held in close confidence. Then he realized that the idea of *lendépendans,* far from elating his interlocutors, made them tremble. *Lendépendans?* No more DOM Overseas Department status? So no more Social Security or minimum wage or housing subsidies? No RMI or CNAF or CNAV or GRISS or CREA or IRCANTEC or ASSEDIC? How would the days go by without Dannon yogurts, Président camembert, Lesieur cooking oils, Sopalin paper towels, Lustucru pasta, Heudebert biscuits, Astra margarine, Lu cookies, William Saurin cassoulet, Jacques Vabre coffee, Amora mustard, Ariel detergent, Garbit couscous . . .?

At that, Boris was seized with a righteous anger and started insulting these cowards who kept singing the evil stepmother's

praises. Leaving the militiamen stuck to the spot in their surprise, he climbed back into his car and, still at breakneck speed,
headed toward the Fleurie complex.

16

Since the beginning of the strikes, electricity had totally deserted the Cadenat neighborhood where, once and for all, the
power had been cut off. There too, as in the Place des Écarts,
the dogs reigned supreme. When the weather got too hot for
their liking, they'd sleep on the sidewalks, sprawled in the
shade of the houses. If the breeze got chilly, they'd wake and
prowl around, a vicious, ferocious troop, perpetually starving,
voraciously nosing through the trash piled up just about everywhere, since the sanitation services weren't running there either. You couldn't even count anymore the number of children
they had bitten, chased, and scared during playtime. Once, they
had even devoured a baby asleep in its crib. Between the foul-
ness and the darkness, the Cadenat residents didn't know what
to do. First, in protest, they had written letter after letter to the
Electric Company, to City Hall, to the Sous-Prefecture, to the
Prefecture. They had even organized a march through the city
streets. Then they had thrown up their hands, resourcefulness
taking the place of anger. First the men had bought bars of
ice at the service stations. Alas! When these closed down one
after the other, the women set themselves to salting and drying
fish, and red meat when there was any, following old recipes
preserved since the days of wartime isolation under Governor
Sorin. They began canning tomatoes, okra, and breadfruit. In-
geniously, starting at seven o'clock in the evening people would
hang huge acetylene lamps from their balconies. It didn't
completely chase away all the shadows; a ballet of phantoms
seemed to dance in the streets. Even so, it was better than total
obscurity. The *bòbòs* were aggrieved. They complained that
it was bad for business. The bourgeois never ventured near
them anymore: instead of getting a welcoming pair of thighs
and consenting breasts for their trouble, they were liable to get
mugged in all this darkness.

Dieudonné almost slipped when he entered the stinking, impenetrable bowels separating Lakou Ferraille from the street, and cautiously felt his way up the worm-eaten stairs. A cat sitting on its behind was meowing. Once he got to the second floor, room number 5, he pounded on the bulky doors with all his strength, then pressed his lips to the slats in the wood.

"It's me! Let me in," he commanded.

It wasn't long before he heard a creak and the clink of the latch, then the key turned in the lock. Ana appeared, a candle in hand, smaller, thinner, and more worn-out than he remembered her. She stood on tiptoe, embraced him awkwardly, and whispered passionately, "I wasn't asleep, I was waiting for you. I knew you would come."

Without responding, he followed her inside, which was also more cramped and modest than he recalled, while she scurried to light more candles and perch them here and there on the furniture throughout the room. Soon it resembled a mortuary chapel with shapes and objects shifting indistinctly in the half light. Right away, Dieudonné noticed the bassinet, sheltered under mosquito netting next to the bed, and he turned to Ana:

"You had a baby?"

She nodded. "A boy!" she specified, proudly.

He looked at her hard. "Who's the father?"

Since her eyes suddenly filled with water and she kept silent, he asked her rather curtly, "Why didn't you say anything to me?"

She burst into tears outright. "I didn't know if you'd be happy, and then, being where you were, you had other problems to think about! OK, so this isn't America. They don't kill people for just anything. But you were facing a heavy sentence."

While she was talking, he went over to the bassinet, looked at the little sleeping bundle without showing what he was thinking and asked, "What's his name?"

"Werner . . ."

He spun around abruptly to face her. "What kind of a name is that? I would have wanted my child to be named Wesley . . ."

She murmured apologetically, "How could I have guessed? Werner was the name of the father I adored, who I lost too early."

He softened and sat down on the bed. It was then that she realized his clothes were torn and stained with blood, his face swollen. She went into a panic. "What did they do to you? Let me take care of you."

He smiled sadly. "No, thanks! You know Vodou, too?"

Vodou? She didn't follow him, but let it go. She sat down close to him and, not knowing how to make him happy, suggested, "You want me to put some hot compresses on it?"

He stretched out, laid his head on a pillow, and closed his eyes with a sigh of fatigue. Even though she wanted to, she didn't dare touch him, but murmured, "Did you get my packages? Did you read the books I put in? I bet you didn't even open them! José Saramago: *The Gospel According to Jesus Christ.* What a masterpiece, isn't it!"

Couldn't she shut up? Her voice was as unbearable to him as a Good Friday *rara.* How cruel it was to find her alive when the one he adored was cold, lost forever. Where was her grave? It wouldn't be hard to find it. In the Port-Mahault Cemetery, in certain aisles, the *békés* have their family crypts, monumental crypts covered in black-and-white marble flagstones, adorned with artificial flowers and pearl crosses. In the frames, photographs of slick, proudly mustachioed Matamoros, powerful during their lifetimes, and languid women, so pale beneath their straw bonnets, reminded anyone who doubted it that death respects no one. Most likely she was laid to rest there. Unless she was in Saint-Léger-des-Feuilles in the same crypt as her aunt and godmother Yolande. Dieudonné recalled the little cemetery, perched balancing on the mountainside under the canopy of catalpas. His eyes filled with tears. So many times, in jail, he had imagined this burial. He would picture himself throwing roses on the casket. Red roses as symbols of love. White roses to beg forgiveness.

The nasal sound of Ana's voice struck his ears again. "Tell me, what was it like?"

He stared at her stiffly and she hastened to explain, fearing a misunderstanding: "No! Not that . . . I mean prison. It wasn't too hard? People say the new Basse-Pointe penitentiary is ultramodern. Televisions in every room . . ."

He interrupted her. "I'm dying of hunger."

Straight away, she busied herself, running around, quickly opening the cooler, the food safe, the dresser, looking for a glass, a plate, and silverware in a feverish commotion. He followed each of her movements, irritated to find her so common, so dull, almost ugly in her bargain-basement nightgown.

The last time he had seen Loraine, it was the middle of the night, the very evening of Luc's departure. He couldn't wait any longer, and was coming back to her in his thirst, his heart palpitating. He didn't think he had betrayed her. For what had happened with Luc belonged to another circle, another place inside himself, a peripheral, unimportant place, really. A little desire. A little pleasure. A lot, even. None of that lasts. The neighborhood was asleep, with the exception of the panting pack of watchdogs on the lookout in the yards. Like a burglar, he had circled the villa, testing the entry points one by one. As he expected, the bathroom window had not resisted his push and, straddling it, he had landed on the plush, blood-red carpet covering the floor. In the living room, the lights were on and the television was talking out loud to itself. Loraine was in bed, with a half-empty bottle of Glenfiddich on the nightstand, next to her gun. She had dozed off in her thick terry robe and was snoring lightly, her mouth half-open, her eyes half-closed as usual. When he had tried to undress her, her eyes had opened, at first fuzzy, at first bottomless. Little by little, as her consciousness returned, anger hardened and darkened them. She stood up and seized her weapon, hissing:

"Did you forget? I told you to keep your filthy self out of here."

What a surprise! For him, once Luc was back on his plane, once the Angel of Evil was busy conquering other victims—for it was Luc who deserved that name, not poor Rodrigue, who was himself a victim—everything would go back to the way it was before. Dumbfounded, he had stammered, "But he's gone!"

She had sat down, shouting, "Idiot! You think I don't know he's gone?"

Suddenly, waves of tears had flowed down her cheeks, giving her the baby face she must have had when she was six—and it was pathetic to see her childhood portrait reemerging in the worn contours of her fifty-year-old features. She had continued plaintively, speaking for her own benefit, "He's gone, and like every time, he refused to tell me when his flight was or let me take him to the airport. I had to say good-bye at the house. I know that after leaving me, he was going to celebrate New Year's with friends. That's fine with me. Youth is youth. God knows when I'll see him again. Sometimes, he turns up just for a weekend without telling me in advance and then leaves again before I've caught my breath."

Overwhelmed with emotion, Dieudonné had stretched out a hand to caress her. At his touch, she had recoiled, pointing her weapon again, screaming, "Don't touch me!"

There was a silence. To put herself out of reach, she had scrunched herself up on the other side of the bed. Finally, she set her weapon down, and began again in a barely distinguishable monotone, as if she were entirely possessed by her grief, entirely possessed by a past in which she played no role:

"Luc was my student at the École des Arts Plastiques. And I have never known a more talented student. It was even more of a miracle because he landed there after coming from a hole in the wall, Morne Vert, where he had taken some drawing lessons with a priest in the presbytery. Blown away, I got him his first scholarship, which got him on track. He finished first in his class at the École des Arts in Martinique. Then I helped him get another grant, a Guggenheim, and he left for the United States. One day, I assure you, his name will be well known. And the people in this country who keep denigrating themselves will be completely astonished to learn that they've produced a genius, that Gauguin was reincarnated on Morne Vert like the Dalai Lama in the mountains of Tibet. A year ago he had his first exhibit in SoHo—there were tons of articles in the papers, and to celebrate it I joined him in New York. I wanted to buy him an apartment too. He never asked me for anything. He never asks me for anything. People who say he's with me for the money aren't just bad-mouthers. They're imbeciles who think slavery's still alive today, who can't conceive that a *nègre* in this country can really truly love a *békée,* that a young man can love an older woman. Who want to issue commandments, to put rules on everything, even the heart, even sex. We looked all over Manhattan, from the Village to the Upper West Side, from Riverside to FDR Drive. Finally, we decided on a penthouse all the way downtown, on Water Street. On the 34th floor. We made love under the curious eyes of the Empire State Building, against the backdrop of streets streaked with headlights. At lunch, I'd go meet him at his school and the Americans, shameless as they are, would ask him, 'Is she your mother?' He'd say yes, then run and kiss me on the mouth. You should have seen their faces! You see, Luc is the gift the Good Lord gave me at the very last moment, when I had given up expecting anything from life anymore."

Under this painful blow, he couldn't help but whimper, "And me, then? What am I to you?"

"Come sit at the table," ordered Ana, barging rudely into his musings.

She had fixed a tuna sandwich and tomatoes with salt—an American's idea of a meal—and he attacked it reluctantly. At that moment, Werner cried out from his cradle. She rushed to him, took him in her arms, then brought him to Dieudonné. From the way she was carrying him, you could tell how proud she was. In her eyes, he was her most beautiful creation, the one that gave meaning to an otherwise ordinary life without rhyme or reason. You have to admit she wasn't wrong. He was a magnificent child. Plump and firm, cheerful, with almond-shaped eyes. He had Dieudonné's very dark skin, and his *kako*-colored eyes too. From his mother, his curls had the gift of a golden sheen. Dieudonné grabbed his little hand clumsily. Babies made him uneasy. Was it their nostalgia for their mother's womb, paradise they would never regain, that made them nervous, edgy, and unpredictable? What's more, he pitied them deeply, thinking of the miles of ocean these solo sailors had to cross, tossed about on the swells and troughs, on waves waiting to gobble up their frail skiffs. However, at least this one had his mama, who would know how to protect and guide him. Unlike Marine, Ana had an education. And besides, she was born on the side of the conquerors. She only needed to take Werner back home for his life to be transformed, for thousands of doors to open up for him. He pressed her harshly.

"Why do you stay in this country? Why don't you go back home, to the United States?"

She fumbled, flustered.

"I've never really considered the United States my home, which is nothing new. It's a place where everyone comes from Elsewhere, clings to an Elsewhere. Some come from Ireland, some from Portugal, others from Russia, but all cherish the fantasy of their ancestral homeland. But I know that it's just a dream, that I could never go back to Germany. I could only go back to the US. There are so many universities there that I'd end up finding a position in anthropology someplace in the middle of nowhere. But that narrow, confining life I lived my whole childhood scares me."

He snickered. "And things are different here?"

She stammered, putting forward the thin arguments she had made to herself a hundred times, aware that they were barely even good enough for a tourist brochure. "Well, first there's the beautiful setting. Sometimes, when everyone in the *lakou* is still asleep, I take Werner on a walk all the way to the shore. You can't make out anything. The scenery seems to be wrapped in a ball of cotton. All of a sudden, the sun rises. The cotton ball rips open and the scenery lights up."

He listened, a little mockingly, while making his way unenthusiastically through the sandwich. Werner, who wasn't getting any attention, started crying. Ana broke off and busied herself again, uncovering a beautiful, firm breast that surprised Dieudonné. Loraine's breasts, by contrast, were withered, limp waterskins. She would make fun of them, in her usual way: "You see, they're cushions that have worn out from too much use. Too many men have laid their heads there to cry, pretending to confide their heart's innermost secrets to me, while it was all just lies."

A mother tenders her breast to her baby. The father looks on. Isn't that the picture of happiness? A conventional, deceitful picture. In reality, everything happens differently. The father doesn't love the mother, doesn't love the baby.

While the child was sucking noisily, Dieudonné tried to dredge his memory. Really, he had actually slept with this woman? He had taken pleasure in it? This child was his? By his sperm? Even if he could recognize his own features, his eyes, his mouth, he didn't feel the slightest affection for this little howler. Not the slightest feeling of responsibility. No impulse in his heart or his body. This detour led him back to Milo Vertueux again. So, it was him! The secret had been well kept. He had never had any idea. When he was a little boy, the desire to give a name to his father used to eat him alive. As he grew up, though, he had gotten over this itch. Now, more than the urge to kill him, the thought of all the damage caused by his absence and his failure to acknowledge paternity possessed him uncontrollably. Had that filthy scumbag felt guilty about Marine's death? After Hugo, he was all over the television, the radio. Did he feel more concern for the devastation done to the banana farms than for the devastation he had done to his former mistress's life?

Arbella foolishly maintained that he wanted to make amends. That would be easy, wouldn't it, if life could be sewn back together like a rip in a piece of clothing!

At the same time, a bitter feeling of jubilation started to permeate him. He wasn't just some nobody. Without suspecting it, he had ties to the world of the wealthy. Is that why he had never hated it like Rodrigue or Boris, who, in different ways, dreamed only of destroying it? He on the other hand just lived his life, focused on himself, feeling no rage or envy toward anybody. As a child, the son of the maid, he wasn't embarrassed among the children of doctors, business managers, and airline pilots with whom the Cohens rubbed shoulders. Once, when one of these charming fair-haired tykes had refused to play with the little black boy, he had just gone on his way, leaving it to David and Benjamin to fight for his honor. He had always suspected— and his relationship with Loraine had brought him proof—that loneliness and mourning dwell in both the *kaz-nèg* and the master's house, that anguish and insecurity lie down to sleep in majestic four-poster beds just as they do in *kabanns* made of piles of rags. Nothing can protect against the rabid bite of that bitch that is life. He pushed back his plate.

"Listen, I'm going to lie down for a while."

Again, she was quick to offer help. "Are you sure you don't want me to make you some hot compresses? The warm water will relax you."

He declined with a wave of his hand. Far from pleasing him, her attentiveness and subservience irritated him and he couldn't help noticing the contrast. He had always served women. Marine first. Then Loraine, who was able-bodied but incapable of pouring herself a glass of water, pushing a button on the television set, changing a CD. He tried to take off his shirt, then gave up since it was sticking more and more firmly to his wounds, and stretched out fully clothed instead. As he was closing his eyes, about to sink into sleep, Loraine's voice again slung the arrow that had irreparably planted itself in the middle of his heart: "Luc is the gift the Good Lord gave me at the very last moment, when I had given up expecting anything from life anymore."

He fell asleep crying, repeating his everlasting question. "And me, then? What am I to you?"

Still at the table, with Werner in her arms, Ana watched this stranger getting into her bed. What had she expected? That he would take her in his arms murmuring words of love? That he would hug his son to his breast in a surge of paternal feeling? Only in Hollywood movies do things like that happen. Reality is more bitter. Yes, for her part, she had been thinking only of him. Yes, for almost two years, week after week, she had lovingly wrapped and shipped him packages. Yes, day after day she had followed his trial, getting irritated with Mr. Serbulon's stupid, black-and-white picture of things. Clearly, though, the brief time they had spent together held no value for him. Did he even remember it? An emission of sperm. An egg fertilized deep inside a vagina. That's all there is to it. Now, she seemed to be in his way. Would he stay with them, make a life with them? She put the sleeping child back in his cradle, blew out all the candles except the one on the nightstand, and sat back down in the dimness, her head between her hands. It wasn't surprising that Dieudonné had found her skinnier and aged. It hadn't been easy, the year she'd had.

Despite all the talk across the world about women's liberation and the right of every individual to make her own decisions
about motherhood, a foreign woman shouldn't be like a fallen
woman. She shouldn't be schlepping around a belly bought
on credit, a gift from who knows what tramp. As soon as her
condition became visible, Ana's American friends had fled. It
wasn't just that she was pregnant. A tenacious rumor was going
around that, O shame of shames, the father was that homeless
guy, Boris. People had seen him in Lakou Ferraille. People swore
that they were getting together on the *Belle Créole*. Overnight,
half her students left her school. The chamber of commerce
ended her contract, while the businessmen who had sung her
praises now closed their offices to her. Not only had she experienced loneliness and exclusion, but she would also have died of
hunger if it weren't for some translations she did bravely by cor-
respondence. Only the *bòbòs* and her friend Eudoxia had stood
faithfully by her. You would have thought the child to come was
one of their own, and the fact that his father was unknown had
nothing to do with anything. Not once did they get themselves
a *krèye* of fish without offering Ana a coney or a red hind, not
once did they buy a bag of rice without saving a few pounds
for her. They had split their yams and dasheens, shared their
portions of pigeon peas and sweet potatoes. During the final
months, they had taken shifts sleeping in her room. When her
labor pains started, the whole group had gone with her to the
maternity ward and waited in the hall on their high heels until
a tight-lipped midwife informed them that the baby had come
without a hitch, and that at nine thirty in the morning, Werner
Alexander Rumpf had made his entrance into our world. They
had clapped their hands, crying out:

"¡Es un niño, un niño! Qué maravilla!"

This had led to joyful celebrations that were repeated when
Ana came back home and even more so again, a month later,
on baptism Sunday at Saint-Laurent, the neighborhood church.
In a garnet-colored taffeta suit, Eudoxia had held the little one
while he chewed on the blessed salt, and the godfather was
Isaac, the renter from number 17, a Saint-Lucian house painter
and sometime dealer. After she got pregnant, Ana had tried to

build up a clientele again, ruining herself paying for brochures and leaflets, mailing them, or tasking the *bòbòs* to slip them to their customers. All that in vain. When businessmen did return her calls, it was to treat her unceremoniously as a *dame-gabrielle* and put their hands on her backside in a crude way of indicating what they hoped to get out of her. If she had weathered the winds and tides, it was thanks to Dieudonné. She didn't know how many years he'd be in prison. Ten, fifteen. When he got out, his shock of hair graying, she would be there to take him in. She would succeed in proving to him that all manner of women flower under the eye of the sun. Not just depraved ones like Loraine. Not just deceptive, vicious, crooked ones. But also valiant, upstanding ones. Yet now that he was here, so close to her, she realized that there were no ties between them. Neither she nor Werner occupied the least little place inside him. Maybe they'd never be able to clear a path to his heart.

She started to cry, paradoxically finding some comfort in these silent tears she shed so rarely, in this weakness that she never wanted to admit to herself. Then she pulled herself together, so thoroughly trained was she to "think positive!" The father, in the image of the son, was sleeping under her roof. Just as she had hoped, Lakou Ferraille had been his chosen refuge.

In the morning, it would be high time to make plans for the future.

She blew out the candle and went back to bed.

17

"Midnight," Milo said to himself. "He won't be coming now."

He felt incredibly relieved, like someone witnessing the failure of an action he didn't want to take, of something he was constrained to do. One by one, he turned off the living room lights and started up the stairs. In his villa, which he was very proud of, the bedrooms, six in all, each flanked by its own bathroom, were located on the second floor. A spiral staircase led to the garret where two comfortable studios were set up. Before her death, the mother he had idolized had occupied one of them. But she had always remained the *moun-bitation* that she was, a vegetable farmer from Grands-Fonds accustomed to hard labor, and had never gotten used to the ostentation and luxury of the place.

Contrary to what he had assured Arbella, Milo hadn't admitted anything to his daughters. Even if he had wanted to, that confession would have been difficult. Every time they saw Dieudonné's face on television or in the pages of *France-Caraïbes,* the four adolescents would get worked up with excitement:

"Isn't he handsome! He looks like Lenny Kravitz!"

Who was Lenny Kravitz? wondered Milo. He never understood anything in his daughters' conversations. Mona, the eldest and the prettiest, but also the most *mal sòti,* the darkest, who took after Milo's mother, would fly into a rage:

"As soon as they get handsome like that, they run after white women! Girls of color aren't good enough for them anymore! They have to have blondes! And too bad if they're fat cows. Because you have to admit, that old *békée* was a fat cow."

Maryvonne, the youngest, didn't agree, and thought that Loraine, despite her age, still had class. She thought she looked like Glenn Close in *Fatal Attraction.* Glenn Close! Mona protested. No, better to be deaf than to have to hear something so idiotic! The debate got more and more heated until their father, who couldn't take it anymore, made them shut up.

In fact, it is safe to say that Milo lied to Arbella all down the line. All those years, he had never written one word to Marine offering support for their son's upbringing. In truth, it was Arielle, his wife, a scrupulous Christian who attended Mass every morning, confession every Friday, and Holy Table every Sunday, who had convinced him that he must expiate his sin. From the time she had arrived from her native Martinique and married him, some twenty years earlier, kind souls torn between malevolence and compassion had informed her in hushed tones of this unacknowledged and totally abandoned bastard. That hadn't put her off Milo. Men aren't women. If the latter owes it to herself to remain intact, what man enters marriage without carting his lot of bastards behind him? She had merely done her duty and continually reminded him, "You are responsible. On Judgment

Day, the Good Lord will open His Book and ask you to account for yourself. What will you tell Him in your defense?"

After Marine's unfortunate accident, she had pressed him more strongly. A few years later, after her death, Arielle got impatient and even more insistent. In vain. The recent drama featuring Dieudonné had changed her sermons and pious exhortations into imprecations, so much so that Milo had ended up taking the road to Arbella's place. Underneath the surface appearance of a union without cracks, a respectable couple unanimously respected among the local bourgeoisie, Milo and Arielle formed a rather curious hitched team. Milo lived in terror of Arielle. This thundering man, built like a giant, who called French prime ministers by their first names and had prefects over for dinner, was afraid of this tiny little thing and the way she saw straight through the vanity, cowardice, and selfishness of his actions. This man who had been so cavalier in his youth gave up cheating on her, for as soon as he went on the littlest jaunt, her intuition would alert her and she'd summon him before her like a schoolboy. He only felt he was the master when they made love, which, given their age and her increasing piety, was, alas, becoming rarer and rarer. Milo came into the bedroom where Arielle, her silky hair moisturized for the night and rolled into four knots making her look at once like a little girl and an old lady, was reading *The Imitation of Christ*. He sighed. "You see? He didn't come."

Arielle closed the holy book, put her glasses in their case, and said tenderly, for the mystery of it was that she cherished Milo as much now as on the first day of their marriage, despite his load of faults, "That suits you, doesn't it?"

Since she had seen through him, he decided to be sincere and admitted, "Yes, I'm not ready. I'm doing this because you've filled my head with all this talk about the Good Lord, the Good Lord. But I don't feel anything for him. You don't call a boy your son when you haven't seen him grow up, when, really, you don't know him!"

He didn't add that his relationship with Marine had hardly left him good memories. True, she was one hell of a black woman! When she was young, she could have set a font of holy water on fire, and their nights blazed with sparks. But she was quick-tempered and demanding, always picking a fight, always accusing him cruelly of lying, of not keeping his word, of not sticking to his promises. When they broke up, she had him followed by one of her Malabars of a brother whose hand never left his cutlass. When he married Arielle, she had threatened to set fire to his plantations. At that point, he had warned her he could use his connections to have her put in an insane asylum or in jail. A threat for a threat! He went to the window and looked out at the street, lit up by powerful floodlights posted on top of the walls surrounding the villas. Holding their dogs on a leash, the guards kept their fingers on the trigger. The scene was nightmarish. You would have thought filming for an American action movie was about to start: *Mission Impossible* or *Mission to Mars*. For crying out loud, what good was this administration? Instead of sending police and gendarme reinforcements, the CRS riot police, or the army if necessary, instead of throwing Benjy in jail along with the other troublemakers of his ilk, this government was negotiating and—a new word—dialoguing, and finally, had tasked two leftist parliamentary deputies with writing a report on the situation in the Caribbean! Really? Power wasn't power anymore! They hadn't needed kid gloves to liquidate the independentist rebels of the '60s. Arrests, heavy sentences! If this had happened during the term of his personal friend the late president, Milo would have been on the phone with him long ago to tell him what actions to take. Unfortunately, these new representatives didn't listen to anyone, and thought they knew everything. Communists and environmentalists were laying down the law in the National Assembly!

Behind him, Arielle inquired, "Did you talk to Julius Rangoon? Did you suggest that he do his community service with him?"

Could anyone match that woman's obstinacy? Milo turned to face her and dug in. "No, I didn't say anything to Julius. First I have to see this Dieudonné, and talk with him! Who's to say that he'd want to work in farming? It's no joyride, I assure you. It means getting up at four in the morning . . ."

She interrupted him.

"He knows something about working the land. He was a gardener, wasn't he?"

Milo snorted derisively. "Seriously, a gardener? A pretext for getting himself into villas and fucking the women who weren't too turned off by him! Surely it wasn't a vocation. The youths today are lazybones who don't want to do anything! All that interests them is cruising in BMWs and calling people on their cell phones!"

Milo never lost an opportunity to remind Arielle, a pure blossom of the urban mulatto bourgeoisie, of his own peasant childhood. He boasted of having slept four hours a night for years, of getting up before dawn to water the stock and put them out to picket in the savanna through blades of grass wet with dew and sharp as razors. Then, he would go water hectares of lettuce, tomatoes, cabbages, and carrots. Often, all he had to fill up his stomach were mangoes. When he had started sixth grade at Victor-Schœlcher school, the students pretended to hold their noses because of his smell. Up until he turned twenty, people called him "*bitako.*" According to Milo, the race of those intimately familiar with the traditions of the land had ended with him. Because the thought had always preoccupied him, he asked, gravely, "And another thing, aren't you afraid of what he did to that woman? You'd let him prowl around our daughters? I have to tell you, frankly, I don't like that idea at all."

Arielle turned off her bedside lamp, lay down on her side, and declared, resolutely, "Our Lord Jesus Christ forgave Peter, who denied him three times!"

Milo protested, "The Good Lord also commanded, 'Thou shalt not kill!'"

She responded in the most surprising, even shocking way a Christian like her could. "I think she deserved to die the way she did."

He stared at her, floored, and she explained herself steadily.

"It's not because she was a *békée*, despite all the harm those people did to us and never acknowledged. Back home, in Martinique, I would hear *békés* boasting, 'We've done a lot of good for this country!' They were completely convinced of it too. If I say that, it's because she was a bad person."

How could she be so sure? He had followed the trial a bit, and that wasn't the impression of Loraine he had come away with. What he saw was a woman who was washed up, spoiled by heavy drinking, idleness, and too much money. If, like his own mother, she had been forced to do battle to feed her son, she would have seen life through different eyes. He was not at all persuaded by Mr. Serbulon's scenario. Mistress, slave—that was all in the past now. Society had changed, and at the height of the twentieth century, nobody believed in that nonsense anymore. Milo had his own theory. The lawyer had insisted on the fact that money wasn't the motive for the crime. The proof, according to him, was that the contents of the safe were untouched. That didn't mean anything. Maybe Dieudonné was just incompetent and couldn't manage to pull off his scheme. Mr. Serbulon had skirted around an important fact—by design, most likely—which was that Dieudonné's best friend, a certain Rodrigue, was a top-notch armed robber. A few days before the Allée des Amériques drama, he too had committed burglary and murder. These misdeeds had to have been connected. Probably the two partners in crime had dreamed up their heinous acts and planned everything out together. Yet Rodrigue had been sentenced to twenty years in prison without any high-profile trial. And Dieudonné had been acquitted! Why were there two weights, two measures for this pair of crooks, these dangerous good-for-nothings?

Eventually, he got undressed and climbed into bed.

By his side, engulfed in her pillows, Arielle kept quiet; he knew she was reciting her nightly prayer. What a misfortune it was when the Good Lord carved out a space in the conjugal bed, lying down between a wife and her husband.

Just as he was about to fall asleep, troubled and vexed, Dieudonné's face came to rest on his subconscious like a photograph tacked at its four corners to a wall. It had not escaped him that Arbella, who felt little tenderness for her grandson, had nothing planned for his future. For the first time, he wondered whether Arielle wasn't right to underscore his responsibility in this drama. His own father hadn't counted for much in his life. He was an influential banana grower that he saw at church on Sundays, dignified and paunchy, as befit his position, accompanied by his wife and his string of legitimate children. When he had started making a name for himself, this prominent figure had at last taken an interest in him. They had a falling out a few years later when Milo created the Food-Crop Producers Association and the father found himself decidedly overshadowed by this peppy son. If his father's indifference and then his about-faces had never really affected Milo, it was because, through it all, his mother had lavished him with devotion. But the unfortunate Dieudonné didn't have a place in anyone's heart.

Reluctantly, Milo promised himself he'd return to Arbella's the next day.

Carla's first labor pains started a little before midnight. All day long, she had been dragging her heavy, uncomfortable belly. She had drunk gallons of water, for she was constantly thirsty. A fire in her throat. When everything went into motion, she didn't panic. For at least a week, her hospital bag had been ready. Alcohol-free eau de Cologne, baby powder, Diadermine skin cream. The cotton bodysuits and blue baby clothes, the sonogram having left no doubts. Mystery was out of style, so Boris and Carla were aware it would be a boy. The booties, the Pampers diapers. She had already given birth twice. But this time would be different. Thinking about the worried troop that had escorted her to the hospital in Bologna, she felt she had never been so alone as she was now. Where was Boris? Why wasn't he with her? The maternity wards are full of fathers who want to share everything with their companions. Her first husband, Aldo, out of desire to compensate for his inability to carry their children, to feel them moving deep inside and then part with them in a bloody epilogue, hadn't left her for a second. From the first contractions up to the delivery. But when, one time, she had asked Boris to stay with her in the delivery room, he had responded curtly,

"Men where I'm from don't do that!"

She had consoled herself after this rebuff by telling herself that his brusqueness must be hiding fear. Fear of women's

uncontrollable sex! That contradictory organ, a source of pleasure at first, but then horror too, at the end of the day.

To give birth so far from home! Without any relatives or
close friends to look over her. Without her native language to
express her suffering, forced to speak her pain in a borrowed,
foreign idiom. The faces of her mother, her aunts, the whole
brood came back to her. Unfortunately, the ones who loved
her couldn't be near. She would be surrounded by people who
didn't care one way or another.

In the beginning, everything enchanted Carla. A dip in the
sea, the scent of the sand baking in the sun, the almond trees,
the mangoes tasting of the ocean, the bananas melting in her
mouth. Even the sound of zouk music playing all day long
didn't bother her. The graceless villa where she had moved in
with Boris a couple doors down from Benjy delighted her. She
lovingly tended to its flower beds, planted arums and ginger
lilies, cultivated a vegetable garden. But then, unexpectedly,
everything had changed and she found herself in hell. It wasn't
the situation of the country that weighed on her, the strikes
launched at the drop of a hat, the shortages, or even the violence. On the contrary, she thought that a people had the right
to use any weapon to gain its freedom. For too long, this country had been under tutelage. It had to emancipate itself. The
problem was that nothing tied her to Boris anymore. The man
she had discovered and loved was a crazy poet, an incorrigible
dreamer, a marginalized figure. But she found herself married
to the spitting image of a civil servant, sententious, convinced
he was working on a crucial mission. Had he forgotten that the
most crucial mission is fidelity to one's self? She had taken a
dislike to Benjy as if he were responsible for the changes in the
one she loved. However, deep inside, she knew this wasn't the
case. It was because of her, because of her well-being, because
of their unborn son that Boris had gone through such an ugly
metamorphosis. What horrifying choices life forces on you! On
the one side, creativity, whimsy, and freedom. On the other, bu-
reaucratic constraints and oppressiveness. There was no way
out of this trap.

When her contractions intensified, she called Inis, the only person with whom she had some semblance of intimacy. Having to share their husbands with the PTCR, that capricious and demanding mistress, had brought these two women together when they otherwise had few things in common. The one was European and an intellectual, proud of her long career as a journalist. The other was a mother without much education who had never left her spitball of a country and was completely devoted to raising her boys. On weekends, to escape loneliness, Carla would go with Inis to the deepest parts of Haute-Terre, to Maraval, where Inis's mama, a single mother, lived with one of her sisters, who was divorced, and her daughters. There in that rural village, hidden in the *pié-bwa* of the dense forest, she found herself among women without a man, who lived taking pride in lusterless tasks: cooking, raising children, keeping house. The days were spent sitting together around a table, making children recite their lessons, correcting homework. In the evenings, they'd take a walk down muddy paths under a canopy of tousled trees. They'd have different stews for supper. And exchange recipes. Inis's mother had taught her how to make stock, and goat colombo. Carla had introduced her in turn to the savors of olive oil, lasagna, and artichokes alla romana. And each time, she wondered whether this was fundamentally what happiness was, if her quest for the perfect companion wasn't unrealistic.

Even though she hadn't even had two hours' sleep, Inis arrived smiling, and, without any unnecessary talk, grabbed Carla's things and helped her out of the house. The guards interrupted their rounds to light their way and escort them to their car. Inis took the wheel. At first, for a second, the headlights illuminated a stampede of brazen rats as big as cats. It was a bleak view. Rats were proliferating everywhere. In broad daylight you could see them running single file or in couples. The doctors feared them more than the dogs, predicting they'd bring horrible epidemics. In the absence of trash collection, they recommended spreading quicklime on rubbish piles. Unfortunately, the lime provided by the quarries in the North was starting to run out. Crafty little rascals were getting rich by going

to buy it in the Dominican Republic and reselling it at top dol-
lar. Next the car dove into the trench of darkness that was the
highway. To distract herself from the pain, Carla made an effort
to think about her child, who she imagined was suffering as
much as she was, frightened, crouched deep in the refuge he had
thought was forever but that nature was inexorably forcing him
to leave. How could she explain to him that once his terrible
journey was complete, the warmth of his mother's breast would
be waiting for him? She ran a hand over the bump of her stomach as if the little stranger she was carrying could feel her caress.
They crossed the Petit-Paradis neighborhood. The flaming car
tires on the sidewalks lit up the night and recalled the old days.
When Port-Mahault was just a pile of soapbox cottages, every
night whole neighborhoods went up in smoke. It was the terror
of those poor people who'd risk their lives to save a mean straw
mattress, a table, a wooden dresser, and the flames illuminated
faces in tears, but fascinated nevertheless by this reminder of
original fires. The massive block of the hospital, glowing with
all its lights on its hill, towered over the city. It wasn't guarded
since it sheltered only sickness, suffering, insomnia, and death,
commodities coveted by no one. An old watchman, bundled up
in wools, was sleeping next to the open gate. He roused himself
to inspect the car. Then, at the sight of Carla, he let them race
up to the entrance to the maternity ward. The whole ride, the
two friends had stayed silent, aside from Inis's ritual questions:
  "How do you feel?"
  Or:
  "You're not in too much pain?"
  Yet they didn't need to talk. Never had they felt so close,
together in this territory that belongs to women alone, that
only their feet can tread, keenly aware of every little bump in
the terrain. Carla no longer had any thought for Boris. As a
man, at present, he was frankly in the way. An intruder. He
had no place inside the circle closing in on her and her child.
The maternity ward was the pride of Port-Mahault for, long
decrepit and badly equipped, it had been entirely remodeled
a year earlier. The lobby was decorated with a mural by Roro
Xantippe, who was considered a national painter, representing

a mother, a magnificent black woman in an orange boubou, her newborn at her generous breast and other children of various ages clinging to the folds of her garment. It was obvious that, through this maternity ward, the artist had wanted to glorify the country and its too-often-unsung African origins. Though he was a mulatto, Roro Xantippe had painted many a *Baby Jesus, Holy Family,* and *Christ* in the most beautiful black, to the public's satisfaction. In the emergency room, the nurse's aides took charge of Carla with a wholly professional indifference, which paradoxically reassured her, for it assigned her a role with no surprises in the drama in three acts that humanity has played out again and again since the world has been the world: birth, growth, death.

One of them asked, "Has your water already broken?"

And when she nodded yes, overwhelmed now, hiccupping and doubled over in pain, the other, reflexively, gave her a smile to comfort her:

"Things will go very fast, then."

Dorisca took care not to let the door slam behind her, and stepped out onto the sidewalk. She had put her Doc Martens back on her painful feet and was limping.

"Hey, where do you think you're going at this hour?"

The young folks who were betting it all playing cards were calling out to her affectionately, for she was, as she had said, everyone's child. In the beginning, people were suspicious of these Haitians who spoke a funny Creole. Then, they had discovered that the husband knew remedies for all manner of *bouden* aches, for the hot and cold, and especially for the frequent illnesses that attack men's *koks* and leave them limp as a rag; that the wife cooked an excellent potato bread that she'd sell for next to nothing. They had ended up growing attached to this odd little Dorisca girl. Ever since her uncle had died and her *ninnaine* only had one idea in her head—meeting back up with him at midnight—the whole neighborhood took care of her. People would feed her; people would wash her clothes; people would resole her shoes. When she stank too much, they'd scrub her down with a wisp of herbs, like a floorboard.

Dorisca pretended not to hear their exclamations and quick-ened her step, briskly rounding the corner of the Rue des Sol-dats. Poor Dieudonné! Where was he? You could bet that he wouldn't go finish out the night with a grandmother who, ac-cording to *France-Caraïbe,* had kicked him out at the age of sixteen. He wouldn't go to his godmother either, who had never held him close to her heart. He didn't have much choice: he'd most likely return to the Mégisserie marina, to the *Belle Créole.* She trotted all the way to the Amandiers complex, and there she ran into the Leopards. The Leopards were a gang of boys who put on American airs by donning baseball caps and wearing T-shirts curiously sporting the slogan "I love L.A.," a city they had never visited. Aside from that, they hadn't done much to attract attention and limited themselves to mugging imprudent night owls. At the moment, they had just trapped a broke guy who hadn't taken the trouble to lock the doors of his old beater and they were now sharing out the meager booty: a wallet without any credit cards or cash, some spare change left forgotten in the glove box. She sat down next to Lenny, the leader, who, to dis-tinguish himself from the rest of his troops, was sporting a tri-color beanie in place of a baseball cap. Pushing it back revealed the beginnings of some locks, reddened with sweat and dirt, as well as a prominent forehead, rounded like a pebble. Dorisca said to him, reproachfully, "What you did before, a little while back, wasn't right. Beating up my friend."

Lenny took his hash cigarette out of his mouth, handed it to her, and, while she was inhaling, eyes closed, he protested, "Since when is he your friend? Isn't he that bastard who killed the *békée?* There's no justice in this country. They let a guy like that out. They lock poor souls up in jail for smoking a little weed."

"It was a crime of passion," explained Dorisca, leaning for reference on her favorite newspaper. "The jury is always more lenient with that kind of thing. And besides, she was a *békée* who drank and sat around doing nothing! And here, people don't like *békés* to start with!"

He repeated, in a comical tone, "A crime of passion . . . ? What the hell is that?"

On that note, he burst out laughing, imitated by his follow-ers, who didn't know what was going on but were laughing from afar all the same. Irritated, Dorisca gave his joint back to him, got up with dignity, and moved off. Behind her, he shouted, "Be careful. One day you'll regret it. Some criminal is going to force his iron rod into you know where and you'll be left with only your two eyes for crying."

She didn't answer.

Dorisca had no memories of Haiti. Through her relatives' stories, she had put together her own idea of it. It was a cruel and colorful land. The dead marched alongside the living. The Tontons Macoutes on dictators' payrolls assassinated a zombi-fied populace. And yet, Vodou still staked its sliver of rainbow light there. People still danced the merengue and the compas-color while eating pork grillot with djon-djon rice. After the death of her mother and father, the family had planned to send her and Max, her twin brother, to an aunt who had gone into exile twenty years previously, and who was living safe in Brook-lyn. But another aunt, her godmother, had become attached to Dorisca and refused to be separated from her. And so Max had left all by himself. She had cried a lot over it at the time, because twins, Marassa, are no ordinary people. In fact, they are a single soul divided into two distinct bodies, a single mind in two sepa-rate envelopes of flesh. If one twin is hurting, the other automati-cally suffers. People maintain that they die on the same day, that they follow one another into the invisible. Max had come out first to do a sweep and make sure that nothing would put his sister at risk. From that moment on, he had never given up his role as a protector. When they were first separated, he faithfully kept in touch with her, describing to her in detail the marvels of life. He had walked through the crown—yes, the crown!—of the Statue of Liberty, had looked through the hole in her eye—yes, her eye!—and from there he had defiantly stood up to Manhat-tan, carved into potato plots by the straight lines of its streets and avenues. He had roller-skated between the feet of the buses, right under the noses of the yellow taxis. He had attended a Fu-gees concert in Central Park. More than two thousand people, all speaking Creole. Then these missives had stopped and she

went through torture, picturing him dead already. There are
so many crazy people in the United States! People who empty
their clips into innocent customers sitting at McDonald's. After
a few months, though, the flow of letters started up again, written now on thick letterhead, stamped with incomprehensible
words. American English, probably. Max explained that he had
been sent to Diagnostic, a detention center for boys too young
for prison. What was he guilty of? A trivial thing. At school he
had flaunted a revolver and threatened one of his classmates on
the playground.

Ever since her godmother had left her to her own devices,
Dorisca no longer set foot in school. And yet, back in the day,
she had been a good student. She had even skipped a year. The
teacher would read her French homework aloud, compliment-
ing her on her imagination. But now she no longer had a taste
for anything but drifting. During the day, she slept her fill. At
lunchtime, she'd go eat with a neighbor lady or another, whoever had cooked extra rice or fish stock. In the evenings, she'd
start her peregrinations. She had begun to like Port-Mahault,
which she couldn't stand in the beginning, finding it so small
and ugly in comparison to Jacmel, and especially to New York,
though she had only seen it in her dreams. Port-Mahault's tow-
ers, turns, dead ends, and *lakous* held no more secrets for her.
She was intimately familiar with the old neighborhoods with
their pink and blue postcard houses, ringed with wrought-iron
balconies. The modern neighborhoods, the HLM housing projects with their identical facades. The last remaining "islands of
insalubrity," as the city pompously called them, where running
water was unknown to the needy, who did their business in
tomas as in the olden days. For her, the newspapers from France
and Canada were full of nothing but lies: Port-Mahault wasn't
dangerous. If, during the daytime, Port-Mahault was preoccupied with its merchants, often Haitian matrons, offering for sale
everything under the sun that can be sold, its Lebanese shop
criers trumpeting discounts, the *bitakos* come to window-shop,
and the schoolchildren skipping school, at night it was a party,
with the moon and the stars as accomplices. Dorisca knew how
to get into the Alhambra Cinema Theater to see Bruce Willis

movies without paying. She stood in line at the mobile pizzerias, run by peddlers with butterfly- and bird-tattooed biceps, their mouths full of laughter and jokes. Next, she'd drink to her favorite, the Neptune, with a can of Coca-Cola or nonalcoholic beer sold by other peddlers, just as tattooed and just as joking. People from Port-Mahault called these merchants *blancs-gâchés,* botched whites. Just like the ones all along the seafront who sold T-shirts and the thousand and one objects you could fashion from coconut shells. "Botched"? Why "botched"? Did it mean that people resented the look they had about them? That they reproached them for having lost the luster that their brothers still had, those *métro* civil servants and *béké* storekeepers? Dorisca beat the *gwo-ka* drum with the amateur *tambouyés.* The highlight of the night consisted of chasing away the dogs amassed in the concert gazebo. These were truly pitched battles, for the curs, who, as everyone knows, are Satan incarnate, howled, scratched, bit, and refused to go along with it. Some *tambouyés* brought balls of poisoned meat and it was great fun to see the famished beasts throw themselves onto it then stiffen and die doing grotesque entrechats. When Dorisca had gotten drunk enough on the rhythm of the *toumblak,* she went to shoot dice with the dealers and sniff around just about everywhere with friends. At times, morning found her in houses she wasn't quite sure how she had gotten into, sleeping next to strangers. Outside, the air smelled wet. You could hope for cool weather, since the sun was balking at getting up. And then it changed its mind, jumping brutally out of bed. On its orders, the sea and the sky got bluer and bluer, while the mountains, somber green fortresses, mated and rose up to block the horizon. Yet all of that couldn't console Dorisca in her loneliness. More than ever, she missed the warmth of a family, the affection of her twin brother.

She headed toward the Mégisserie dock. She pressed ahead, almost running, because of this crazy idea that had sprouted in her mind. Not so crazy, actually! The Cuban *balseros* and the Haitian boat people, if they're lucky, manage to reach America, even if, up close, it has nothing in common with the land of their hopes. Why not them? Dieudonné kept repeating that the

Belle Créole was an extraordinary sailboat, a queen of the seas. Of course, with all the time that she had spent worrying herself sick sitting at the dock, she must have lost some of her get-up-and-go. But, rest assured, as soon as she heard the song of the wind again, the call of the open sea, she'd rush forward like a raging horse and cover miles.

She would see Max again. She would get to know New York.

And the image of her brother and that of the unknown city blurred together in a symbol of her dreams and desires.

18

For Dieudonné, seeing the *Belle Créole* again was like reuniting with a woman you love after a long separation. He had a lot to apologize for. He hadn't come back to her until three in the morning, after he had really gauged how fragile his ties to others truly were. No family. No friends. Except for Ana, everyone had dropped him. Not that it surprised him. When he was in the Basse-Pointe prison, he frequently had a dream that, he could see now, was prophetic: one morning, he would get out of jail only to find himself in a maze, searching for hours for the exit. In the end, he always died all alone without ever finding it.

At three o'clock in the morning, a relative peace reigns over land, sea, and sky. On land, robbers have finished robbing, rapists have finished raping, and murderers have finished murdering. At sea, the waves no longer whip the ship hulls. They just lick them like a bitch nuzzling her pups. The sails flap silently, for the wind has stopped making them sing. In the heavens, the hour belongs to the stars. Dieudonné sat down as always with his back against the boom. A crescent moon had hoisted itself high up there. It gave no light and contented itself with watching over this peace. Suddenly, the pale glow of the stars darkened and rain began to fall. It was just a drizzle, but he had to run and take shelter inside. In the galley, the stench was so thick that he quickly came back out onto the bridge. No longer paying any mind to the water soaking his back and shoulders, he sat down again at the foot of the mast. He had left Lakou Ferraille with his shoes in his hand like an unfaithful man returning from an escapade and taking pains not to wake his companion. Despite himself, when it came time to unlatch the heavy doors and turn the key in the lock, his courage had faltered. He had turned back toward the shape asleep on the bed, toward the bassinet, and then, seized with fear, he had ploughed headfirst outside. A *bòbò* braving the night dangers to walk the streets as in the good old days mistook him for a criminal and, terrified, flattened herself against the wall. When he came to Rue Sully-Lancrerot he had seen the dogs. The same ones. How did he recognize them? He couldn't have said. They were motionless, waiting for him, their muzzles turned toward him, sniffing the air as if they were trying to pick up his scent. Trembling, he hadn't dared move. This time, too, the pack had scampered off in another direction and done him no harm. It was better this way. Ana thought she loved him. So at first she would cry, and rage against him too, taking him for just another Milo Vertueux, one of those irresponsible men, such a common species in the world, who never lift a finger for their children. Bitter, she would end up getting back on a plane headed for the United States and it was best that way. There, she'd hole herself up like a dying animal. No visitors, no friends. Nobody. Then the day would come when she'd thank him for leaving her free, for having spared her child the name of a murderer as his inheritance. The night was snatching him up, kneading him in its voracious gullet. Fragmented memories, imprecise, disjointed pictures followed by blanks, played over and over in his mind. After being pushed so far down into the depths of his being, that evening had lost the stark outlines of reality.

The heart! The heart! Of what material is it made? How does it stretch far enough to harbor such contradictory desires and emotions? On New Year's Eve, he had gone to Fifth Avenue. He had made an effort to look his best. He had smoothed his hair with cologne, and slipped on his best pair of jeans and a garnet silk shirt that one of his uncles had given him for his twentieth birthday. That uncle had always spoiled Dieudonné. He had always loved Marine, the family said, and channeled this affection into her son. Unfortunately he lived in the Côtes-d'Armor. Married to a woman from Lille, he never came back to the country to visit. Why had he gone to meet up again with Luc, after almost wringing his neck ten days before? Because he knew this strangling meant nothing at all. It was just a defense reflex against what he knew to be ineluctable between them. At the same time, deprived of Loraine, nothing made sense anymore. He couldn't sleep, and spent his nights torturing himself with burning images: Loraine and Luc walking arm in arm, down the Allée des Amériques. Loraine and Luc making love. Sleeping in one another's arms. And we must add that he felt very alone, so alone on the threshold of this new year with nobody—even mechanically, even grudgingly—to wish him health and happiness. Boris had left his bus stop for a time to spend the holidays with Benjy and his wife and children. Arbella, who was a good cook, had made a pork stew and pakala yam gratin. The family was planning to celebrate over at Fanniéta's, but, like every year, no one wanted him there. He could still see the look on their faces when he had shown up last year at midnight to take his place at the table.

Port-Mahault was doing its best to welcome the new year ahead. That season marked the first of the big electric company strikes. For, recently, the PTCR had hardened its position. Each time the current deigned to come back on, lanterns and streamers clamoring "Happy Holidays" would light up over the streets. It was also the start of the sanitation strikes. For New Year's the municipality had contracted with a private cleaning service. No trash bags nor detritus stood guard the length of the sidewalks. A street-cleaning truck as massive as a Nazi tank had washed the roadways and the air smelled clean and fresh. Fifth Avenue, the nightclub for those who know how to have fun, as the television guaranteed, looked nothing like the common joints Dieudonné frequented from time to time. Like the Sphinx, for example, where he had sometimes gone with Rodrigue. Instead of one huge space resembling a hangar, fairly stark, badly lit, and decorated with crude garlands, it was a room as tiny as a bijou apartment, covered with mirrors and red wall hangings, and the lights were dimmed so low that you couldn't see past the end of your nose. The dancers were crushing each other on the floor to the sounds of African American music. Sorry! No zouk or zouk love. After much hesitation, Dieudonné approached the bar and timidly addressed one of the bartenders mixing cocktails. They scared him with their epaulet-studded uniforms, like the ones sailors wore. Of them all, this young *métro* was sporting a less formidable expression than his coworkers, despite his hair, which was standing up straight like a rooster's, only green. He gestured that he couldn't hear anything with all the noise, and Dieudonné had to shout his question, bringing out into the light of day what he had holed up deep inside himself:

"I'm looking for Luc Alliot . . . the painter."

In turn, the barman shouted, "Go ahead, man! Am I stopping you?"

Then, laughing at his own great joke, he took pity on Dieudonné's distressed expression and added, "I haven't seen him yet."

Disappointed, Dieudonné headed for the "Exit" sign, spelled out in English in blood-red letters, crossed the threshold, and found himself back on the sidewalk. Fifth Avenue was located in a somewhat seedy neighborhood of garages and warehouses. At this hour the surroundings were plunged in darkness, and its neon sign emerged from the obscurity like a phosphorescent island. Behemoth security guards, armed to the teeth, turned the gleam of their flashlights on everything that moved, and the mangy dogs, far from strutting their stuff, hugged the walls. One of these guards ordered Dieudonné sharply, "Don't hang around here!"

The latter, feigning obedience, crossed the street and stayed there pacing the area, his eyes glued to the light of the sign. How long? The bells of the Saint-John-de-Obispo Cathedral rang midnight. He reflected sadly on all the people kissing each other, wild with happiness and anticipation, champagne flowing. And he, with no one by his side. He was thinking of leaving when a group descended noisily from a chrome-bedecked SUV. These guys and girls could have stepped out of a Benetton ad because none of them was the same color: one pale, another a good deep black, another either *chabin* or mulatto. However, if you could tell them apart by their skin and their hair, curly, coily, or outright kinky, they were alike in the exuberantly cheerful, effervescent, and nonchalant way they inhabited their clothes. The girls bared their endless legs and their shapely cleavage. With a shiver, Dieudonné recognized Luc. Dressed entirely in white, seductive, just as the devil must have looked to Jesus in the desert. Luc gave him that smile that said he was the person most dear to his heart. He introduced him warmly to his friends and swept him along, scolding him gently all the same in his usual way: "You look magnificent. But you're always making that gloomy face! Tonight's New Year's Eve, for God's sake! We're all here to have fun! Do what everybody's doing! Have fun!"

They went inside and Fifth Avenue's muzzle closed its scarlet gums and palate around them. Dieudonné was so rarely among people his age that the scent and warmth of these young folks went to his head like a new wine. Usually, the few times he ventured into dance halls, following a pattern traced by his shyness, he sat as close as he could to the dance floor and let the music sink into him, nothing more. That night, Luc wouldn't hear of it. Each time Dieudonné made as if to stop, Luc pulled him back to the floor, into a human magma as scorching as the one swelling all down the slopes of the Stromboli. He, the guy who never touched a drop of alcohol, who constantly tried to put the brakes on Loraine, was now constantly refilling his own glass. With anything and everything. Champagne. Gin. Whiskey. A green-colored cocktail christened "The Tsunami." He had never felt so good, so outside his body, which he had left behind like an ill-fitting envelope, at last in unison with the world. His mother had never lost her legs or her beauty or her life. Loraine hadn't thrown him out like a dog. Life was like a coral necklace fastened around his neck by a deep-sea diver.

Around two in the morning, the high-decibel racket dimmed and it got quiet. The dancers formed a ring as a group invaded the floor. Six girls, two guys, their kinky hair dyed blonde, dressed in identical shiny leather outfits, with those ubiquitous Nikes on their feet. The "All Blacks." Despite their American name, they were local rappers, all born in Port-Mahault or its surroundings. Punctuating their words with jerky gestures, like robots in sci-fi films, they started singing. In Creole? In an English marked by an even more approximate accent than Boris's? In both languages? Apparently it hardly mattered, given the cries, the shrieks, the foot-stomping and the transports of the audience. Next to Dieudonné, two young girls were swooning against their partners, sobbing nervously. It was obvious that despite their ridiculous looks, these artists spoke to the crowd's soul, capturing its moods perfectly. Dieudonné had never been interested in music. At times a memory of the beguines Marine used to hum in the rare moments when her heart was joyful would float pleasantly through his mind.

Nèg ni môvé man-nyè
Nèg ni môvé man-nyè

Rodrigue and Boris alike were passionate about Cuban music: mambos, boleros, pachangas, guajiras . . .

Dos gardenias para ti
Con ellas quiero decir

As for the sounds of the blues that Loraine used to listen to, always the same ones with their funereal voices, Lena Horne, Billie Holiday, Dinah Washington, Sarah Vaughan, they exasperated him. To his surprise, these deliberately discordant, baroque—some would say barbarous—tones stirred something deep within him to expression, as if the music were summoning some part of himself that had never before had its say. Luc alone seemed dissatisfied. He was shrugging his shoulders and making a face, protesting, "That is bullshit, man! They're just imitating the African Americans!"

They stayed at Fifth Avenue until morning. After a certain point, however, everything came unglued in Dieudonné. His consciousness of time, of where he was ceased. He was nothing but a patchwork of impressions and sensations anymore. Bolts of light blinded him, bursts of laughter, sound, and voices deafened him. This bitter taste in his mouth was the taste of happiness.

Brutally, the biting air on his face brought him fully back to consciousness. He realized that daylight had broken; they were aboard the SUV, which was zipping along speedily. Everyone around him was completely sacked out, slouched over every which way. Luc, alert and lucid for his part, was behind the wheel. Dieudonné felt wonderful. He could have wanted life to last forever and ever, to stay for always on this unbroken road seemingly stretching to infinity. Judging by the countryside, flat as the flat of the hand, with the ponds popping up all over the fields and the windmills looking just like burial mounds of gray stone in the tide of sugarcane washing around the vehicle, he guessed that they must be in the Salines basin. Luc spoke to him in a grave voice.

"You're not going to keep scratching the earth for her *ad vitam aeternam*. How much is she paying you?"

" . . ."

"You realize what's going on, right? Don't let yourself be exploited. Loraine has that in her blood. It's hereditary—as soon as she can, she takes advantage. She only respects people she can't drive up the wall. Me, for example. I've thought about your case: I'm going to put a word in with a good friend, Cyrille Sirius, the director of the tourism bureau. Don't act standoffish with him. He loves good-looking boys. If you play your cards right, he'll get you a job in a hotel or a restaurant . . . It would be better than what you're doing now, at least."

At one point, they crossed Blanchette, the former capital, its wooden houses with their multicolored shutters grouped around the church. They entered a wooded area and dark-green blotches smudged the air. At last, the car stopped in front of a fairly ordinary villa with its wraparound veranda and its concrete gutter, bristling with the usual television antennas and surrounded by a jumble of trees. Through the mix of banana, mango, and calabash trunks, you could glimpse the sea, at this hour a leaden gray, like a piece of sheet metal. New Year's or not, fishermen were rowing furiously toward the open water to earn their daily bread.

The group split into two. One half went inside the house. The other sprawled out on the beach, and some curled up in the sand to sleep.

"How about a swim?" cried Luc.

He threw off his clothes and started running, totally naked, toward the sea. In the nude his body was surprising, for he was a lot more muscular than you'd expect. A compact torso, rounded buttocks, tight, well-defined abs. You could sense that he was in love with his body, and so he forced it to accomplish innumerable feats, looking after it as you look after an expensive piece of equipment. Dieudonné lowered his eyes and hesitated, overcome by modesty. But everyone around him was undressing as though it was natural. He ended up following suit. In turn, naked as the day he was born, he marched toward his favorite lover. She took him in her wild arms, rubbed up against his most private parts, offering up that heady intoxication without compare. After the excesses of the night before, it was like a purifying bath. No longer caring about the others, he moved off at a vigorous stroke. On this side of the country, the sea resembled a rodeo horse, rearing, swelling, and bucking with waves to unseat a rider. Beyond the illusory line of the horizon, receding bit by bit, the sun was starting to sling its arrows. They landed haphazardly in the disheveled mass of clouds. And the formless world, emerging from the shadows, began to take shape. What had Loraine done after Luc left her to go to Fifth Avenue? Most likely she had gone to bed in the deserted, glacial lair of her bedroom and drunk her fill? He, on the other hand, if she had only wanted, would never have left her alone at a time when everyone around was celebrating joyfully. He would have listened to her ramblings and lamentations yet again, then he would have tucked her in like a baby. He would have tried to invent funny stories to distract her. Instead, this heartless guy had selfishly chosen to go have his fun. Why, from one end of the earth to the other, do humans celebrate the new year with such fervor? Simple-mindedly, they hope it will bring them what the year before, and the year before that, obstinately refused to give them. Happiness, happiness. Money. Security by the handful! He almost ran into a boat, and the two toothless, bearded fishermen, worthy in every respect of appearing on a postcard in the "Picturesque Caribbean" series, greeted him, smiling. Yet their eyes remained hard and piercing, like shards of flint. Undoubtedly they took him for an intruder violating the woman they wanted to keep for themselves alone. Exhausted by his night of revelry, he suddenly ran out of breath, and, floating on his back, eyes closed, he let himself drift and bob at the pleasure of the currents. Through the lattice of his eyelashes, the outlines of shapes began to stand out against the ever-deepening blue of the sky, dissolving and reemerging again. Tails of scarves, bows of ribbon, circles, trapeziums, animals: a whole new whimsical bestiary.

After a time, he caught his breath and came back to the beach. His heart filled with elation. In a few days, Luc would be leaving. Then he'd have Loraine to himself again. No doubt she would cry over it. So he'd console her, hugging her to him, hurt and lonely, and the memory of their weeks apart would fade. At the same time, a hunger had awakened inside him that he could not name, that he did not want to look in the face. He wasn't sure he could settle for his former life. On the veranda, a tireless few were dancing to the sounds of Marvin Gaye. Around Luc, a group of guys, still naked, was sprawled out again in the sand under an almond tree. They were drinking from coconuts that one of them, also naked, was opening skillfully with a single machete blow. And this impudent display of *koks,* some bellicose, some proudly holding their heads high, some limper, others downright lazy, reminded Dieudonné of his livestock on Morne Lafleur and that bittersweet time when he was a god among his creatures. Where was Marine hiding? Some people firmly maintain that the dead don't leave our earth; they have too much of a taste for it; they carry on fighting to clear a space for themselves among the living. But he had never seen his mother again, not even in a dream. Sometimes, he missed her so much that he thought he glimpsed her silhouette rounding a street corner, among the crowds at the market or the throngs at carnival. It was only ever a mirage vanishing in the desert.

When he approached, Luc signaled to him to come stretch out next to him, and, taking the others as witnesses, affectionately declared, "Guys, when I'm gone, I'm entrusting this little fella to your care. Loraine's got him in her claws and I'm very afraid for him."

He added, sardonically, "He's in love with her!"

The whole group guffawed as if it were the funniest joke imaginable. One of the guys, the one opening the coconuts, questioned Dieudonné. "Do you know who Loraine is?"

Since Dieudonné said nothing, he moved into an explanation. "Let me tell you."

He set about informing Dieudonné of every minute detail. Loraine had worn out three husbands and no one knows how many lovers. If he was to be believed, all the boys in the present company had enjoyed her favors. She had a weakness for painters, but it was enough to declare oneself an ARTIST. Any guitar-strummer who came around had a shot. Toumblak, who toured the world with his *gwo-ka* music, had sojourned at length in her bed. Élias Reclus, who all of Paris had admired in *Black Battles with Dogs* at the Théâtre de la Farandole, had too. The game was who could boast of squeezing something, extorting something out of her. Ferociously. Without the least remorse. For, in a way, this money, these gifts, these recommendations, these words put in at the right place and time, miraculously changing destinies, were their due. Loraine was only paying a small part of the considerable debt accumulated on the part of the Race, over the centuries of slave trading, slavery, exploitation of every type and humiliation of every sort. Dieudonné didn't understand or share this rancor. Neither Marine nor Arbella ever really talked to him about the past. When he saw other blacks, Africans or Americans, in movies or on television, he knew that a unique heritage united them. He knew that long ago, they had been brothers and sisters, fruits of the same womb, before a cruel force dispersed them across the four corners of the world. How exactly had that happened? He didn't know and hardly cared. That past was nothing compared to the present he was living with its torments and deprivations. To the tune of "La Tonkinoise," Luc sang, "*Mais c'est moi qu'elle aime le mieux!* But it's me she loves the best. Because deep down she's scared of me."

He laid his head on Dieudonné's thigh. "You see, in the beginning she wanted to manage me: 'You have to paint like this. You have to paint like that.' I sent her packing."

Everyone approved.

"She has to be put in her place."

Shouldn't he have made a statement, got up, left? No, he shot nothing back. He listened to these indescribable words, held back by what? Cowardice, the fear of finding himself alone again, and above all, the unavowed, unavowable desire to stay within the circle of warmth and light emitted by Luc.

Wrapped in a pareo, one of the girls came running, unfazed by all these undressed boys. It was because she belonged to this new generation, the one that fears nothing, has sex at the age of twelve, takes the pill, and knows she is equal to men. She scolded them: while they were sitting there idle, swapping stories and drinking coconut milk, other people were going to a lot of trouble. Maxo had covered miles to buy bread and croissants. Célia had cooked a conch pie. She herself had made coffee. In short, a sumptuous breakfast awaited those with the strength to get up. Obediently, all of them clambered to their feet and put on the clothes scattered all around in the sand.

The sun had embarked on its ascent and no longer held any surprises for anyone. It had only risen midway. Yet already they were tired of it, of its unbearable presence. The sand was already burning hot under their feet. An oily light, as thick as an egg yolk, was spreading and spattering one side of the clouds. Luc straightened up, leaning on Dieudonné's arm, a simple and apparently banal gesture that nevertheless sealed the silent agreement concluded between them.

19

A tap on the shoulder brought Dieudonné back to the darkness of the present. He jumped into the air as if a snake had brushed him, and beside him, he could make out Dorisca, planted there pluckily like Charlie Chaplin.

"What are you doing here?" he roared.

You would have thought he had forgotten her kindness earlier and the effort she had made to tend to him. It wasn't her fault if her *ninnaine* had broken up the party and kicked him out. She only wanted to help, with her Vodou, her oil, her massage, and her candles. Dorisca, who must have expected more gratitude, immediately teared up, and stood there shifting from one leg to the other. Seeing her distress, he softened. "One day, traipsing around at all hours of the night like this, you're going to get what you're looking for."

She sniffled. "I already told you I'm not afraid. Nobody will touch me." Then she added passionately, "Let's go away."

He questioned her gruffly. "Go where?"

She stammered, aware of her stupidity, "To America."

He burst out laughing. "You're crazy! This boat hasn't been to sea for years. If there's any good advice I can give you, it's to go home."

She didn't move and he said mockingly, "You think you're the next Tabarly, honestly! You want your solo title too!"

She persisted. "I want to go to New York to be with my brother again."

At that, she started to cry tears she had been holding inside her and that came pouring out now, bathing her cheeks. "I don't want to stay here anymore. I don't want to live like this anymore. Without anybody to take care of me. Since my *ninnaine*'s husband's been gone, she doesn't have any time for me anymore."

He interrupted her brusquely. "You already told me that! Listen, if you want to join your brother, I'm not the one to help you. All you have to do is go to school and study. If you do good work, you can get a scholarship and leave for New York. I have a friend who did that. A painter who's becoming well known in the field. His name is Luc Alliot."

He realized, saying it, that his voice was taking on a ridiculously affected, proud tone, and he repeated savagely, "Go away, do you hear me?"

She was in his way, in a nutshell. She had come and inserted herself in the middle of his thoughts and he had the urge to grab her by the shoulders and push her unceremoniously toward the boarding ladder. Why had he, someone who never talked, who never confided anything in anyone, told Loraine every last detail of what had happened at Fifth Avenue and, afterward, with Luc? To hurt her, no question about it. He had wanted to repay evil with evil. She had drawn blood with her sentence, that sentence that was still drumming in his ears, still burning his heart, tearing him apart like a dagger:

"Luc is the gift the Good Lord gave me at the very last moment, when I had given up expecting anything from life anymore."

Mixed in with that maybe was also the stupid desire to show what he was worth. We'll see what we'll see! Oh no, I'm not as insignificant as you think! When he had whimpered, "And me, then? What am I to you?" she had laughed insultingly. Her lip had curled into a rictus of viciousness and scorn. Throwing herself back onto her pillows, she had fixed her harsh eyes on him and enunciated her words. "You? You're a common nobody. You're just black trash, a *petit nègre* full of bitterness and spite like all of your kind. You need the cudgel, which you'll remember for all eternity."

Shouldn't he have understood that she was talking crazy? Because she had drunk too much. The half-empty bottle of Glenfiddich testified to that. Because she felt too alone during the holiday season. Because she was too down over Luc's departure. Maybe she didn't believe a single word coming out of her mouth and was just trying to goad him into forgetting his perpetual reserve.

"You're like a wilk," she often teased him. "Always deep inside his shell. I'll get you out of there, yes I will!"

Instead of keeping quiet and consoling her, he had started talking. While he was draining himself of his story, as the words took shape, arranging themselves into sentences and paragraphs, he had struggled against a feeling of unreality. Had all of that really happened? Did what he was saying capture reality? Hadn't he dreamed that afternoon, that night in the bedroom, deep in the tulle mesh bowels of mosquito netting in the stifling air that the fan failed to stir? The moon had watched them, perhaps shocked by so much passion, because they left the windows and blinds wide open, hoping to catch a breeze on their sweaty skin. The song of the sea had deafened them, raging, as if the official mistress was railing against her betrayal. And yet, he hadn't betrayed her either. He hadn't done anything but snatch a crumb of happiness from life. After lovemaking, they had chatted, which was new for Dieudonné, and enchanting. Night after night, Loraine would turn her back to him, dropping a quick good-night over her shoulder. Once or twice, she had fallen asleep under him, delivering her ravaged face up to his love, and he had covered it with kisses. Luc had told him a story much like his own. He had never known his father. When he was five, his mother had left to look for work in France, abandoning him to his grandmother, who, before dying, had entrusted him to his godmother. His mother had married a white man and he had some rosy blonde half brothers. All he knew of them were their photos. No doubt once he was internationally recognized, all these people would be trying to grab on to his coattails. That would be the day! He was living for that vengeance alone. He felt no gratitude toward Loraine. Like his friends, he thought she was just paying a small part of the reparations due.

The next day, they had all gone in a group to the airport. Around him, people were laughing and joking, knowing they'd see each other again after a short time apart. In New York. In Paris. In London. He alone felt like he was forever losing what could have been, if fate hadn't decided otherwise. Luc, sensitive to his disarray, tried to console him in his usual playful and affectionate way.

"Come see me in New York. You'll get to know what a real city is, you, the guy who has never gotten out of his hole. At lunchtime, people crowd together like acoushi ants in the streets. It's best to come in winter. Because you've never seen that, except in the movies. You haven't seen the sky darken in the middle of the day and the flakes fall in a flurry of confetti. A city dressed in white. White rooftops. White tree branches. White streets and sidewalks, and you play leapfrog with the snow piles. Silence sets in, the silence of beginnings. At times, the river freezes as far as you can see and the boats stop in place, stuck in this sea of ice."

Despite himself, Dieudonné's whipped-up imagination started galloping like a horse: me, Dieudonné Sabrina, boss of New York! The yellow taxis line up to salute me. The skyscrapers bow at my feet. Watch out, here I come! However, he knew quite well these were just empty words. Luc, spoiled child that he was, had used him for his own pleasure, to spice up his vacation. As soon as he was on his Boeing, his headphones on his ears, he'd forget him.

Loraine hadn't interrupted him a single time. Transformed into a statue, she hadn't moved a single muscle. When he stopped, she stammered out, "You're lying!"

At the same time, her eyes contradicted her mouth, betraying the fear lodged in her heart. Isn't that what she had been dreading from the start? Isn't that why she had pushed Dieudonné pitilessly away? Because she knew her Luc! She knew he swung both ways, seducing everyone who came near him, men, women, a string of tortured people on his left and right. At that point he had snorted meanly, piling on the details: Luc's address in New York, his telephone number, the name of the gallery where he was exhibiting, as if at all costs he had to stamp his tale with a seal of authenticity. That's when she had seized her gun again, raised it and fired, all while her eyes were rambling, not only out of anger, but also in a kind of desperate craze. One bullet had lodged itself in the wall above his head, one in the floorboards. A brief struggle had ensued, during the course of which he had done nothing but defend himself. To save his skin.

That's how it had happened. Self-defense, Mr. Serbulon would have argued, if he had known the truth. And he wouldn't have been lying. In her pain, in her drunken stupor, Loraine would have shot him down like a dog. Yet to admit that would have been the ultimate betrayal. That's why, after four days of reflection, he had turned himself in to the Cadenat commissariat like a guilty man. That's why he had kept silent, letting the lawyer construct his absurd theories. White against black. The sadistic mistress against the docile slave. Who, one day, pushes back. A baptism of blood. I ask you, can you kill your life?

"Last year, you remember? Two pleasure boaters drifted all the way to Florida. They talked about it in *France-Caraïbe.*"

Dieudonné jumped, startled, then came back down to earth and found himself with Dorisca again. In her desire to convince him, she was still whining, lifting her begging face to him. And to say he had thought she was pretty. To say he had imagined her as his little sister. He made a gesture of exasperation.

"Stop saying such stupid things. Go back home, I'm telling you."

Despite himself, he was shouting. In the half-deserted marina, the echo of his voice came back to them amplified. So she obeyed. He heard her uneven footsteps on the dock. As she was about to disappear, gulped up by the shadows, he felt a little remorseful and almost called her back. Then he thought the better of it. Where he had decided to go, she couldn't come along. No one could. With Dorisca gone, he remained immobile, sitting in the same place. Around him, the black night was whitening imperceptibly. Pale threads were appearing here and there, mixed into the sky's somber infinity. The giant uterus of the other side was preparing to expel the day. Because, in the end, what could he do with his life? Leave for Cuba like Boris was proposing? Do community service like Mr. Serbulon was suggesting? Meaning, packaging pineapples or bananas, packing bottles of rum or shrub in homegrown parcel post crates? These were all ridiculous ideas.

He realized that a resolution had taken shape in him. It had been born and had matured all through this endless ramble, maybe before, during his months at Basse-Pointe, maybe even before that, the night of the crime itself, when, silently, he had watched the blood redden the bed sheets before dripping onto the floor. So much blood in a woman's body! Paralyzed, he had stayed there, unable to admit that she was no more, that her hoarse voice wouldn't give him orders anymore, that he wouldn't press himself up against her anymore. And so, this resolution was raising its head again, a hard seed lodged in the middle of his consciousness. He got up, at once feverish and calm. He began by turning on the signal lights, surprised to see them shine docilely after all this time, red portside, green starboard, white on the prow. Only the mast signal refused to obey. Similarly, the weathervane was stuck. Oh well! He checked the tank and poured in the splash of diesel left at the bottom of a stray gas can. For delicate maneuvers such as exiting the marina, Vincent Cohen, a cautious skipper, always used the motor.

Dieudonné decided to do so as well. While he busied himself, you would have thought the *Belle Créole* understood his intentions. She was trembling, vibrating from the hull to the rigging and stem to rudder, snorting and sniffing the air. Dieudonné started the motor, which, after a few coughs, began to purr. Gently, he untied the *Belle Créole* from the dock, felt her shudder, and coaxed her like a fiery-spirited horse you want to keep calm. To the right and left, as the monohull glided along the surface of the sea, the shorefront villas of the Mégisserie slipped by, their lights off, like tropical versions of Venetian palaces. At the back of the bay, Port-Mahault's inky houses and palm fronds stood stacked in a jumble. On the left, you could make out the dock bordered by almond trees and some sorry-looking cargo piles.

In the past, on board the *Belle Créole* Vincent Cohen used to treat him like an adult and let him take a shift. Even at night. Only the wind could be heard ruffling the mainsail and the jib. The world seemed to stand still. Except for Marine, who was afraid of the sea and never came near the *Belle Créole,* all his goods were under his feet. Aline Cohen and the children slept in the fore and aft cabins. And so, aware of his responsibilities, he made an effort to remain vigilant and not go off dreaming, his head in the clouds. After taking his turn to nap, Vincent would come join him with a mug of coffee and they stayed side by side for long stretches without talking.

When he had passed the green buoys, he shut off the motor and prepared the rigging. He turned the stem to face the wind, then grappled like a devil with the mainsail and the jib because the roller furling systems no longer worked; the drum was blocked. He managed to hoist them after a fashion, burning his hands on the halyards. Yet far from paining him, these forgotten movements, recovered instinctively, brought his childhood back to him, rallying the excitement of times lost, rekindling his vitality of old.

Abruptly, everything was as before. The sails ended up unfurling. The sky cleared, a hem of light skirted the clouds drained of rain, the quarter moon came out of its hiding place to show itself without shame, and the fog rolling on the horizon dissipated while the space all around him crooned that song, unforgettable once heard.

When they reached the open sea, the boat began to list.

20

Where could Dieudonné possibly be if he wasn't at his grand-mother Arbella's? Where had he run off to? The militiamen confirmed that he had headed toward the city. He didn't have any friends in the city. He barely knew anyone there except his aunt and godmother Fanniéta, who had never held him close. So where could he be?

Boris decided to call a truce with his anguish for the span of a meeting, and ended up going to the Fleurie complex. All the windows were lit up and the tenants were calling out to one another from balcony to balcony. Since they took care of their security themselves, a group of men in athletic wear, holding dogs on leashes and comically armed with clubs and machetes, were strolling around the parking lot.

The Fleurie complex, ten identical five-story buildings, each bearing the name of a flower, the usual regulars, Bougainvillea, Hibiscus, Ginger Lily, Mussaenda, Alamanda, Poinsettia . . . , was one of the first HLM projects in Port-Mahault, built not long after the war by a philanthropic governor appalled by the housing conditions. It must be recalled that Port-Mahault at that time was nothing but a pitiful pile of shacks. Up until the 1950s, the vast majority of the country's residents, even the fortunate ones, had never tasted the delights of running water, all-purpose sewers, or electricity. Most significantly, they had no knowledge of the privacy provided by water closets, those places where anyone can hole up with a book when nature requires it. That's why the Fleurie complex was first besieged by influential individuals who were in good with the municipal council members responsible for allocating the residences. Over the years, obviously, its prestige had eroded. The never-repainted walls were covered in graffiti, the trash cans were overflowing and jammed, and the elevators didn't budge from the ground floor. Those with sufficient means had abandoned the place and built themselves residences in the country. However, a dozen tenants, like Roméo Serrutin, who could have made his home elsewhere with all the money earned by his wife, a gynecologist from Toulouse, were obligated by political belief to openly disdain material success and to remain in these uncomfortable apartments.

Boris had barely entered the living room when he caught the unpleasant whiff of catastrophe. Not only was Benjy's absence glaring, but, well after midnight, three half-empty bottles of rhum agricole stood on the table. The members of the PPRP were drinking their rum straight, and chomping on their smokes with an attitude that portended nothing good. He thought he should apologize for being late. However, he noticed that no one was paying the least attention to him, that no one heard him. Roméo Serrutin lifted a face furrowed with wrinkles and anxiety.

"You didn't hear the news?" A pause. "Benjy just called. He's not coming. They've made him step down! José Merlot is replacing him!"

In his heart, Boris knew that such a catastrophe had been about to hit any day now. For many long months, Benjy had been having the utmost difficulty mobilizing his troops. The reason for this sorry situation was that it had become obvious to everyone that he no longer believed his own recommendations. Besides, what exactly was he recommending? He had done nothing but pivot lately. At the last minute, he had thought of sequestering the owner of Auto-Caraïbe after the unjust layoffs of two workers. Then he had hesitated and gone back on his decision. This had given the owner plenty of time to jump on the first plane to Paris. A first-class winner, a strikebreaker, had come over to replace him. Furious, he jumped up.

"We won't let them do it! It's not legal!"

"What do you mean it's not legal?" Roméo Serrutin replied in a tired voice. "On the contrary, it's absolutely legal. They convened a special meeting. All the members of the executive committee were present. A quorum was attained."

Boris sat back down. "But you're not going to just sit there, are you?"

The others looked him up and down, for none of them cared much for this ex–homeless poet and moralizer. "And what do you suggest?" Évariste Philomène, the PPRP's treasurer, questioned him sardonically.

Boris had a fertile brain. From the time he was a schoolboy, he had never run short of ideas. When he didn't know a single word of his lesson, he could dazzle the class with his inventiveness and dupe the teacher with brio. In a flash, he hatched a proposition. This kind of power play could only be met with a power play. In a few hours it would be time for his editorial on Solèye Lévé. All they had to do was show up at this station and the PPRP's at the same time and, speaking together in one voice, inform the residents of Port-Mahault of the actions taken by this handful of machinating cowards. Everyone loved Benjy. Without a doubt, the country would insist he be reinstated as head of the trade union confederation. These words got a lukewarm reception. Unlike Solèye Lévé, the PPRP's station, Radio Van Doubout, Headwind Radio, was just a ghost of its former self; in the 1960s, the heyday of the battle for *lendépendans,* thousands of listeners kept an ear glued to their programs. It had no audience anymore. Three times a day, an uninspired host did nothing but stumble monotonously through a news bulletin in Creole. The PPRP members exchanged unenthusiastic glances. One of them listlessly remarked, "We'd have to agree on what to say."

"What's the worry?" Boris replied loftily. "We'll improvise!"

We'll improvise? You don't improvise in politics! In the end, though, Roméo Serrutin got up, promptly followed by his soldiers.

"Let's go!"

The little troop went down the stairs and disbanded as they made their way to their cars. Just as he got behind the wheel of his Toyota again, Boris had an epiphany. The *Belle Créole!* How could he have been so blind before? Dieudonné, abandoned by all, had taken refuge on the *Belle Créole.* In the life of an individual or a collective group, there are fundamental moments, major decisions that must not go unmade. We could dissertate endlessly about it here. What if Boris had put general interest first? What would have transpired if he had gone directly to Radio Solèye Lévé? What if he had been able to deliver an invigorating editorial on the spot, stirring up all the country's men lying sluggishly abed in their *kabanns* beside their wives, or more likely one of their mistresses, and enjoining them not to let themselves be manipulated? Indeed, despite the early hour and their desire for a steaming mug of coffee and a cold shower, perhaps they would have marched through the streets and avenues of Port-Mahault chanting, "Benjy! Benjy! Ban nou Benjy! Lagé Benjy!" Perhaps it would have been an excuse for a riot, which the CRS riot police, armed with helmets and shields, would have repressed with force and bloodshed? Perhaps José Merlot would have gotten scared and reinstated Benjy? Rumor had it that the man had no balls, that he was always of the same opinion as whoever had spoken to him last. But instead of running to Radio Solèye Lévé, Boris, worrying only about Dieudonné, rushed like mad to the Mégisserie marina.

A marina is a little like a sweetheart's smile. If her gums are deserted, if incisors, canines, or molars are missing, loose, rotten, or pulled out, the absence doesn't go unnoticed and the wave that plugs the hole serves as a gravestone. In the toothless cave that the Mégisserie had become, Boris couldn't tell at first that the *Belle Créole* was missing. He paced the length of dock number 2 several times. Then he had to yield to the evidence. The monohull had disappeared. It had been moored there. There, next to a rental catamaran that nobody rented anymore. He had set sail. Where had he gone off to? Dieudonné was crazy to go out to sea in a tub that hadn't sailed in so many years. What was he searching for? Death? Yes, that was indeed what he was after. Death. His only friend had abandoned him. He believed that absolutely nothing was keeping him here on earth anymore. Death. Like a madman, Boris ran again to the end of the dock, scrutinizing the troughs and bumps of the endless surface. Maybe he could catch the escapee unawares? If so, how would he bring him back to dry land? Unfortunately, his eyes saw nothing.

The small hours were clearly ending. Nature thought the period of mourning had lasted long enough. Now she wanted to dress herself in blue, green, and mauve, in the carnival colors of tropical daylight. Relegated to a corner of the sky, the weak quarter moon was getting ready to topple over onto the other side of the earth and give his seat to the sun. However, Boris did not detect these first signs. Night and pain were in him. Thousands of thoughts jostled in his mind. Where could he find the coast guard? Did that type of emergency assistance exist in the country? If so, how would you alert them? How should he set about searching for Dieudonné? He felt guilty, impotent, and defeated all at once.

21

The following facts belong to history. Written history, for it's been ages since our history was passed down orally. Those who keep rehearsing the opposite just love basking in their own words. Two historians, university professors of great talent, wrote a work titled *May '99* in order to relate the events of what they emphatically called an aborted "revolution."

Let's spend a moment on this word: revolution! It is beautiful. It is formidable. It inspires terror. If all this had taken place under a dictatorship like the ones in African countries, or in Haiti, an island just next door, a tireless agitator and strike leader like Benjy or an inexhaustible windbag with Marxist pretensions like Boris would undoubtedly have been put down like dogs. One night, someone would have found their lifeless bodies on a deserted beach and the next day their friends and relatives would have taken the road to exile. In a country such as the one in question, there exists a certain amount of respect for human life, a certain conception of freedom of speech— you know, that sacrosanct notion called democracy! So, those who didn't share the opinions of the two rogues contented themselves with sidelining them, never touching a hair on their heads. Or perhaps they did not seem sufficiently dangerous. Since, you might rightly object, even in democracies political assassinations exist. Who will cast the deciding vote? In any case, everything happened just as we have reported. No bloodshed. No arbitrary imprisonment. No forced exile. And our two nationalist historians had a great deal of trouble imposing their point of view.

Despite its beautiful name, Radio Solèye Lévé was not much to look at. It was located on the eighth floor of an exceedingly shabby residential building, one of those blocks built in a rush during the first years of the exodus toward cities. It was tucked away in a two-bedroom apartment rented by the PTCR. When Boris, his mind whirling, finally arrived a few hours later and headed for the miraculously functional elevator, he was surprised to run into municipal police officers in their flat-topped caps, their right hands menacingly positioned at their hips.

"ID," they barked in a single voice.

Boris, who took pride in being known throughout the country from north to south like the mythic three-legged witch, la Bête à Man Ibè, vainly refused to carry such trivial objects around with him. So he ignored the injunction and made as if to continue on his way. Consequently the henchmen seized him brutally, handcuffed him, and pushed him to their van parked near a bare croton hedge, and the vehicle took off like a shot for the main precinct. The whole scenario was resolved. During this time, José Merlot was reading his harangue over the airwaves in his hermaphrodite voice. Unfortunately, we have no copy of this speech. But we do know that it detailed the makeup of the PTCR's new board and announced that work would resume that very morning in most sectors affected by the strike. It gave assurances that within a few days, life would go back to normal.

People were certainly surprised by this about-face. Yesterday, they were swearing management's days were over. Today they were making a pact with them. But it was barely four o'clock in the morning. It was still dark outside. The women hadn't yet gotten up to make coffee. The children were sleeping. In a flurry of telephone calls, the men were exchanging confused questions.

"Ka ka passé?" (What's going on?)

"An pa konnèt!" (I don't know!)

Some got up the courage to pull their clothes on and flock to the street corner, lighting their first cigarettes to dispel the muddle of sleepiness with nicotine. They couldn't believe their foggy eyes: were those cops, zooming up and down the streets in their vans? They could guess what was about to transpire, then. Deep in their hearts, this sudden display of energy by the powers that be did not displease everyone. Because the majority of people were exhausted. Exhausted by the state of the country, by all these strikes, these managerial sequestrations, this chaos with no clear end point in sight. However, their approval would have remained private and lukewarm if it weren't for one seemingly minor detail that changed the minds of those who were still waffling. Around five o'clock, the sanitation trucks that nobody had seen for months and months came out of their hangar, and these forgotten mastodons hurtled victoriously through Port-Mahault's arteries. When a team of workers in protective white masks attacked the mounds of trash blocking the sidewalks, shouts of joy went up that quickly became an ovation. Because more than poverty, which can be remedied through government subsidies, more than illness, which can be treated through medical evacuation to the Hôpitaux de Paris, more than death itself, which reunites blacks and whites, racism over and done, this country's inhabitants feared dirtiness. Dirtiness carries with it the memory of the congested slave ships, plantations, and slave quarters. Dirtiness is the mark of inferiority. That's why some people maintained that Benjy's resignation prompted jubilation among the populace. That's what the newspapers wrote, not only those who were openly affiliated with management, but also other, more moderate outlets aiming for objectivity who had always criticized the social dysfunction produced by the strikes and claimed that Benjy had no overarching project. Another noteworthy fact is that among the intellectuals who had praised him to the skies, none took Benjy's defense. Quite the contrary. *May '99*, the work mentioned above, barely conceals its critique. The prologue reminds the reader that, if the Cuban revolution succeeded, it was because Fidel and his *barbudos* knew how to win the support of the people. For nothing is possible without the people! A word to the wise!

During this time, Boris was wringing his hands sitting at the precinct. At his request, the police officers had agreed to call his house. But to his great surprise, no one was there. Where was the Angel Carla? It could only mean one thing: if she wasn't at home, she must be at the hospital. Her labor pains had started. The concern Boris felt for Dieudonné was compounded now by a new anguish. He knew how much Carla feared giving birth. The reason she had given was that she wasn't so young anymore, old enough to be a grandmother, she'd say, laughing, since her daughters were eighteen. At first fooled, Boris understood now that it was about something else altogether. You don't change countries or languages easily. Only the naive believe it, and his wife's loneliness, which he was discovering months late, devastated him. How had she gone on all this time, at his side, without him suspecting a thing? What kind of a man was he? At once a bad friend who wasn't there for his own, and a bad husband who deserted his post. He took pride in working for the well-being of some abstract whole, all the while beings of flesh and blood that he purported to hold close were withering and suffering beside him. He would devote himself to making amends for all his weaknesses and mistakes. From now on he would take such care of Carla! He would swaddle her in comfort! But in Dieudonné's case, could he still make amends? A terrible feeling of foreboding filled his heart.

In the cell next to his were two cross-dressers who had gotten into a knife fight in a bar but for the time being were snoring side by side like two brothers, stupefied by alcohol vapors. The police had put him with an old teacher they arrested almost daily, because ever since his wife died, he was nuts and would pee from his balcony onto little girls passing by in the street. He had recognized Boris straight off and was sharing some distressing remarks with him.

"You're an idealist. You want to change this country. You're not the first. Take a good look: the list is long, starting with Aurélien Aurélianus, whose mother was a slave and who the whites sentenced to life in prison because he had led the insurrection in the South. But just like him and just like everyone else, you'll fail too. Also, you think people like you because they're all smiles with you. But I'm telling you they hate you. Your books, your poems, especially the ones in French—behind your back people poke fun at them. Your posture and your ideas turn people off. Your wife's Italian, from what I've heard? If there's a piece of advice I can give you, it's to take her and get the hell out of here. Rome, Milan, Venice! Those are the places where you should live. Not in a hole like this where people only care about ox and goat cart-pulling races."

To avoid hearing the rattle of this voice drilling in truths better left unsaid, Boris stretched out on the bench and tried to doze off. But each time he closed his eyes, he'd just become prey to a string of dreams, nightmares, all revolving around Dieudonné and Carla. Sometimes they'd be lost in the middle of the ocean, just like boat people. Side by side, they were huddling half-naked in the net of a catamaran cast adrift. Their lips were black. Their faces looked like parchment. Their bodies were fleshless. They were trying in vain to escape the murderous stare of the sun. Sometimes, the ocean became a desert. As far as the eye could see flocked deceptively gentle dunes of white sand. There too, the sun was a warden without mercy. They were suffocating from thirst. Then the ocean changed in turn into a forest as impenetrable and inhospitable as the one densely covering the inaptly named Chauve Mountain, which was not bald in the least. In the sultriness, every tree distilled a poison, every branch hid a trap. Thus, he saw those he loved either burned to a char or hanged upside down from the tops of the *pié-bwa,* like the maroons tortured to death in the olden days.

Those who haven't been caught unawares by dawn breaking over the sea can't imagine the wonderment that surprises the eye. It's a symphony in white. It's as if sparkling cotton balls have suddenly spilled across the ocean, piling up in a fleece all the way to the horizon. The sky is like an immense basin of milk where clouds, just as so many ewes, come crowding to drink. A deathly pale light filters through from all the corners of infinity.

Dieudonné, who had ridden the waves so many times before, had never grown tired of this spectacle. In the past, so that he could enjoy it with him, Vincent Cohen used to come get him from the aft berth where he slept with the other boys.

Dieudonné would follow him all the way to the ship's prow, shivering because at that hour the wind blows icy cold. As in the past, he sat squatting at the pulpit for a long while, and stayed there, filling his eyes. The marvel doesn't last long and its brevity enhances its otherworldly magic, for you could doubt what you had seen. You might wonder whether you hadn't witnessed a mirage, like those brought forth by the sand in the desert.

When the sun's disk turned an ordinary red and began its usual ascent, Dieudonné came back to the helm. Where was he? None of the navigation instruments on board were functional. From deep inside a drawer he had ferreted out a nautical chart, but he hadn't bothered to take his bearings. Judging by the pelicans' and cormorants' flight, which indicated land was near, he guessed he must be off the coast of the two San Diego cays. A few hours earlier, the radio had crackled out some news, but he hadn't really gathered much from it. With the barometer blocked, he didn't know what sort of weather was coming. A tropical wave? A depression? Or a stretch of good weather? But this vulnerability, in the middle of the capricious ocean, suited him. It wouldn't take much, the wind rising, the peaceful surface of the water suddenly swelling, bristling with trenchant waves and troughs, for him to be swept away to the land from which there is no return. Wasn't that what he wanted? What he desired with all his might? He had nothing left to do in a world without her in it. What memories of her could he keep to light up his remaining days? They hadn't experienced a single night of great passion. They hadn't exchanged any tender words. She had never said, "I love you." There was no trace of a precious, intimate conversation for him to hang on to. She had died locked in violence, maybe in hate. And so, he was going to go back to the one who had never mistreated or scorned him, the one who had never been wrong about him. She would hold him close and he would suffocate in her arms. Maybe, in the unknown awaiting him, he would find Marine again. Arbella and Fanniéta, who always went to confession and communion but had shut him out of their hearts, had put him off religion and all its trappings. They had never shown him what love means. Yet maybe beyond the world our eyes can see, there's an invisible place of peace and happiness where those who loved each other a great deal and never stop longing for one another can spend eternity together. Who knows!

He hadn't brought any provisions with him. Hunger, thirst, and all this blue penetrating the eye would quickly get the better of him.

EPILOGUE

From torturing himself so much, Boris ended up falling asleep, a light, feverish sleep broken by periods of wakefulness during which he whimpered like a small child. He heard the cross-dressers leave, still insulting each other despite the threats from the police, and swearing they'd meet again in their bar and fight to the death. The old teacher was dozing too, muttering incomprehensibly. Finally, around noon, an officer turned the key in the lock and Benjy's massive silhouette appeared, blocking the light coming into the cell. He came in and sat down on the bench next to Boris and without a word held out a pack of cigarettes. For a time, the two men smoked in silence, despite the protests of the old teacher, who, awake now, was calling them every name in the book. Benjy didn't seem very sad about what could be considered a degrading loss. On the contrary, he seemed relieved and raring to go. More relieved and raring to go than he had been for a long time, with a sort of sparkle in his eye.

"Maybe now we can start living?" he suggested.

"What do you mean by that?" asked Boris wanly.

He shrugged his shoulders. "I don't know. Screw our wives, take our kids to the pool, pig out with our friends."

With sadness, Boris asked, "Is that what you call living?"

The other turned to look at him. "If not that, then what?"

He was addressing him as his former master, expecting a definition, a lesson, or one of those luminous comparisons only Boris knew how to make so well. Even though at present, disoriented, the master was sure of nothing, and doubted everything.

"Frankly," Boris sighed, "I don't know anymore now."

Benjy stood up. "Let's get out of here. What we need is a good shot of rum!"

As they left, they bid good-bye politely to the old teacher, who didn't bother to answer and kept on yelling. Out in the station's large hall, the officers returned the personal effects they had confiscated from Boris: a half-empty pack of cigarettes, a wallet containing two wrinkled 50-franc bills, some Lotus tissues, an Intensity ballpoint pen, some blank note paper folded into quarters on which he had started to scribble his speech for Radio Solèye Lévé. Then, the officers gave the two men their regards with a remnant of respect. Hadn't they for a time symbolized the change that the country needed so badly?

Once outside, Boris was seized with dizziness and nearly fell. Was it the broad daylight? The lack of sleep? The anguish? Without a word, Benjy took his arm like an invalid's and they went on their way, Boris leaning heavily on him. You would have thought they had switched roles. Since childhood, it was Boris who had been the leader, the one whose fertile brain was crawling with ideas. Not a single deed, good or bad, wasn't first thought up by him. And here he was, sapped of energy, trailing behind. He was clinging to Benjy as a sinking swimmer clings to a buoy and everything was churning in his head: Carla in the hospital, Dieudonné on board the *Belle Créole,* the PTCR on the road to perdition.

Port-Mahault was being reborn. In just a few hours, the sanitation department had accomplished miracles. The Boulevard des Canettes was shining like a new penny. Not only had the piles of rubbish that had so long offended the eye disappeared, but also the municipal street-cleaning trucks had poured gallons and gallons of water where it was needed, and swarms of sanitation employees had wielded their scrub brushes and disinfectant. Consequently the sidewalks and pavement were glistening with cleanliness. While this metamorphosis was taking place, however, a simultaneous spectacle lost no time leaving its stamp of horror. En masse, the dogs were chased from the Place des Écarts and every nook and cranny they had been occupying with impunity up to that point: empty lots, corridors, abandoned houses. Teams of exterminators in white masks, dressed like *jab* devils in their red outfits, followed in pursuit, lassoing them and stuffing their heads into plastic bags filled with chloroform, and dragged them, still twitching, to the new waste incinerator located on Morne Bouchot. A smoke black as ink came pouring down on the city while the stench of this charred flesh rapidly became unbearable. At this, even the most hardened souls began to miss the cavalcade of beasts that had nonetheless repulsed them so strongly before.

Benjy dragged Boris toward the narrow Rue du Docteur-Lévy. "There used to be a bar on this street," he said confidently. "After work, I'd go there with José Merlot!"

He wasn't mistaken. The bar was wedged between a jewelry store guarded like Fort Knox and a Lebanese shop brimming with all manner of textiles. Which meant that you could easily pass by its facade and never see it. It was uncreatively named "Le Rendez-Vous des Amis," The Hangout. It was a single long, narrow room without windows, already filled with barflies getting drunk, the dim light serving as their accomplice. Since the electricity had come back on, the stereo was competing with the television; the first was belting out zouk music, the other a Brazilian film whose long-haired actors were talking love, kisses, and caresses at the top of their lungs too. Recognizing Benjy and Boris, the clients gave them that look reserved for stars who aren't stars anymore, for athletes with mono, and politicians who have lost power despite all their fraudulent electoral manipulations. Nevertheless, with the exception of the owner, out of discretion no one approached them. The owner brought them a bottle of Feneteau les Grappes Blanches with a sober but sympathetic remark: "It's the best I've got."

The two pals thanked him with a nod, then shamelessly filled their glasses to the top with rum. Contrary to what Boris was hoping, the burn that went down his throat and stomach stirred up his pain again. His eyes filled with salt water. "I'm in agony," he murmured. "Dieudonné has disappeared!"

Benjy, clearly feeling better and better, filled his glass again and drained it in one go. For a second it knocked him stupefied; then, coming back to his senses, he asked, "What do you mean, disappeared?"

In a few sentences, Boris breathlessly explained the calamity he feared lay ahead. The *Belle Créole* was no longer at the dock, which meant Dieudonné had gone off God knows where. In a tub like that, chances were slim that they'd find him alive. Benjy jumped up. "So we need to alert the marine rescue service, the nautical brigade, and the police's coastal observation branch as quick as we can."

"If something happens to him, I'll never forgive myself," Boris went on, still slumped over the table, his head in his hands. "I'll always feel guilty."

"We'll all be guilty," replied Benjy, pulling him to his feet. "You, me, his grandmother, his godmother, the country."

They headed for the exit, followed by the clientele's pitying eyes. Still sober, the owner gave them a smile and merely remarked, "Already?"

Benjy nodded yes distractedly. Suddenly, as he stepped out onto the sidewalk, he exclaimed, "I almost forgot! Inis wanted me to tell you that she took Carla to the hospital last night. This morning at 9:27, your son was born. He weighed six pounds two ounces. City Hall has reopened in time for you to go claim paternity," he added.

"Six pounds two ounces," Boris repeated. "He's not very big!"

At this, the thought of Dieudonné very likely lost at sea ran together with that of this scrawny newborn, all he had been able to sire, and Carla, whose suffering he hadn't shared, and he burst into tears like a child.

Around noon, *Fleur des Tropiques,* a catamaran belonging to the Marissol brothers with three hundred passengers traveling from Martinique aboard, caught sight of a wreck impaled on the rock known as La Baleine off the coast of the San Diego cays. Since leaving Fort-de-France, they had been sailing for seven hours. Thus a profound torpor had descended upon the boat. In the blink of an eye, everything changed. Those who were dozing woke up and a crush of people scrambled to the upper deck; the weak and the sick found their legs again, the luckier among them arming themselves with binoculars, the shorter people cursing the taller ones blocking their view. A single question was on everyone's lips: How could anyone run aground on this rock? This wasn't the month of September, that hurricane midwife, but the end of the dry season. For days, even weeks, the weather bulletins had been repeating themselves:

waves calm, no hazards; moderate trade winds; brief, insignificant showers. It was true that at high tide the water covered the rock, making it invisible. But there were plenty of isolated danger buoys all around it. And even without that, everyone who had sailed in the region was familiar with this bad tooth lodged in the gums of the sea and carefully avoided it. Unless the skipper had been particularly inexperienced or clumsy, how was such an accident possible?

One morose soul ventured to ask whether this might not instead be an intentional shipwreck? The act of some desperate person? Unthinkable, everyone replied. Who would be crazy enough to do that? The speaker held his ground: Not a local, everyone knows that's not in our customs, but a European, a foreigner! Those people aren't like us. They kill themselves over the least little thing! A heartache, a failed exam, a domestic squabble. Apparently, France holds the pathetic record for adolescent suicides. But they're a quarrelsome people. Yet another passenger, outraged, was quick to contradict him, recalling to everyone's memory that suicide was not the privileged domain of white people alone. Under slavery, blacks had committed mass suicide to escape servitude. These semihistorical debates and discussions went on for the remainder of the trip. Even so, *Fleur des Tropiques* finished its course without a hitch and docked, and at that point, the captain alerted the nautical brigade. Around two o'clock in the afternoon, then, a police speedboat set out for the open water. The sea was still calm. No wind. No drizzle in sight.

The gendarmes easily identified the wreckage: it was the *Belle Créole,* a boat up for sale with a spot at dock number 2 in the Mégisserie marina. Everyone knew that for a time, it had been used as a squat for a gang of wrongdoers, drug traffickers, who were now under lock and key, and for many years to come, thank God, along with the sadly famous Dieudonné Sabrina, unfortunately freed thanks to his lawyer's tricks. Since there was no risk of pollution or environmental damage, the gendarmes decided after careful reflection to sink the wreck. At that spot, the depths reached twenty meters. It would make the fish happy.

On the other hand, even though the divers brought in as reinforcements later spent hours circling the area, they found no body. As if the sailboat had detached itself from the dock and come to these parts to run aground all by itself. As if a ghost had taken the helm.

Despite this, the people of Port-Mahault understood quite well that Dieudonné had been on board. They were too taken with stories of extraordinary events to judge it just a banal accident, to think that the *Belle Créole,* uncontrollable after all those years of inaction, had merely played a fatal trick. The majority were of the opinion that Dieudonné had deliberately wrecked himself on La Baleine and that his body was drifting twenty thousand leagues, wrapped in the shroud of the sea. For that, some people pitied him. What death is worse than death by drowning? He who perishes that way has no coffin, no wake, no burial. Only sorrowful sharks ring the remains. However, this unusual, showy manner of getting life over with came across as theatrics and in general people disliked it. After all, there are less ostentatious ways to kill yourself: powders, drops, barbiturates. People also saw ingratitude in this end. Ingratitude toward his own, who, despite everything, were thrilled to get him back and live out their lives with him: his grandmother, his godmother, two worthy women that the scandal-hungry newspapers had said so many bad things about. Ingratitude toward Mr. Serbulon especially, who had gone to all that trouble for nothing. It was as if, in spite of his lawyer's efforts, Dieudonné was declaring himself guilty and inflicting on himself the punishment he had been spared.

A week later, the family had a Mass celebrated at the Saints-Innocents Chapel, near Morne Julien. The ceremony drew no more than a handful of people. If Fanniéta's ferreting eyes, and Hélène's especially, spotted Ana there with her son in her arms and were taken aback—Whose child is that?—they did not see Milo Vertueux kneeling in the last pew, his head in his hands.

His wife had convinced him that everything that had happened had happened because of him.

GLOSSARY

alouvi grand falle (variant: *agoulou granfal*)   A glutton, a voracious person.

bakoua   A straw hat made from leaves of the *bakoua* (screw pine, *Pandanus utilis*) tree.

béké (masculine), *békée* (feminine)   White Creoles and their present-day descendants. The "Grands Békés" are those families with the most powerful economic interests in the Antilles.

béni-rété   A marriage ceremony formalizing a common-law union.

bitako   A country bumpkin, an oaf.

bòbò   A prostitute.

bouden   The stomach.

brevet   A French national diploma awarded on successfully passing examinations at the end of junior high school (typically completed at age fourteen or fifteen).

bwa-bwa   A puppet or effigy (paraded during Lenten Carnival celebrations).

chabin (masculine), *chabine* (feminine)   A black person with light skin and red or golden naturally textured hair.

Chantez Noël   A festive Advent gathering of family and neighbors to sing Christmas carols together.

compas (variant: *konpa*)   A Haitian dance music that became popular in the 1950s and influenced the development of zouk.

da   A nanny.

dame-gabrielle   A prostitute.

Dé mo, kat'pawol   Briefly, in a few words (literally, "two words, four remarks").

doktè fèye   A healer who works with medicinal plants.

doudou   Dear, sweetie.

gadèdzafè   A seer or medium who helps resolve problems.

grand grek An intellectual, a well-educated person.

Grande Békée See *béké*.

gwo-ka A large traditional drum, played with the hands.

hak Nothing.

HLM (Habitation à loyer modéré) Rent-controlled housing.

jab (masculine), *jablesse* (feminine) A devil, a she-devil. On Ash Wednesday, women dressed as *jablesses* in black and white (the colors of mourning) burn the effigy Vaval, marking the end of Carnival and the beginning of Lent.

ka A large traditional drum, played with the hands; also called a *gwo-ka*.

kabann A bed made of rags.

kako Cocoa, cocoa-colored.

kaz-nèg A hut or cabin; historically, slave quarters (which continued to be occupied by plantation workers after emancipation).

kimbwazè A magico-religious practitioner with powers to heal, to do harm, and to divine events.

kok A cock.

kokdjèm A gamecock.

koudzyé A look, a glance.

krèye A group, collection, or batch.

lakou A group of *cases* (traditional cabins) sharing common spaces (courtyard, gardens). *Lakous* in Guadeloupe were typically family groupings and served as a way to pool resources and maintain property.

lendépendans Independence.

lewoz An evening of *gwo-ka* drum music.

lolo A small general grocery store.

LTS (Logement très social) Subsidized housing for very low-income households.

makoumè A homosexual.

mal kadik Epilepsy.

mal-nèg A manly man.

mal-sòti Literally, "badly come out"; said of a newborn with dark skin.

mambo A Vodou priestess.

mayolè A traditional stick-fighting dance accompanied by drumming and singing.

métro (*métropolitain*)   A person from the "métropole," or mainland France.

mi ta-w, mi tan mwen   Said of a woman's seductive, swaying gait (literally, "Here's one for you and one for me").

morne   Regional term for a hill or small mountain.

moun-bitation   A country dweller (from *moun,* person, and *habitation,* or plantation).

nègre   In the Antilles, the term *nègre* (Creole, *neg*) can mean a person, generally speaking, or a black person more specifically, depending on context. The term does not ordinarily have the negative and outmoded connotations that it does in mainland France (where it is the historical equivalent of the English term *Negro* and can also function as an insult), though it can take on pejorative connotations in certain contexts, or when combined with other adjectives (*neg-kongo,* for example, used historically to designate indentured Congolese workers, and, in contemporary times, to disparage a person's looks or character). The terms *grand* and *petit* are associated with socioeconomic class and take on positive, neutral, or negative connotations depending on the speaker and context; *Grands Nègres* designates upper- and middle-class elites, and *petits nègres,* the poor, working class.

négropolitain (pejorative; portmanteau derived from *nègre* and *métropolitain*)   An Antillean living in mainland (*métropolitain*) France.

ninnaine   Godmother.

petit nègre   See *nègre.*

pié-bwa   A tree.

pièce d'Inde (historical)   Term used to describe a young, healthy, robust slave (and thus a slave of high monetary value).

poto mitan   A center post; figuratively, a matriarch who holds the family together.

rara   A wooden rattle used to call the faithful to vespers on Good Friday.

razyé   Wild grasses, bushes, and herbs (*razyé* are also associated with traditional medicine).

rhum agricole   Rum distilled directly from fresh sugarcane juice (rather than from molasses, as is common outside the French Caribbean tradition).

RMI (Revenu minimum d'insertion)   A French welfare benefit ensuring that households attain a minimum monthly income. This benefit program was replaced by the RSA (Revenu de solidarité active) system in 2009.

sousoun klairant   Made of shiny material.

tambouyé   A drummer.

titane (bal-titane)   A ball, traditionally held in the daytime.

tomas   Chamber pots.

toumblak   A drumming rhythm associated with joy and celebration; also, the dance performed to this rhythm.

zindien (masculine), *zindienne* (feminine)   East Indian–Antilleans.

AFTERWORD

Dawn Fulton

The Belle Créole stands apart in Maryse Condé's work for
its focus on contemporary Guadeloupe. With a literary corpus
of novels, plays, and short stories whose settings shift from the
seventeenth to the twenty-first century, from the Caribbean to
Africa, Europe, and the United States, Condé is known perhaps more than anything else for an expansive and sometimes
restless sense of movement. Migration, transnationalism, and
globalization are terms that surface regularly in criticism on
Condé's work, as well as in her own extensive set of critical
essays and anthologies. But *The Belle Créole,* her twelfth of
sixteen novels, is a work that stays put geographically. In this
respect it can be compared to the author's sixth novel, *Traversée
de la mangrove* (*Crossing the Mangrove*), whose Guadeloupean
setting was characterized as a literary "return" to the author's
native island at the time of its publication in 1989, after a series
of novels set entirely or primarily in Africa or the United States.
In contrast to *Crossing the Mangrove*'s kaleidoscopic structure,
giving voice to twenty-one different characters, however, *The
Belle Créole* presents a notably tighter focus on its protagonist,
Dieudonné, and his contemporary political and cultural moment at the turn of the twenty-first century.

Guadeloupe, a French- and Creole-speaking archipelago
with a population of just over four hundred thousand, has always held a somewhat thorny place in Condé's literary oeu-
vre, one that in many ways mirrors its place in the author's
biography. Intersections between Condé's life and work are another signature trait: the autobiographical impulse of her writing is at times explicit in such works as *Victoire, les saveurs
et les mots* (*Victoire, My Mother's Mother*), a tribute to the
author's grandmother; *Le coeur à rire et à pleurer* (*Tales from*

the Heart), essayistic sketches drawn from Condé's childhood in Guadeloupe and Paris; or *La vie sans fards* (*What Is Africa to Me?*), which recounts the author's young adult years as a mother, wife, and teacher in Guinea, Ghana, and Senegal. But autobiography is also woven into Condé's fiction, particularly in her début novel, *Heremakhonon* (1976), whose embittered young narrator leaves her native Guadeloupe behind for an unsettling encounter with postindependence West Africa. The negative portrait of the Caribbean in this first novel, coupled with Condé's disparaging comments in interviews and essays, made for a sour start to the relationship between this new writer and her birthplace.

It is likely that Condé's sense of belonging in Guadeloupe came up against the socioeconomic and cultural dynamics of her family life. Born in 1937, the last of eight children, to parents who had fought hard to gain a foothold in Guadeloupe's nascent black bourgeoisie, Condé describes herself as a precocious witness to the complexities and contradictions of her parents' relationship to French culture. Still a French colony at the time of the author's birth, Guadeloupe, along with neighboring colonies Martinique and French Guiana, was to gain status as an Overseas Department (Département d'Outre-Mer) in 1946, thanks to the efforts of the Martinican statesman and poet Aimé Césaire. While this move offered economic security to postwar Guadeloupe, giving its inhabitants French citizenship and political representation in metropolitan France, many saw it as a disappointing compromise that undercut any hope of the island's independence. For the young Maryse, however, departmentalization meant the confirmation of her parents' wholehearted identification with France, justifying their disinterest in African history or culture and their refusal to allow their children to speak the island's native Creole.

This injunction against speaking Creole was to have long-term political and artistic consequences for Condé, functioning in some ways as a marker of her estrangement from intellectual communities in the French Antilles. Born with the Atlantic slave trade, Caribbean Creole languages developed as a means of communication among multiple African language groups and

European languages that had not yet been unified. After aboli-
tion and the end of the plantation economy, Creole continued to
be used in everyday Guadeloupe, but it had second-class status
in a context where French dominated the media, politics, and
education. For middle-class black Guadeloupeans of the postwar period like Condé's parents, the language was associated
with poverty and slavery and was thus incompatible with their
self-image. In subsequent decades, however, intellectuals and
poets in Martinique and Guadeloupe mobilized to affirm the
legitimacy of Creole alongside French, endeavoring to codify
its written form, publishing literary works in Creole, and in-
stituting a doctoral program in Creole studies at the Université
des Antilles in Schoelcher, Martinique. Although these initial
efforts struggled to find an audience, recent years have seen a
renewed interest in Creole among younger generations in Guadeloupe and the increasingly widespread use of the language in
the media.

Creole plays a key role in Condé's fiction, its usage modulated
to the varied registers, discursive modes, and socioeconomic
conditions portrayed in a given text. Thanks to its geographical
stability, *La Belle Créole* sits at the far end of this spectrum, with
an infusion of Creole words, phrases, and locutions sustained
throughout the text and notably left untranslated by the French
publisher Mercure de France. For this reason, the novel might
belie the controversy sparked earlier in Condé's career, when
in the 1980s and 1990s the author ruffled feathers by taking
issue with what she considered the binary thinking that aligned
the Creole language with the colonized and the French language with the colonizer. Directly contradicting the tenets of the
Créolité movement and its Martinican founders Jean Bernabé,
Patrick Chamoiseau, and Raphaël Confiant, Condé refused to
claim victimization by the French language. Poetic license, she
maintained, confers dominion over language; thus she writes
not in French or in Creole but in an expressive mode forged of
her own voice. The phrase "j'écris en Maryse Condé" (I write
in Maryse Condé) has become a refrain invoked—often with
humor—by Condé herself and others in discussing this aspect
of her work (see, for example, Pfaff, *Nouveaux entretiens,* 64).

The polemics surrounding Condé's use of Creole in her work also highlight the question of authenticity that has been at the heart of the fraught relationship between the author and Guadeloupe. In the decades following African independence movements when Condé was beginning to publish her fiction, the rising interest in so-called postcolonial literature placed a premium on "authentic" narratives of oppressed peoples, of rural spaces and local cultures. But Condé's own story and the narratives she created did not always fit these parameters. Instead, she wrote of culturally assimilated yet psychologically untroubled black subjects, of political corruption in postcolonial Africa, of cosmopolitan black women who eschewed solidarity with the working classes or fell in love with white men. This friction became especially pronounced in the responses to her fourth novel, *Moi, Tituba . . . sorcière noire de Salem* (*I, Tituba, Black Witch of Salem*), which was instantly hailed by luminaries of African American studies, feminist studies, and postcolonial criticism as the triumphant redress of a subjugated black female voice, only to be unveiled by the author as a parody (see Pfaff, *Conversations,* 59; and Scarboro, 212). For these and other uncommon portraits of ostensibly marginalized subjects, Condé gained a reputation for political incorrectness and iconoclasm across cultures.

Condé left Guadeloupe at the age of sixteen to study in Paris, then to study and teach in Côte d'Ivoire, Guinea, Ghana, Senegal, and the United States, and it would be thirty-three years before she would return to live in her homeland. In the decades following that return, however, she split her time between her house in Montebello, Guadeloupe, and her teaching appointments at various universities in the United States, including the University of California at Berkeley, the University of Maryland, the University of Virginia, Harvard University, and finally Columbia University, where she taught until her retirement in 2005. Even in recent years, despite a health condition that has placed significant constraints on her trademark mobility, Condé has maintained her links to the island, making the long trip there from her current home in Gordes, France, numerous times. While through her critics' eyes it may seem as if she is always leaving Guadeloupe behind, one could also say that she is always returning to it, and that in fact her portrait of this foundational space is all the richer for her repeated departures. Just as her own childhood confirms that there is no single narrative of Guadeloupean experience, her fiction undoes the notion of cultural authenticity, elaborating instead a range of idiosyncratic, unpredictable Caribbean lives and perspectives.

The Belle Créole is an exemplary work in this respect. Beginning with its title, the novel seems to hold up a series of clichéd, easily digestible images of Guadeloupe only to turn them on their heads. "La Belle Créole" is a phrase that would be at home in the French Caribbean tourism industry: literally, "the beautiful Creole woman," it suggests at once exoticism, femininity, and aesthetic appeal, a formula apt to attract the potential foreign patrons of a restaurant or hotel. Thus while the novel's title is partly a reference to the character of Loraine Féréol de Brémont ("Creole," in addition to referring to the island's language and culture, can also be used to designate the *béké* class of slave-owner descendants), it is significant that it is the name chosen for their treasured sailboat by the Cohen family, outsiders who fall in love with the area only to abandon it—and the boat—for more prestigious opportunities. In recounting this abandonment and the sailboat's subsequent degradation and destruction, Condé seems to gesture toward the way Guadeloupe is often viewed in metropolitan France—as a beautiful vacation spot that is at once exotic and accessible for French-speaking Europeans—while tracing the destructive effects of this touristic impulse.

Like the sailboat, the city of Port-Mahault belies romanticized visions of Caribbean spaces. In Condé's narrative, the union strikes, political discord, and heat wave in turn-of-the-twenty-first-century Guadeloupe combine to form a quasi-apocalyptic vision of accumulating garbage and stench, crime and violence, and vicious dogs prowling the streets. The exaggerated squalor in this portrait pointedly counters the images of calm blue waters and pristine beaches generally associated with the Caribbean, defying a consumerism that prefers such aesthetically pleasing vistas to modernity, politics, or human beings. And yet even this juxtaposition is anything but simplistic, as the novel's concluding scenes suggest. The scrubbing of the streets signaling the end of the strikes and the horrific mass killing of the dogs seem to restore a sense of order in the city but are met with an uncertain mixture of relief and regret by the city's inhabitants: "Even the most hardened souls began to miss the cavalcade of beasts that had nonetheless repulsed them so strongly before" (179). For native Guadeloupeans, too, there are conflicting images of what constitutes—or should constitute—"authentic" Caribbean life.

With the novel's central narrative, the story of Dieudonné, Condé also points to the role of cliché in the contemporary legacy of the island's long history of slavery and colonization. The cynical juxtaposition of appearance and reality is dramatized by the opposing narratives of the young protagonist and his lawyer, Serbulon. In the face of his client's virtual silence, Serbulon puts together a story infused with Guadeloupe's history of violence and oppression, a story that holds up its characters as present-day manifestations of this collective past. Through Serbulon's lens, Dieudonné is a slave violently separated from his African homeland, transported across the Middle Passage, and subjected to the dehumanization of the plantation. Loraine is the cruel master, the embodiment of centuries-long abuse and exploitation who deserves the punishment of death for her crimes. The defense thus makes Dieudonné a hero for all black Caribbean people, symbol of a successful slave rebellion and champion of human rights and justice: "The cruel *békée* mistress. The defenseless slave. The mistress humiliates and wields the whip. One day, the slave frees himself. By killing. A baptism in blood" (30).

What Condé's novel recounts is, of course, a story that bears little resemblance to this courtroom narrative. Loraine does display a healthy dose of cruelty and remains staunchly embedded in the power hierarchies guaranteed by her genealogy, but her relationship to the *béké* community is fraught with ambivalence, and her feelings for and behavior toward Dieudonné have only partly to do with race. In the end the character is more likely to incite pity than fear, and Condé's portrait—while less than sympathetic—nonetheless strains the plausibility of positing Loraine as a representative *béké* master. Dieudonné, on the other hand, while regularly subject to the racial and economic inequities of a postslavery society, is victimized less by the labor structures that inhere in his relationship with Loraine than by his Oedipal, obsessive love for her. Further, he fails or refuses to see himself as a member of an oppressed class ("Oppressed by who? By what?" [53]), and, if he is indeed responsible for his mistress's death, he executed her on anything but heroic terms.

By methodically taking down the scaffolding that would support Serbulon's narrative of events, Condé points to all that must be approximated, glossed over, or left out in such historically and politically infused readings of Caribbean experience. The tongue-in-cheek references to the renowned Martinican intellectuals and activists Aimé Césaire and Frantz Fanon in Matthias Serbulon's assessment of his own legal argument ("Matthias had been proud of his line of argument, which he deemed Césairean, or even Fanonian" [30]), meanwhile, slyly bring the fields of critical race theory and postcolonial criticism into the discussion, suggesting that some of the progressive arguments around human rights and slave reparations that have drawn heavily on the scholarship of Césaire and Fanon may not have been immune to similarly reductive reasoning. Everyday people are not spared either in Condé's critique, however, since in the end the lawyer's argument is successful: the one-dimensional image cut from cardboard versions of history sets his client free. Fed by the sensationalist media, the jury of peers and members of the community in Port-Mahault buy the story just as the intellectual Left might, making a hero of the hapless Dieudonné.

Parody, irreverence, and playful cynicism are ever-present in Condé's fiction, keeping the reader off balance and undercutting self-righteous doctrine across the political spectrum. And yet this derisive spirit is not borne from a lack of political conscience or of ethical seriousness. The vision of Condé that emerges from her body of work is that of an author who is an attentive and trenchant witness to her contemporary moment and to its underlying histories. Her novels have taken on slavery and the slave trade, US puritanism, French metropolitan racism, the rise and fall of the Bambara Empire, South African apartheid, and, more recently, twenty-first-century Islamic radicalization in *Le fabuleux et triste destin d'Ivan et d'Ivana* (*The Wondrous and Tragic Life of Ivan and Ivana*), a novel inspired by events surrounding the terrorist attacks in Paris in 2015. And, nearly a decade after its publication, *The Belle Créole*'s evocation of the 1999 strikes in Port-Mahault seemed to take on a prescient note, as if anticipating the general strikes that began in Guadeloupe on January 20, 2009, and lasted forty-four days, spreading to Martinique and to Reunion Island in the Indian Ocean and receiving unprecedented international media coverage.

As a public intellectual, Condé plays a role that is often as political as it is artistic. She was selected in 2004 by then French president Jacques Chirac to be the inaugural president of the Comité pour la mémoire de l'esclavage (Committee for the Memory of Slavery), an organization instated in the wake of the so-called Taubira Law that in 2001 recognized slavery as a crime against humanity. She is also a member of the pro-independence political party, the Union Populaire pour la Libération de Guadeloupe (UPLG; Popular Union for the Liberation of Guadeloupe), recently traveling to Guadeloupe to preside over the fortieth-anniversary celebration of the party's founding. The critique of political ideology in her work is thus anything but apolitical; instead it marks an effort to bring depth and nuance to such arguments. Just as she warns against notions of feminism that entail a blind embrace of anything a woman does on the sole basis of her gender, Condé demands a frank assessment of success and failure in any struggle for equality. Thus *The Belle Créole* derides the hollowness and opportunism of its fictional independence movement, and Condé herself speaks frankly about the fading relevance of the UPLG in twenty-first-century Guadeloupean politics even as she celebrates its historical importance (see Condé, "Giving Voice").

In literary terms, this is perhaps the most significant dimension of Condé's work: the insistence on probing the contradictions and incongruities of her portraits and characters. The figures she creates in her novels are famously not heroic, yet they unfailingly speak to us, draw us in, incite our compassion, frustration, fear, and empathy. Often these characters struggle against the very criteria that might propel them to heroic status, striving to find their own way amid social, political, and cultural pressures that seek to define them by their race, gender, sexuality, or class. We see *The Belle Créole*'s Dieudonné, for example, unable to live up to the tale of postcolonial triumph told by his lawyer and the media, and at the same time unable to shake free of the loss of his cherished mother, of his feelings of abandonment by his ersatz family, of his unrequited love for the woman who humiliates him. In the end the inexorable humanity that draws the reader back again and again to Condé's work lies precisely in these singular instances, in the rejection of the cliché, in the defiance—proud or hopeless—of the individual whose path cannot be drawn by collective history.

For Condé, writing and literature are also a medium of transcultural exchange. The Guadeloupe she presents in her novels encompasses the multifaceted histories of its native inhabitants but also highlights the experiences of the island's cultural outsiders, from the Indian, Chinese, Syrian, and Haitian immigrant communities featured in *Traversée de la mangrove* to such characters as the Italian journalist Carla and the German-born, US-educated Ana in *La Belle Créole*. Cuba, Haiti, France, the United States, and Africa are frequent references in this culture, which through Condé's eyes is opened up to the world outside its borders. Speaking of her genealogy as a writer, Condé credits the particular capacity of literature to cut across national and cultural boundaries with her first glimmer of the possibility of becoming a novelist. Upon reading the French translation of Emily Brontë's *Wuthering Heights* at the age of ten, Condé recounts, she was struck by the similarity between the desolate landscape of the Yorkshire moors and the ruins of a plantation sugar mill in Guadeloupe, and drawn in unequivocally by the tragic passion of Heathcliff and Cathy. "That's the power and magic of literature," she writes, "it knows no borders, it is the realm of hard to reach dreams, obsessions, and desires, which unites readers through time and space" ("Giving Voice," par. 7).

If this act of cross-cultural reading marks the start of an illustrious writing career, it is also noteworthy in that it highlights the enduring importance of English and Anglophone cultures in Condé's work. During the several decades that she spent teaching at universities and colleges in the United States, Condé lectured and published in English, becoming a key voice in the field of cultural and literary criticism where the English language was dominant. It was her early experience of US racism when she first moved to Los Angeles that led her to turn her attention to Puritan culture in seventeenth-century Massachusetts and to study the history of the Barbadian slave Tituba whose story would inspire her novel *I, Tituba, Black Witch of Salem*. The language of the civil rights movement punctuates *Les derniers rois mages (The Last of the African Kings)* with its portrait of the African American historian and ideologue Debbie Middleton, and the strained politics of race in US academe come to the fore through the eyes of Marie-Noëlle, a professor of literature from Guadeloupe teaching in Newbury, Massachusetts, in *Desirada*. Brontë's *Wuthering Heights* itself became a more direct inspiration for Condé's work in her monumental novel *La migration des cœurs (Windward Heights)*, a transposition of the British classic's setting to late nineteenth- and early twentieth-century Cuba and Guadeloupe. What the author terms her "cannibalization" of the European literary tradition appears in most explicit form here but is present to various degrees in the references within her novels to works familiar to readers of Anglophone literature: Shelley's *Frankenstein* in *Célanire cou-coupé (Who Slashed Célanire's Throat?)*, for example, or Faulkner's *As I Lay Dying* in *Crossing the Mangrove*.

Condé's work "speaks" to an English-language audience, in other words, and *The Belle Créole* is no exception, with its playful references to Lawrence's *Lady Chatterley's Lover* in Ana's characterization of Dieudonné's story (63), to Shakespeare's *Othello,* which writer-activist Boris describes as the story of "a man who had gotten up the courage to kill the woman who had betrayed him" (23), or even to the seemingly remote spaces of the New York art world and Hollywood cinema. Widely translated into such languages as Japanese, Spanish, Portuguese,

German, Italian, Dutch, and Hebrew, Condé's work has been embraced with particular warmth by her Anglophone readership, sometimes finding more success in English translation, she notes, than in the original French (Pfaff, *Nouveaux entretiens,* 124). Of course, the work of the author's second husband, Richard Philcox, is important to note here: Philcox, to whom Condé has been married since 1982, is a British translator who has brought the great majority of Condé's literary and critical works to the English-speaking world and in doing so has played a key role in the international reputation earned by Condé.

That reputation has been confirmed not only by the prestigious university positions Condé has held but also by the prizes, awards, and honors she has received across four continents. The list is a long one and includes the Grand Prix Littéraire de la Femme for *Moi, Tituba* (1987), the Prix de l'Académie Française for *La vie scélérate* (1988; *Tree of Life*) the Hurston/Wright Legacy Award for *Célanire cou-coupé* (2005), and the Prix Tropiques for *Victoire, les saveurs et les mots* (2007). She received a Guggenheim Fellowship in 1987, and was named Commandeur de l'Ordre des Arts et des Lettres by the French government in 2001 and Chevalier de la Légion d'Honneur in 2004. Still, the absence of some of the major literary awards from her list of accolades has not gone unnoticed by Condé. In a book-length collection of interviews published in 2016, Françoise Pfaff concludes the wide-ranging conversation with questions about goals and future projects, asking the author if there is one thing she has always wanted but never achieved. Condé's response is simple: the Nobel Prize (Pfaff, *Nouveaux entretiens,* 192). Two years later, Maryse Condé was selected as the winner of the New Academy Prize, known more commonly under the designation "alternative Nobel," as it was conferred in a year when the Nobel Prize in Literature was not awarded because of a sexual misconduct scandal involving the husband of a member of the Swedish Academy, which awards the prize.

The populist bent of the New Academy Prize, with an initial selection process by Swedish librarians and a public poll included in the deliberations, along with the particular attention paid to gender equity in the wake of the Nobel-associated scandal, seem particularly fitting to honor Condé and her work. There is a flavor of triumphant defiance in the very existence of this prize, built from the ground up with word spread through social media and funds raised through Kickstarter, its successful campaign confirming a widespread determination to refuse to let literature pay the price for the crimes of the elite. Condé, for her part, has conveyed a deep sense of appreciation and even fulfillment at this tribute. Now able to write only by dictation, the author seems truly gratified by the international recognition represented by this prize. "The award came to me as a total surprise," she writes. "Besides being proud and happy, I felt relieved. For the first time, I was at peace with myself" ("Giving Voice," par. 2). Describing her as "a grand storyteller," New Academy Prize jury chair Ann Pålsson affirmed that her work "belongs to world literature" and praised her ability to mingle magic, terror, dreams, and love: "Respectfully and with humor, she narrates the postcolonial insanity, disruption and abuse, but also human solidarity and warmth. The dead live in her stories closely to the living in a multitudinous world where gender, race and class are constantly turned over in new constellations" (Chela, par. 3).

In addition to traveling to Stockholm to receive this award in December 2018, Condé made the trip to Guadeloupe to celebrate the historic moment with her compatriots amid great fanfare. Significantly, she has placed Guadeloupe front and center in her acceptance of the prize, construing the award as a simultaneous recognition of her work and of her native island. In the same breath as her grateful acknowledgment to the committee, she moves to share the prize with friends, family, and "above all the people of Guadeloupe." Indeed, in the author's responses to the award, we see a poignant rehearsal of the struggle evoked in *The Belle Créole,* the battle of images that the perennially exoticized Caribbean seems fated to confront. In the essay "Giving Voice to Guadeloupe," adapted from her acceptance speech for the New Academy Prize, Condé notes that the only mentions of Guadeloupe in the international media occur "when there is a hurricane, or a transatlantic yacht race like the *Route du Rhum,* or when a celebrity visits, even posthumously—like the rock star Johnny Hallyday." Thus she is proud, she says, "to be one Guadeloupean who has made her voice heard," thanks to the awarding of the New Academy Prize (par. 18–19).

For the reader of Caribbean literature, it is difficult not to hear in this evocation of voice and collective identity an echo of the often-cited words of Aimé Césaire in his foundational poem of the Négritude movement, *Cahier d'un retour au pays natal* (*Notebook of a Return to My Native Land*): "My mouth shall be the mouth of those calamities that have no mouth, my voice the freedom of those who break down in the solitary confinement of despair" (45). And yet this is a phrase that Condé herself has critiqued for its potentially prescriptive vision of the role of the Caribbean poet (Condé, "Order," 122). Even as she calls up the concept of the writer as force of solidarity and representation, then, Condé adds an important and defining edge of contention to this image in her closing words: "This gives me hope that Guadeloupe's voice, despite the island's misfortunes, remains powerful, remains magical, and still has the power to say no" ("Giving Voice," par. 19). With every affirmation of Guadeloupean identity and experience, Condé's work seems to tell us, come beauty and enchantment, but also discord, rebuttal, contradiction. Condé's Guadeloupe is ever a site of both homecoming and departure, a native land cherished against the grain.

BIBLIOGRAPHY

Césaire, Aimé. *The Collected Poetry*. Translated by Clayton Eshleman and Annette Smith. Berkeley: University of California Press, 1983.

Chela, Efemia. "Maryse Condé Receives the New Academy Prize in Literature, aka the 'Alternative Nobel.'" *Johannesburg Review of Books*, November 5, 2018. https://johannesburgreviewofbooks.com/2018/11/05/maryse-conde-receives-the-new-academy-prize-in-literature-aka-the-alternative-nobel/.

Condé, Maryse. *La Belle Créole*. Paris: Mercure de France, 2001.

———. *Célanire cou-coupé*. Paris: Robert Laffont, 2000.

———. *Le cœur à rire et à pleurer, contes vrais de mon enfance*. Paris: Robert Laffont, 1999.

———. *Crossing the Mangrove*. Translated by Richard Philcox. New York: Doubleday, 1995.

———. *Les derniers rois mages*. Paris: Mercure de France, 1992.

———. *Desirada*. Paris: Robert Laffont, 1997.

———. *Desirada*. Translated by Richard Philcox. New York: Soho, 2000.

———. *Le fabuleux et triste destin d'Ivan et d'Ivana*. Paris: Lattès, 2017.

———. "Giving Voice to Guadeloupe." *New York Review of Books*, February 6, 2019. https://www.nybooks.com/daily/2019/02/06/giving-voice-to-guadeloupe/.

———. *Heremakhonon*. Paris: Editions 10/18, 1976.

———. *Heremakhonon*. Translated by Richard Philcox. Washington: Three Continents, 1982.

———. *I, Tituba, Black Witch of Salem*. Translated by Richard Philcox. New York: Ballantine, 1992.

———. *The Last of the African Kings*. Translated by Richard Philcox. Lincoln: University of Nebraska Press, 1997.

———. *La migration des cœurs*. Paris: Robert Laffont, 1995.

———. *Moi, Tituba, sorcière . . . noire de Salem*. Paris: Mercure de France, 1986.

———. "Order, Disorder, Freedom, and the West Indian Writer." *Yale French Studies* 83, no. 2 (1993): 121–35.

———. *Tales from the Heart: True Stories from My Childhood*. Translated by Richard Philcox. New York: Soho, 2001.

———. *Traversée de la mangrove*. Paris: Mercure de France, 1989.

———. *Tree of Life*. Translated by Victoria Reiter. New York: Ballantine, 1992.

———. *Victoire, les saveurs et les mots*. Paris: Mercure de France, 2006.

———. *Victoire, My Mother's Mother*. Translated by Richard Philcox. New York: Atria, 2010.

———. *La vie sans fards*. Paris: Lattès, 2012.

———. *La vie scélérate*. Paris: Seghers, 1987.

———. *What Is Africa to Me?* Translated by Richard Philcox. New York: Seagull, 2016.

———. *Who Slashed Célanire's Throat?* Translated by Richard Philcox. New York: Atria, 2004.

———. *Windward Heights*. Translated by Richard Philcox. New York: Soho, 1998.

Pfaff, Françoise. *Conversations with Maryse Condé*. Lincoln: University of Nebraska Press, 1996.

———. *Nouveaux entretiens avec Maryse Condé*. Paris: Karthala, 2016.

Scarboro, Ann Armstrong. Afterword to *I, Tituba, Black Witch of Salem*, by Maryse Condé, translated by Richard Philcox, 187–225. New York: Ballantine, 1992.

CPSIA information can be obtained
at www.ICGtesting.com
Printed in the USA
LVHW010758280721
693844LV00013B/1830